Tuareg

First published by O-Books, 2009
O-Books is an imprint of John Hunt Publishing Ltd., Laurel House, Station Approach,
Alresford, Hants, SO24 9JH, UK
office1@o-books.net
www.o-books.com

For distributor details and how to order please visit the 'Ordering' section on our website.

Text copyright: Alberto Vázquez Figueroa 2008

ISBN: 978 1 84694 192 4

A CIP catalogue record for this book is available from the British Library.

Design: A. Smith
Cover design: Marc Armangue

Artwork by Amanda Robinson at www.amandadesign.co.uk
© Cover Image: Pascal Maitre
Translated by Vicky Collier

www.albertovazquezfigueroa.com
Translation © Desperado Management, London

Printed in the UK by CPI Antony Rowe
Printed in the USA by Offset Paperback Mfrs, Inc

We operate a distinctive and ethical publishing philosophy in all
areas of our business, from our global network of authors to
production and worldwide distribution.

Tuareg

Alberto Vázquez Figueroa

Translated from the Spanish by
Vicky Collier

BOOKS

Winchester, UK
Washington, USA

To my father

'Allah is Great. Blessed is Allah.'

'It was a long time ago now. A time when I was young and my legs carried me over sand and stone for days at a time, without tiring, and I received news one day that my younger brother was ill. Although three days of travel stood between my jaima and his, the strength of my love for him was enough to overcome any apathy and I set off without trepidation, being, like I said, young, strong and fearless.

Night was closing in on the second day of my journey, when I came across a cluster of high dunes, some half a day's walk from the tomb of the holy man Omar Abraham. I scrambled up to the top of one to see if I could spot a settlement and somewhere I might take shelter, but I saw nothing and decided to stay put for the night, shielded from the wind.

The moon must have been very high in the sky - lucky for me that Allah had wished it so on this particular night - when I was awoken by a blood-curdling scream and terrified, I curled up into a small ball of panic.

Then the terrible screams started up once again, but this time they were followed by such a wailing and a moaning, that it felt like the howls of a soul suffering in hell had penetrated through to this very world.

Soon after that I heard a scratching noise in the sand nearby, then the noise would stop and start up again further away, so that I was able to predict its whereabouts. This happened some five or six times over, whilst the heart-breaking sobs continued, and I recoiled, paralyzed and shaking with fear.

But my troubles didn't stop there, as a huge sighing sound suddenly filled the air and something or someone started to throw fistfuls of sand into my face. So begging forgiveness from my ancestors, and beside myself with fear, I jumped up and started to run as if Satan, the stoned demon himself, was on my tail. I didn't stop running until the sun came up and I could no longer see any sign of those towering dunes.

I arrived at my brother's house, and praise be to Allah, he was sufficiently recovered to be able to listen to the story of my terrifying night. And whilst I was retelling the story by the warm glow of the fire, just as I am recounting it to you now, a neighbour told me what had happened, according to what his father had told him.

And he said this:

"Allah is great. Praise be to Allah. Many years ago there were two powerful families, the Zayed and the Atman. They hated each other vehemently and so many lives had been lost between the two families that you could have dyed all their clothes and livestock with the red from all their spilled blood. A young Atman had been the last victim of the feud and revenge hung heavy in the air."

And it was there, among those dunes where you slept, not far from the tomb of the holy man Omar Ibrahim, that the Zayed tribe were once settled. Only all the men in the camp had been killed and just a mother and child remained there, living peacefully, because even though the families loathed each other fiercely, to kill a woman was still considered a heinous crime.

But one night their enemies appeared and after tying up the mother, who sobbed and wailed, they took the little one away to be buried alive in the dunes.

Her ropes were strong, but it is well known that a mother's love is stronger still, and the woman managed to break free. But when she got outside they had disappeared and she could see nothing more than a line of high dunes stretching out to infinity. So she took off, throwing herself from one dune to the next, moaning and crying out in the knowledge that her son would be suffocating at that very moment and that she was the only one that could save him. And suddenly dawn was upon her."

They say she continued like that, searching desperately for her son, for the rest of her days and that her madness was a gift from the merciful Allah, to ease her suffering and help her to forget the evil of man's ways.

The old man paused.

'And no one knew what became of the poor woman and they say that her spirit still roams the dunes, not far from the tomb of the holy man Omar Ibrahim, still searching and lamenting her misfortunes. It was there that you slept without knowing it and there that you met with her.

Blessed is Allah, the Merciful one, that he let you out safely and that you are here now, with us, by the warm glow of the fire. Blessed is Allah.'

When he had finished his tale, the old man took a deep breath and turning to face the youngest in the group, those who were hearing the story for the very first time, said:

'See how hate and struggle between families leads to nothing, nothing more than fear, madness and death. I can tell you one thing for certain and that is in all the years that I battled with my own men against our eternal enemies from the North, the Ibn-Aziz, I never saw anything that justified such treachery. In the end one pillaging is paid for with another and the deaths in each group had no price and only served to create a spate of new deaths. The jaimas were left empty of strong arms, and the children brought up without the sound of their father's voice.'

For a few minutes nobody spoke, out of respect, as the lessons of the story told by the ancient Suilem were absorbed and his listeners considered its message, all of them aware that the venerable man had sacrificed some hours of sleep for their benefit and was now weary.

In the end it was Gazel, who had heard the tale a dozen times before, who signalled with a gesture of his hands that it was time for everyone to retire and go to sleep. Then he went off alone, as he did every night, to check that the livestock had been brought in and the slaves had finished their work; that his family was resting in peace and order prevailed over his small empire, made up of four camel-hair tents, half a dozen woven cane sheribas, a well, nine palm trees and a handful of goats and camels.

Then, as he did every night, he slowly climbed to the top of the tall, solid dune that protected the settlement from the east winds, and by the light of the moon, looked out over the rest of his empire. This was his dominion, the desert that stretched out to infinity. Gazel Sayah ruled over this vast area of sand, rock, mountain and stony ground with absolute authority, being the only inmouchar to have settled there and owner of the only known water source in the region.

He liked to sit there on top, to give thanks to Allah as he counted the thousand blessings that filled his thoughts: the beautiful family he had been given; the good health of his slaves; the wellbeing of his livestock; the fruit from the palm trees and the highest of all his fortunes, that of being born a nobleman amongst nobility in the powerful town of Kel-Talgimus, one of the veil people, the indomitable Imohag, or, as they were known to the rest of mankind, the Tuareg.

There was nothing to the south, the east or the west that set a limit to the land under Gazel's rule. Gazel "the Hunter" who had, over time, left the settlements behind him in order to set up camp in one of the desert's furthest confines, where he could feel utterly alone with his wild animals. There he lived side by side with the roaming addax, that grazed on the plains for days at a time; the mouflons from high up in the remotest mountains that rose up between the seas of sand; wild donkeys, wild boar, gazelles, and never ending numbers of migratory birds. Gazel had fled the advances of civilization, the influences of invaders and their indiscriminate killing of the sand beasts and he was well known throughout the Sahara and all around, from Timbuktu to the banks of the Nile, for his generous hospitality. But while Gazel Sayah's hospitality went unequalled, so did his wrath and he was equally well known for having stopped slave caravans and mad huntsmen who had dared to enter his territory, dead in their tracks.

'My father taught me,' he used to say, 'never to kill more than one gazelle at a time, even if the herd was on the move and it would take another three days to find it again. I can easily go on a trip for three days again, he would say, but nobody can bring a gazelle that was killed in vain, back to life.'

Gazel had seen how the "French" had killed off the antelopes from the north to extinction, and the mouflons in much of the Atlas, and the beautiful hamada addax that came from the other side of the great Sekia, which thousands of years ago used to be a mighty river. That was why he had chosen this stony corner of the plains, with its endless sand and inhospitable mountains, a fourteen-day walk from El-Akab, because only someone like him would dare to take on such an inhospitable land, in the most inhospitable of all deserts.

The days when the Tuaregs were true warriors - ambushing caravans and attacking the French military with their war-like cries, sweeping the plains like fierce winds, pillaging and killing and in combat with anything that stood in their way - were long gone. They had been proud of their reputation as the "desert bandits" or "masters" of the Saharan sands, from south of the Atlas to the shores of the river Chad. But the fighting and wars of fratricide were long forgotten now, apart from in the distant memories of some of the older generations. The Imohag race was in decline, as the most valiant of its warriors chose to leave the desert and drive lorries for a "French" patron instead, or joined the regular army or sold candles and sandals to tourists in tie-dye t-shirts.

On the day that his cousin Suleiman left the desert and went to live in the city to sell bricks, driving them around from one place to the next, day after day, covered in cement and whitewash, he knew that he to had to leave and establish himself as one of the last of the solitary Tuaregs.

And it was there, high up on that same dune, his family below him, that he would sit every night and give thanks to Allah one thousand and one times and not once in all those years – so many now that he had lost track - had he regretted his decision.

From the bits and pieces he picked up from passing travellers, it seemed to him that strange things were happening in the world. They brought with them tales of death and war, of rapid change that did not seem to be of any great benefit to anyone and he was happy not to have witnessed the events that they spoke of.

One night, as he sat there, contemplating the stars that had so often guided him through the desert, he saw one he did not recognise, shining brilliantly and moving at a fast but steady, almost purposeful rate, unlike the reckless paths of errant shooting stars that would eventually fade away to nothing. For the first time in his life he had frozen with fear, unable to find in his memory or in the memories of his ancestors a tradition or legend that told of such a star, of one that followed the same path, night after night. They grew in number over the years, until together, they resembled a pack of racing hounds running riot through space and disturbing the ancient peace of the skies.

He would never know the significance of these strange apparitions. Nor would the ancient Suilem, the father of nearly all his slaves and so old, that his grandfather had bought him, already a man, in Senegal.

'The stars have never taken such strange paths through the

sky, master,' Gazel noted. 'Never. This could mean that the end is nigh.'

He had asked one traveller about them, but he had been unable to give him a straight answer. The second traveller he asked had said that it might have something to do with the "French." But Gazel was not convinced, because even though he had heard rumours that the French were making significant advances in technology, he still could not believe they would be mad enough to start putting more stars into a sky that was already full of them.

'It must be a divine sign,' he said. 'Allah is trying to tell us something. But what?'

He tried to find the answer in the Koran, but the Koran did not mention shooting stars that followed paths of mathematical precision, so over time he just got used to their presence, but that is not to say that he forgot about them.

In the clear air of the desert, in the darkness of a land where not a single light burned for hundreds of kilometers all around, the stars looked so close to the land that Gazel would sometimes stretch out his hands as if he was trying to touch the trembling lights that hovered just above him, with his own fingertips.

He remained up there for a long while, alone with his thoughts, and then scrambled quickly down to take a last look at the livestock and the camp and to check for hungry hyenas or cunning jackals that might threaten his small world, before retiring to bed.

At the door of his tent, the biggest and most comfortable in the encampment, he stopped and listened. If the wind had not started up, the silence would have been so intense that it hurt.

Gazel loved this silence.

Every day at dawn Suilem, the old man, or one of his grandsons would saddle up Gazel the inmouchar's favourite camel and leave it at the entrance of their master's tent.

Every day at dawn the Targui would fetch his rifle, mount his white, long-legged mehari and head off to one of the four compass points in search of prey.

Gazel loved his camel, as much as a man of the desert is capable of loving an animal and often depended on him with his life. When they were alone together he would chat to him out loud. He called him "R'Orab, the raven," and made jokes about his snow-white colour, so close to the colour of the sandy landscape through which they travelled, that it often just melted into the background.

There was not a faster or stronger mehari to be found on this side of Tamanrasset. A rich merchant, who was the owner of a caravan of over three hundred animals had once offered to exchange it for five of his choice, but Gazel had turned down his offer. Gazel knew that if anything were ever to happen to him on one of their solitary adventures, "R'Orab" would be the only camel in the world capable of carrying him back to his camp, even on the darkest of nights.

Sometimes, overcome with tiredness and lulled by the animal's swaying gait, he would arrive at the entrance to his tent fast asleep on its back and his family would take him down and put him into bed.

The "French" were convinced that these camels were stupid, cruel and vindictive creatures that only responded to shouting and whipping. A real Imohag knew that a good desert camel, particularly the pure-blooded mehari, that was well cared for and well trained, could be as intelligent and faithful as a dog, but a thousand times more useful in that land of sand and wind.

The French would treat the camels in the same way throughout the different seasons of the year, without understanding that in the rutting season these creatures became irritable and dangerous, especially if the heat intensified with the east winds. This was one reason the French had never made good horseman in the desert and why they had never managed to conquer the Tuareg, who, back in the days of battle and unrest, had always managed to defeat them, despite their larger numbers and more sophisticated weaponry.

The French came to dominate the oases and the wells, and these scarce water sources became their strongholds, which they barricaded in with canons and machine guns, forcing the free and indomitable horsemen, the sons of the wind, to surrender to the enemy they had faced since the beginning of time:

Thirst.

But the French were not proud of having conquered the veil people, because in reality they had not conquered them through open warfare. Neither their black Senegalese men, nor their lorries or tanks were of much use to them in a desert that was still dominated by the Tuaregs and their meharis, from one end of it to the other.

The Tuareg were few and far between, while the soldiers marched in from the cities or the colonies like clouds of locusts, until eventually the day came when neither a camel, man, woman or child could drink in the Sahara without permission from the French first.

So, the Imohag, tired of watching their families dying, laid down their arms and from that point in history they became a people condemned to oblivion; a "nation" that no longer had any reason to exist since the very essence of their existence - war and freedom - had all but disappeared.

There remained some families here and there, like Gazel's family, lost in the desert's confines, but they were no longer made up of proud, tall, warriors, but men that raged internally in the knowledge that they would never be the feared veil people, masters of the sword or spear again.

The Imohag, however, were still masters of the desert, from the hamada to the erg and up in the high, wind-battered mountains, since the real desert was not made up of the wells found scattered through it, but of the thousands of square kilometers that surrounded them. The French had never dared venture too far away from these water sources, nor did the Senegalese Askaris. Even the Bedouins, who despite their keen knowledge of the sands and stony plains, tended to follow the established routes and moved from one well to another, from village to village, fearful of the large and unknown territories that lay on either side of them.

Only the Tuaregs and more specifically the solitary Tuaregs were fearless enough to take on the "lost lands", which were nothing more than a white smudge on the map. They were places where the intense heat of midday would make your blood boil and where not even the hardiest of shrubs grew. Migratory birds even avoided those lands by flying around them, even if it meant adding thousands of kilometers on to their journeys.

Gazel had only crossed that smudge, the so-called "lost land", twice in his life. The first time as a challenge, when he had wanted to prove that he was a true descendent of the legendary Turki, and the second time, as a man, when he had wanted to prove to himself that he was still made of the same stuff as the Gazel who had risked his life as a young boy.

Gazel was strangely drawn to that inferno of sun and heat, to that desolate and maddening furnace. It was a fascination that had started one night, many years previously when, sitting by the fireside, he had first heard the story of the "great caravan" and its seven hundred men and two thousand camels that were swallowed up by a "white smudge" and never seen again.

It had been on its way to Gao in Tripolo and was considered one of the best caravans ever to have been organised by the rich Haussa merchants, guided by men with the highest knowledge of the desert. It carried with it, on the backs of carefully chosen meharis, a veritable fortune in marble, ebony, gold and precious stones.

One of Gazel's distant grandfathers, who was also his namesake, had been in charge of guarding the caravan's merchandise, and he too, along with all his men had disappeared forever, as if they had never existed, as if it had all been just a dream.

Many men had since set off on many a mad adventure since, in search of clues and in the vain hope that they might recover some of the immense riches that it had been carrying when it disappeared. According to the unwritten law, the person who managed to outwit the sand and discover its hidden treasures would be their rightful owner. But the sand hides its secrets well. Sand alone is capable of swallowing entire cities, fortresses, oases, men and camels in one swift, unexpected and violent gulp. With the help of its ally, the wind, a storm of sand could be whipped up enough to turn anyone unlucky enough to be travelling upon it, into just another dune, amongst the millions of other dunes that stretched endlessly through the erg territories.

Nobody knew how many people had lost their lives in search of that lost and legendary caravan and the old men never tired of begging the young not be so foolish as to go in search of it themselves:

'What the desert claims for itself belongs to the desert,' they would say. 'May Allah save those that try to claim it back.'

Gazel only wanted to uncover the mystery that surrounded it and the reason why so many beasts and so many men had just disappeared without trace. It was only when he had found himself in the heart of a "lost land" that he had finally under-stood. In fact, it had made him realise how easy it would be, not just for seven hundred men, but for seven million human beings to disappear into that flat abyss and how surprising it was that anyone, no matter whom, ever came out alive.

Gazel came out alive twice. But there were not many Imohags like Gazel and so the veil people respected the solitary man, "the 'Hunter," inmouchar, who ruled over territories that no one else would have ever dared to claim dominion over.

They turned up outside his jaima one morning. The old man was on the brink of death and the young boy, who had carried him on his shoulders for the last two days, only managed to stutter a few words before passing out.

He gave orders for the best tent to be prepared for them and instructed his slaves and children to look after them day and night in what became, against all logic, a desperate battle to keep the two visitors alive.

It was a miracle that they had survived at all, not being from any one of the desert tribes and travelling without camels, water or guides. It was especially surprising since they had been caught in the heavy and dense sirocco wind that had whipped across the desert in the days prior to their arrival.

They had been, from what he could understand, wandering aimlessly for about a week between the dunes and stony plains, but he still did not know where they had come from, who they were, or where they were headed. It was as if they had arrived on one of those shooting stars. Gazel visited them morning and night, intrigued by their appearance, which suggested that they were city men, their clothes being quite inadequate for the desert and the incomprehensible phrases that they uttered in their dreams. Theirs was an Arabic that was so pure and educated that the Targui could barely discern a word of it.

Finally, on the third day at dusk, he found the young boy

awake, who immediately asked him how far they were from the border.

Gazel looked at him in surprise:

'Border?' he repeated. 'What border? The desert does not have borders… at least not as far as I know.'

'There must be a border,' the other insisted. 'It has got to be near here somewhere.'

'The French do not need borders,' he pointed out. 'They rule the Sahara from one end of it to the other.'

The stranger lifted himself up slowly on to his elbow and looked at him in surprise.

'The French?' he repeated. 'The French left years ago. We are now independent,' he added. 'The desert is made up of free and independent states. Did you not know that?'

Gazel meditated for a few minutes. Someone at some time had told him of a war that was being fought in the north, one where the Arabs were trying to shake off the yoke of the Rumis, but he had not taken much notice since it was a war that had been going on for as long as his forefathers could remember.

Independence to him meant wandering alone and undisturbed throughout his territory and nobody had bothered to come and tell him that he now belonged to a new country.

He shook his head.

'No. I didn't know that,' he admitted, confused. 'Nor did I know that there was a border. Who could possibly create a border in the desert? Who could stop the wind from blowing sand over it back and forth? Who could stop men from crossing it?'

'Soldiers.'

He looked at him in surprise.

'Soldiers? Not even all the soldiers in the world would be capable of protecting a border in the desert and besides, the soldiers are scared of it.' He smiled gently underneath the veil that hid his face and which he always kept on in the company of strangers.

14

'Only the Imohag are not afraid of the desert. Soldiers are like spilled water here, the sand just swallows them up.'

The young boy tried to say something but the Targui reminded him that he was tired and told him to lie back down on the cushions.

'Don't push yourself too hard,' he begged. 'You are weak. Tomorrow we will speak and maybe your friend will also feel better.' He turned round to look at the old man, and for the first time realised that he was not as old as he had initially thought, despite his thin, white hair and deeply lined face. 'Who is he?' he asked.

The boy hesitated for a moment, then closed his eyes and muttered quietly:

'A scholar. He is researching our most distant ancestors. We were on our way to Dajbadel when our lorry broke down.'

'Dajbadel is very far away...' Gazel remarked, but the boy had already fallen back into a deep sleep. 'Very, very far south. I've never been that far.'

He left the tent quietly and once out in the fresh air he felt a sudden emptiness in his stomach; like a warning that he had never before experienced. There was something about those two, seemingly harmless men that unsettled him. They were not armed nor did they look at all frightening in appearance, but a whiff of fear hung in the air around them and it was this fear that he too felt.

'He is researching our ancestors...' the young boy had said. But the other man's face, with its deep lines of suffering, told a different story and they were certainly not the scars caused from just one week of wandering hungry and thirsty through the desert.

He looked into the descending darkness in search of an answer. His Targui spirit and a thousand ancient desert traditions told him that he had done the right thing by putting a roof over the head of the two travellers, because the notion of hospitality was the first of all the Imohag's unwritten rules. His instinct, however, as a man that was used to being guided by a sixth sense that had saved him from death on many an occasion, told him that he was running a huge risk and that the new arrivals would jeopardise the peace that had cost him so much to achieve.

Laila appeared at his side and his eyes warmed as he felt her sweet presence and beheld the startling beauty of this dark-skinned, adolescent girl-woman. He had made her his wife, against the wishes of the old men, who believed it was wrong for an inmouchar of such noble heritage to make a union with someone from the lowly Akli slave caste.

She sat down beside him and turned to face him with her huge black eyes that were always full of light and hidden reflections and gently said:

'These men bother you don't they?'

'Not them...' he replied thoughtfully.

'But something that hangs around, them like a shadow or a smell.'

'They've come from far away. Anything that comes from far away unsettles you, because my grandmother predicted that you would not die in the desert.' She put out her hand timidly, until it touched his. 'My grandmother is often wrong,' she added.

'When I was born they predicted me a gloomy future and instead I married a noble, almost a prince.'

He smiled gently.

'I remember when you were born. It can't be more than fifteen years ago... Your future had not even begun...'

He was sorry that he had made her feel sad, because he loved her and even though an Imohag was never supposed to express too much affection to a woman, she was the mother of the last of his sons, so he opened up his hand and took hers in it.

'Maybe you are right and the old Khaltoum is wrong,' he mused. 'No one will force me to abandon the desert or die somewhere far away from it.'

They remained in contemplation of the silent night for some time and he felt at peace once again.

It was true that the black lady Khaltoum had predicted the death of her father due to an illness, one year before he contracted it and that she had also predicted the great drought that had dried up the wells and left the desert devoid of shrubs, killing hundreds of animals that had, from time immemorial been accustomed to drought and thirst. It was also true that the slave woman often ranted for the sake of ranting and her visions often seemed more the result of senile dementia, than true visions of the future.

'What is there on the other side of the desert?' Laila asked, breaking their silence. 'I've never been further than the Huaila Mountains.'

'People,' came his reply. 'A lot of people.' Gazel meditated, remembering his experience in El-Akab, the oasis in the north, and he shook his head gloomily. 'They like to settle in crowded and small spaces, in narrow, stinking houses. They shout and remonstrate loudly to each other for no reason, and rob and cheat on each other like animals that only know how to live as a herd.'

'Why...?'

He wanted to be able to explain to Laila why, because her admiration for him filled him with pride, but he was unable to give her an answer. He was an Imohag who had been born and bred in the solitude of the wide, open spaces, so, as hard as he might try, he simply could not understand the herd-like instincts that these men and woman from the other tribes possessed.

Gazel embraced visitors whole heartedly and loved to sit round the fire with them, telling old stories and chatting about the idiosyncrasies of daily life. But once the fire had died and the black camel that carried sleep on its back had crossed the encampment, invisible and silent, everybody would retire to their tents and to their own lives, to breath in deeply and absorb the silence.

Life in the Sahara was peaceful and provided an ideal environment within which to explore the self and the universe. The way of life there lent itself to the slow contemplation of the natural surroundings and the unhurried meditation of the lessons of their sacred scriptures. This kind of peace, of time and space, did not exist in the cities or towns, not even in the tiny Berber villages, which were filled with a general confusion of noise and petty problems. To Gazel, the people in these places who fought and gossiped, seemed strangely more interested in everybody else's business and behaviour than their own.

'I don't know,' he admittedly, reluctantly. 'I have never understood why they like to behave in this way, crowded together, all of them so dependent on each other. I don't know...' he repeated. 'I have never met anyone that could answer that question properly either.'

The girl looked at him for some time, perhaps surprised that this man who was her life and from whom she had learned the value of knowledge, was not able to answer one of her questions. From the minute she had been able to reason, Gazel had meant everything to her. First and foremost he had been her master, as a child of the Akli slave race this meant he was, in her eyes, an almost divine being, the absolute master of her life and her contemporaries; master of her parents' lives, their extended families, their animals and whatever else existed on the face of their universe.

He was also the man that one day, when she had reached puberty and with her first menstruation, had made her into a woman. He had called her into his tent and possessed her, making her cry out in pleasure, like the other slave women before her who she had heard at night when the west wind blew. In the end they became lovers and he had carried her with him, as if on wings, swiftly to paradise and back. He was her master, but more so than ever before, because now not only did he dominate her soul, her thoughts and her desires, but he also owned her most hidden and forgotten instincts.

It took her a while to reply and just as she was about to, she was cut short by the appearance of one her husband's eldest sons who had come running over from one the sheribas situated at the other end of the encampment.

'A camel is about to give birth, father,' he said. 'And the jackals are prowling around…'

His fears were confirmed when, on the following day at noon, he saw a long plume of smoke rising up from the horizon, hanging there, motionless, suspended in the sky, despite the fact that he had not felt a breath of wind cross the plains that day.

The vehicles, which must have been motorized vehicles due to the speed at which they were travelling, cut a trail of dirty smoke and dust through the clean desert air.

Then came the faint rumbling of their engines, that soon turned into a roar, upsetting the wood pigeons, the fennecs and the snakes, followed by the screech of brakes, loud, impatient voices and harsh orders as they stopped in a cloud of dust and dirt, no more than fifteen meters away from the settlement.

Every living creature stopped and turned to look at them. The Targui and his wife, his children, his slaves and even his animals all had their eyes fixed on the cloud of dust and the dark brown, monstrous machines, then the children and beasts drew back terrified and the slaves scurried off into their tents, well out of sight of the strangers.

He approached them slowly, his face covered with the veil that distinguished him as a noble Imohag and that was part of an ancient tradition. He stopped half way between the new arrivals and the largest of his jaimas as if to indicate, without actually saying so, that they were not to advance any further unless they were given permission to do so as his guests.

The first thing he noticed about them was the dirty grey of their uniforms, covered in sweat and dust and the menacing metallic glint of their rifles and machine guns. The smell of their crude, leather boots and belts filled the air. His gaze fell on to a tall man wearing a blue djellaba and a dishevelled turban. He recognised him as the Imohag, Mubarrak-ben-Sad, who belonged to the spear people and was considered to be one of the most skilful and meticulous trackers in the desert, almost as famous in the region as Gazel "the Hunter" himself.

'Metulem, metulem,' he greeted.

'Aselum aleikum,' Mubarrak replied. 'We are looking for two men. Two foreigners.'

'They are my guests,' he replied calmly. 'They are unwell.'

The official who appeared to be in charge of the group moved forward a few steps, his medals shining on the cuff of his sleeve, then tried to walk around the Targui, who moved again to block his path.

'They are my guests,' he repeated.

The other man looked at him in surprise, as if he was unable to understand exactly what he had said and Gazel realised straight away that this man was not from the desert and that his mannerisms and the way he looked belonged to other, distant worlds.

He turned to face Mubarrak who had understood and then turned to face the official again.

'Hospitality is a sacred thing for us,' he pointed out. 'A law that is more ancient than the Koran.'

The military man adorned with medals hesitated for a moment, as if unable to believe the absurdity of what he had just heard, then continued forward.

'I represent the law,' he said sharply. 'There is no other.'

He had started to walk past him again, but Gazel grabbed him by the forearm brusquely, forcing the man to look him in the eyes.

'It is a tradition that is some one thousand years old and you are barely fifty years of age. You will leave my guests in peace!'

Following a signal from of one of the military man, the sound of ten rifle bolts clicking into place suddenly filled the air and the Targui realised that all ten guns were pointing at his chest and that any further resistance would be useless.

The military man pushed the hand that still held him back away roughly and continued on towards the largest tent.

He disappeared inside it and a few seconds later a dry, bitter shot rang through the air. He came out and gestured to the two soldiers that were walking behind him to go back into the tent.

When they reappeared they were holding the old man between them, who was sobbing profusely as if he had been woken up from a long and gentle dream only to be confronted with this harsh reality.

They walked straight past Gazel and got into their vehicles. From the cabin the official stared at him severely and hesitated for an instant. For one moment Gazel feared that the prophecy of Khaltoum had been wrong and that he would be killed there and then in the heart of the desert plains. But the man just nodded to the driver and the lorries drove off in the same direction that they had come from.

Mubarrak, Imohag of the spear people, got into the last vehicle, his eyes fixed on the Targui until he disappeared behind a column of dust. In that brief exchange, however, he had seen enough to know what was going through Gazel's mind and what he had seen in his eyes had scared him.

It was never advisable to humiliate an inmouchar of the veil people. It was not advisable to humiliate him and leave him alive.

But nor would it have been right to have killed him there and then, as it would only have unleashed a war between brother tribes and meant the spilling of more blood, just to avenge the blood of someone who had only tried to respect the ancient laws of the desert.

Gazel remained very still, watching the convoy as it moved further away until the noise and the dust had completely disappeared from view. Then, slowly, he turned away and walked towards the largest jaima, which his children, wife and slaves had all gathered in front of. He did not need to go in, to find out what had happened inside it. The young boy was in the same place that he had left him in after their last exchange, with his eyes shut as if he was still fast asleep, the only difference in his appearance being the small red circle on his forehead. He looked at him sadly and angrily for a long time and then called Suilem over.

'Bury him,' he said. 'And get my camel ready for me.'

For the first time in his life Suilem did not do what his master had ordered him to and an hour later he went into his tent and grabbed his feet, trying to kiss his sandals.

'Do not do it!' he begged. 'You will achieve nothing by it.'

Gazel pulled his foot away in disgust.

'You think I will just allow for such an offence to go unchallenged?' he asked angrily. 'Do you think that I could go on living at peace with myself, having allowed one of my guests to be assassinated and the other taken away?'

'There was nothing else you could have done,' he protested. 'They would have killed you.'

'I know, but now I must avenge the insult.'

'And what will you achieve by doing that?' the black man asked. 'Will that bring the dead man back to life?'

'No. But I will remind them that they cannot offend an Imohag so impertinently. That is the difference between your race and mine, Suilem. The Aklis allow themselves to be offended and oppressed and you are satisfied with your role as slaves, you carry it in your blood, from parents to children, from generation to generation and you will always be slaves.'

He paused and stroked the long saber that he had just taken out of the large chest, where he kept his most precious belongings. 'But we the Tuaregs are a free, warrior race, who has remained that way because we have never given in to humiliation or insult.'

He shook his head. 'And we are not about to change.'

'But there are many of them,' he warned. 'And they are powerful.'

'That is true,' the Targui admitted. 'And that is how it is. It is only a coward who challenges the weaker side and that kind of a victory will never make a nobleman of you. And only a fool fights with his equal because only luck will decide who wins that battle. The Imohag, the real warriors of my race, will always take on someone who is much more powerful than they are because if victory smiles on them, their efforts will be rewarded a thousand times over and they can be proud of what they have achieved and carry on.'

'And if they kill you? What will become of us?'

'If they kill me, my camel and I will make a straight run for paradise as promised to me by Allah, because it is written that whoever dies in a fair battle can be sure of reaching Eternity.'

'But you have not answered my question,' the old slave insisted. 'What will become of us? Of your children, your wife, your livestock and your servants?'

He shrugged fatalistically.

'Was I able to defend you before?' he asked. 'If I could not stop one of my guests from being killed then how can I defend my family against rape and murder?' He lent over and with a firm gesture forced his slave to stand up. 'Go and get my camel ready and my weapons,' he ordered. 'I will leave at dawn. Then, pack up the settlement and take it and my family far away to the Huaila guelta, where my first wife died.'

It was always the wind that heralded the arrival of dawn across the plains, as its nocturnal howling became more of a screeching wail, usually about an hour or so before the first ray of light appeared in the sky, some distance away, near the rocky Huaila mountains.

He listened to it with his eyes wide open, contemplating the familiar striped roof of his jaima and imagined the tumbleweed outside, rolling away across the sand. Those vagrant bushes that were always in a hurry, always looking for somewhere or something to attach themselves to, for a proper home and somewhere that would take them in and free them from their eternal wanderings, from journeys without destiny that took them from one end of Africa to the other.

In the milky light of dawn that was filtered through millions of tiny suspended dust particles, these bushes would appear out of nowhere, like ghosts waiting to pounce on man and beast. Then they would disappear, as discreetly as they had arrived, back into the infinite emptiness of a desert without borders.

'There must be a border somewhere. I am sure,' he had said in a voice that was heavy with anxiety and desperation. Now he was dead.

Nobody had informed Gazel of these borders because there had never been any borders in the Sahara until now.

'How could you stop the sand and wind from crossing a

border?'

He turned his face to the night as if searching for an answer, but found none.

Those men had not been criminals, but they had killed one of them and where they had taken the older man was anybody's guess. It was wrong to kill someone in such cold blood, whatever his crime, even worse when that person was under the protection of an inmouchar.

There was something odd about the whole incident, but Gazel could not quite put his finger on it. One thing, however, remained startlingly clear: that an ancient law of the desert had been broken and that, for an Imohag, was unacceptable.

He remembered the old lady Khaltoum and the fear he had felt emanate from her icy hand as she placed it on the nape of his neck. Then he turned towards Laila's huge open eyes, shining widely in the half light, reflecting the dying embers of the fire and he felt sorry for her and the fifteen paltry years she had barely reached and for the emptiness she would feel at night without him. He also felt sorry for himself and for the emptiness he would feel at night without her by his side.

He stroked her hair and her eyes widened like a startled gazelle in open appreciation of his gesture.

'When will you return?' she asked, almost pleadingly.

He shook his head:

'I don't know,' he admitted. 'When justice has been done.'

'What do these men mean to you?'

'They meant nothing,' he confessed. 'Until yesterday, that is. But it's not about them. It's about me. You would not understand.'

Laila understood, but did not protest further. She just moved closer to him as if trying to absorb as much of his strength and warmth as was physically possible. Then she stretched out her hand in one last effort to keep him back, as he stood up to leave the tent.

Outside, the wind was moaning gently. It was cold and he

wrapped himself up in his djelabba as a shiver ran down his back. This often happened to him and he never knew if it was a reaction to the cold or to the black space that stretched out before him. Entering into that black space was like immersing yourself into a sea of black ink. Suilem came out of the shadows and passed him the reins of "R'Orab."

'Good luck, master,' he said and disappeared back into the shadows.

He made the beast kneel down, climbed up onto his back and tapped him lightly on the neck with his heel:

'Shiaaaa…!' he ordered. 'Lets go!'

The animal let out a bad-tempered bellow, got up slowly and stood still on his four feet, face to the wind, waiting.

The Targui pulled him round to face the northeast and tapped his heel, a little more forcefully this time in order to get them on their way.

At the entrance to the jaima he could just make out a shadow that was darker than all the others around it. It was Laila, her eyes shining once again in the darkness, watching as the wind carried the rider and his mount away like tumbleweed and as they disappeared into the night.

The wind's desperate wailings intensified, in the knowledge that the sun would soon be there to calm its anguish.

Even in that early, milky light, Gazel could only just make out the head of his camel, but he did not need any more guidance than that. He knew that he would not meet with any obstacle for hundreds of kilometers either side of him and that being a man of the desert he was capable of navigating his way through the desert with his eyes closed, even on the darkest of nights.

This was a skill that only he and others born like him, amongst the sands, possessed. Like pigeon carriers, like migratory birds or whales in the deepest oceans, the Tuareg always knew where they were and where they were going, as if an ancient gland that had expired in the rest of the human race still remained active, intact and efficient only in them.

North, south, east and west; springs, oases, roads, mountains, "lost lands", rivers of dunes, rocky plains: the whole, huge Saharan universe was embedded in the depths of Gazel's brain, without him even knowing it, without him ever really being conscious of it.

The sun rose and started to pound down on the mehari's back, moving quickly up to its head and getting stronger by the minute. As the wind died down and the tumbleweed came to rest, the sand settled and the earth recoiled. The lizards came out of their hiding places and the birds came to rest on land, not daring to take to the air as the sun approached its zenith.

The Targui stopped his mount and made him kneel down. He then pushed his long sword and his old rifle into the sand as supports next to the saddle cross and stretched a small piece of thick fabric across them to make a crude shelter from the sun.

He crawled under it, lay his head on the white back of his mehari and went to sleep.

He woke up with his nose twitching, as the most yearned for smell in the desert began to fill his nostrils. He opened his eyes but remained there without moving, breathing in the air, without wanting to look up at the sky, scared that it might be just a dream. When he eventually turned to look east, he saw it there, on the horizon, large, dark, promising and full of life. It was different from the other white ones that appeared from time to time, high up in the sky and that blew in from the north, only to disappear as quickly, without even the slightest hint of rain. All the watery treasures of the universe seemed hidden within that splendid, low, grey cloud. Gazel had not seen one quite so beautiful for some fifteen years, not since the great storm that had raged on the eve of Laila's birth; the storm that had made her grandmother predict a miserable future for her because on that occasion the rain that had been so longed for, fast became a flood that swept up jaimas and animals, destroyed crops and drowned a camel.

"R'Orab" fussed about restlessly. He stretched his neck and lifted his nose up eagerly towards the curtain of rain that was moving towards them, breaking up the light and transforming the landscape. He snorted gently and then purred happily like an enormous cat.

Gazel got up slowly, stripped the saddle, took off his clothes and laid them out carefully on some bushes to ensure that they got as much rain on them as possible. He then took off his shoes and stood upright, waiting as the first raindrops began to spot the sand and the land, marking the face of the desert like an attack of small pox. Then it began to fall in sheets and the pitter-patter of drops turned into the crashing sound of water. His senses were intoxicated as the water caressed his warm body and he tasted the fresh, clean water and smelled the sodden, steamy earth underfoot.

There it was, this marvellous and fertile union and soon, with the afternoon sun, the dormant seed of the acheb plant would burst forth violently, turning the plains green and transforming the arid landscape into one of the most beautiful regions on earth. The plants would flower magnificently, but only for a few days, before sinking back again below the surface into another long sleep, maybe for another fifteen years, until they were woken again by another storm.

The wild acheb, when freed by the rains, was a beautiful flower, but it was impossible to grow it as a crop, even when nurtured by the gentle hand of a peasant and watered every day. The plant was just like the spirit of the Tuaregs and the only other living thing that survived in those stony, sandy regions, in a place that the rest of the human race had long since given up on.

The water soaked his hair, washing months, if not years' worth of dirt off of his body. He scrubbed his nails and found a flat, porous stone to rub himself down with, watching as patches of clean skin started to appear. He stood there as the encrusted earth, sweat and dust washed off him and the water that ran off and over his feet turned blue, almost indigo, as the crude dye from his clothes, that had engrained itself into his skin over time, came off.

He remained like that for two hours under the rain, happy and shivering, battling with his desire to just turn around and head home in order to enjoy the water, plant barley and wait for the harvest. He longed to be able to return and enjoy with his own people this gift of water that the marvellous Allah had sent them, which may well have been a message to him, a warning that he should have remained with his people and ignored the insult. But for Gazel, not even all the rain from that immense cloud could wash away the gravity of such an offence.

Gazel was a Targui, unfortunately for him perhaps and the last of the real Tuareg people of the plains, so for that reason alone his honour would never allow him to forget that a defenceless man had been murdered under his roof and another, his guest, been forcefully removed.

So, once the cloud had moved south and the afternoon sun had dried his body and clothes, he dressed again, mounted his camel and set off on his journey, turning his back on the water and the rain; on life and hope; on something that only a few days ago would have warmed his heart and the hearts of those around him.

When night fell he found a small dune and made a hole in it by pushing aside the still damp sand, then covered himself up with dry sand in the knowledge that dawn would bring a frost to the plains and that the wind would turn the water pools on the rocks and tumbleweed, to ice.

The temperature in the desert can vary by as much as fifty degrees, from its maximum at midday to its minimum just before dawn. Gazel knew from experience that the cold could sink into the bones of the unsuspecting traveller, seizing up his joints and making them so painful that they eventually stopped working.

Three hunters had been found frozen on the stony plains in the Huaila foothills and Gazel could still picture their bodies, pressed close together, joined in death, during that same cold winter when tuberculosis had taken their little Bishra away from them. They had almost appeared to be smiling as the sun had dried their bodies and with the process of dehydration, their skin had taken on a strange, leathery appearance, while their teeth had shone brilliantly.

This was a cruel land, in which man could die of either heat or cold in the space of only a few hours and where a camel might search for water without luck for days, only to drown, unsuspectingly, in a well one morning.

A cruel land, without doubt, but Gazel could not imagine living anywhere else. He would never have swapped the thirst, the heat and the cold of his inhospitable land without frontiers, for the comforts and limitations of other worlds without horizons. During his daily prayers, with his face turned east to Mecca, he would always give thanks to Allah for allowing him to live there and for belonging to the blessed race of the veil, spear and sword men.

As he slept he yearned for Laila and when he awoke the hard body of the woman that had pushed against him in his sleep, became nothing more than the soft sand that now slipped through his fingers.

The wind cried out at the hunting hour.

He looked up at the stars to gauge how long it would be before the light erased them from the firmament. He called out to the night and his mehari, who was drinking from the damp bushes, answered him with a soft bellow. He saddled up and set off once again and by mid afternoon he could just make out in the distance, five dark smudges on the stony plains. It was Mubarrak-ben-Sad's settlement, the Imohag of the spear people, the man who had shown the soldiers the way to his jaima.

He said his prayers and then sat down on a smooth rock in order to think through the events that had altered his destiny so cruelly. As he sat there, lost in his black thoughts, he realised that this was the last night of his life that he would sleep in peace.

The following dawn he would be forced to open the lid on the elgebira of wars, on revenge and hate, and no one could say how much violence it would unleash or how many deaths might follow on from this one act of revenge.

He also tried to understand what on earth had prompted Mubarrak to break with the most sacred of Targui traditions, but he could not. He was a desert guide, a good guide without doubt, but a Targui guide was only supposed to guide caravans, track down prey, or aid the French on their strange expeditions in search of their ancestors' relics. A Targui never had the right, under any circumstances, to enter another Imohag's territory without permission and even less so when he was guiding foreigners, who were themselves ignorant of these ancient traditions.

On that same dawn, when Mubarrak-ben-Sad opened his eyes, a shiver ran down his back as the terror that had consumed him in his sleep now troubled him at the waking hour and he instinctively turned his face towards the entrance of his sheriba, fearful of, but almost resigned to what he would see there.

His fears were confirmed as standing there, some thirty meters away, gripping the hilt of his long takuba that he had thrust into the ground, was Gazel Sayah, noble inmouchar of the Kel-Talgimus, waiting for him, ready to call him to account for his actions.

He picked up his sword and moved forward slowly, proud and dignified, stopping some five paces away from Gazel.

'Metulem, metulem,' he said, using their preferred form greeting.

He did not receive an answer and neither had he expected one.

He did, however, expect the to hear the question:

'Why did you do it?'

'The captain of the military outpost at Adoras made me.'

'Nobody can make a Targui do something against his wishes.'

'I've been working for them for three years now. I could not say no. I am the government's official guide.'

'You swore, as I did, never to work for the French.'

'The French have gone. We are a free country now.'

For the second time in the space of a few days he was hearing the same thing and it suddenly dawned on him that neither the official nor the soldiers had been wearing the colonial uniforms they had previously so despised.

None of them had been European and none of them had spoken with the strong accent he had been used to hearing and their vehicles had not displayed the perennial tricolor flag either.

'The French always respected our traditions,' he said. 'Why are they not being respected now, if, moreover, we are free?'

Mubarrak shrugged his shoulders.

'Times have changed...' he said.

'Not for me,' came his reply. 'Only when the desert becomes an oasis, the water runs freely through the wadis and the rain falls as often as we need it to, will the Tuaregs change their customs. Never before.'

Mubarrak kept his calm as he asked:

'Do you mean to say that you have come here to kill me?'

'I am here for that reason.'

Mubarrak nodded silently, in quiet acceptance of his answer, then glanced around him at the damp earth and the tiny acheb shoots that were already pushing their way up between the rocks and the pebbles.

'The rain was beautiful,' he said.

'Very beautiful.'

'Soon the plains will be covered with flowers and only one of us will be around to see them.'

'You should have thought about that before bringing those strangers to my settlement.'

Under his veil, a faint smile played at the corners of Mubarrak's lips:

'It had not rained then,' he replied and then very slowly he took his tabuka out, freeing the metal blade from its embossed leather sheath.

'I pray that this act does not unleash a war between our tribes,' he said. 'We alone must pay for our mistakes.'

'So be it,' Gazel replied solemnly, then crouched down as if ready to receive the first charge.

But it took a while before either of them made a move, because neither Gazel nor Mubarrak were warriors of the sword or spear any longer, but gunmen. The long tabukas were rarely used in battle any more, but brought out during ceremonies or festivals for dramatic effect rather than to draw blood. During these festivities the noise of the swords smacking against the leather shield and the dodges and feints were just theatrical moves as opposed to genuine acts of combat.

But this time round there were no shields or spectators to admire their twists and turns and the flashing blades were not for the benefit of an audience. On this occasion the opponent was brandishing his sword with the intent to kill, before being killed himself.

How to block a blow without a shield?

How to recover a position having fallen backwards or slipped up, when your rival was waiting to pounce?

They studied each other, trying to work out what each other's intentions were, circling each other, one after the other slowly. Men, women and children had started to come out of their jaimas to observe them in silence and dismay, hardly daring to believe that what they saw was for real and not just a theatrical display.

Mubarrak finally made the first move but it was more to test the water, to see whether this really was about a fight to the death.

The answer made him jump backwards as the blade of his furious enemy missed him by only a few centimetres and his blood turned cold. Gazel Sayah, inmouchar of the terrible Kel-Talgimus, wanted to kill him, that was for sure. There was so much hate and such a huge desire for revenge in that single blow that those unknown people that he had given refuge to might just as well have been his very own children, and he, Mubarrak-ben-Sad might just as well have been the man that had assassinated them.

But Gazel did not really hold true hatred in his heart. Gazel was simply trying to do justice and it would not have been right to hate a Targui who had just been carrying out his work, except that his had been a wrong and unworthy line of work. Gazel knew, moreover, that hate, like anxiety, fear, love or any other deep feelings, were not good companions for a man of the desert. In order to survive in that land you had to nurture a temperament of absolute calm. You had to try and be almost cold blooded and cultivate a sense of total self control in order to rise above any sentiment that might provoke an error of judgement. In the desert, you could pay for such mistakes with your life.

Gazel knew that he was taking on the role of the judge and possibly that of the executioner too, neither of whom had any reason to hate their victim. The strength of his blade and the hate it had seemed to carry within it had been more of a warning and a clear response to the clear question that his opponent had asked him.

He attacked again and realised how inappropriate his long robes, his broad turban and his wide veil were. His djelabba wrapped itself around his legs and arms, his thick-soled nails, their straps made of thin strips of antelope leather, made him slip on the sharp stones and his litham prevented him from being able to see clearly and limited the amount of oxygen that he needed in his lungs at that very moment.

But Mubarrak was dressed in the same way, which meant that his movements were equally restricted.

Their steel blades fanned the air, buzzing furiously, slicing through the quiet of the morning stillness and a toothless old woman let out a chilling scream as she begged someone to shoot the dirty jackal that was trying to kill her son.

Mubarrak held out his hand with authority and nobody moved. The sons of the wind had a code of honour that was quite different to the world outside, where moral codes had already been corrupted by treachery and lies. Theirs were different even to the Bedouins, the sons of the clouds and demanded that a confrontation between two warriors was clean and noble, even though a life would be lost during it.

They had challenged each other face to face and they would kill, face to face. He sought firm ground, breathed deeply, cried out and threw himself towards the breast of his enemy, who pushed the point of his sword away with one hard, clean stroke.

They stood quietly once again, looking at each other. Gazel brandished his tabuka like a club, throwing Mubarrak another two-hander and his sword went twisting through the air like a windmill. Any other apprentice of the sword would have taken advantage of this display and lunged at him at once, but Mubarrak preferred to dodge the blade and remain on guard, more confident of his own strength than his skills. Then, brandishing his weapon with both hands he lunged forward with such force that he could have sliced through the waist of a man much bigger than Gazel, but Gazel was nowhere near the end of his sword. The sun was getting stronger and sweat was starting to run off their bodies and their hands, making it harder to grip the swords' metal handles firmly. They lifted them into the air once again and studied each other intently. Then they threw themselves at each other in unison and Gazel managed to pull himself back from the point of Mubarrak's sword, which had ripped his djelabba and scraped his breast, just at the last moment. Then he, in turn, plunged the sword deep into his opponent's stomach and held it there for a few seconds, as he twisted it further in.

Mubarrak remained upright for a few moments, held up mainly by the sword and Gazel's strength, rather than by his own legs, and when he finally pulled out the sword, tearing his intestines as he did so, he fell flat onto the sand, doubled over in pain, but resolved to suffer the long agony of his fate in silence.

Some moments later, as his executioner walked away slowly, neither happy nor proud, towards his mount that awaited him, the old, toothless lady went into the biggest of the jaimas. She took out a rifle, loaded it, walked up to where her son was doubled up in pain and pointed it at his head.

Mubarrak opened his eyes and in them she saw the infinite gratitude that he felt for her as she prepared to free him from the many long hours of suffering he would otherwise have had to endure, without hope.

Gazel heard the shot echo across the plains as he and the camel continued on their journey, but his gaze remained fixed ahead.

He sensed, before he was able to see them, a herd of antelopes in the distance, and he suddenly become aware of how hungry he was.

He had been so worried about his confrontation with Mubarrak that he had only eaten handfuls of millet flour and dates over the last few days, but now his belly ached for a piece of meat, cooked slowly over a fire.

He approached the edge of the grara slowly, leading his camel by the halter, making sure the wind did not carry his scent over to the beasts that he imagined to be grazing on some patches of stubby vegetation growing there in the hollow, which may have once been a pool or small stream and where there were probably still a few patches of slightly damp earth.

A few diffident tamarisks and half a dozen dwarf acacias sprouted here and there and he saw that his hunter instinct had served him well once again. There below him, grazing or basking in the mid afternoon sun, was a family of beautiful, long-horned, reddish-coloured animals, simply waiting to be preyed upon.

He set up his rifle, only loading one bullet in order to avoid the temptation of making a desperate second attempt, once the agile beasts had already started to flee. Gazel knew from experience that this second shot, which was usually a chance shot, rarely hit its target and was simply a waste, especially when ammunition in the desert was as rare, but as vital to survival as water itself.

He let go of the mehari, who started to graze straight away, oblivious to anything but his food, which was succulent and tasty after the rains. Gazel moved forward silently, almost on all fours, moving swiftly from behind a rock to the twisted trunk of a small bush, then from a small dune to another bush, until finally stopping on a small stone mound, from where he could clearly observe the slender silhouette of a great stag that was grazing in the midst of the herd, some thirty meters away.

'When you kill a stag, a younger member of the herd will soon takes its place and mate with the females,' his father had told him. 'When you kill a female you are also killing her children and their children, who you need to feed your children with and the children of you children.'

He got his weapon ready and carefully aimed it at its front shoulder blade, level with its heart. From that distance a shot to the head would have been much more effective, but Gazel, being a good Muslim, could only eat meat from an animal that had had its throat cut whilst facing Mecca and accompanied by the correct prayers, as laid down by the prophet. To kill an antelope there and then would have meant leaving it to waste, when it was much better to run the risk of the animal fleeing wounded, since it was unlikely to get very far with a bullet in its lungs.

The wind suddenly picked up and the animal lifted his head and sniffed the air anxiously. Then, after what seemed like an eternity, but was probably no more than a few minutes, he glanced round at the herd to check for danger before lowering its head once again to graze on the tamarisk.

Once he was certain that he could not fail and that his prey was not going to jump or move unexpectedly, Gazel pulled back the trigger gently. The bullet sliced through the air with a shrill whistle and the antelope fell to its knees as if its legs had been chopped off, or the ground, as if by magic, had suddenly risen up beneath it.

The females looked up at him but remained unperturbed, because although the shot had reverberated through the air, they did not associate the noise with danger or death and it was only when they saw a man running towards them waving a knife, his robes billowing out on either side of him, that they took flight and scampered back onto the plains, disappearing quickly out of sight.

Gazel went over to the wounded animal that was struggling to stand up and follow his family, but something inside had already snapped and its body was no longer obeying its brain.

Only its enormous and innocent eyes reflected the magnitude of its anguish as the Targui grabbed it by the antlers, pulled its head to face Mecca and slit its throat with a sharp dagger, in one clean movement.

Blood came gushing out, spilling over his sandals and splashing his djelabba, but Gazel was oblivious to it, caught up in the moment and satisfied that his aim had been such an excellent one again, having shot his prey in exactly the right place.

He was still eating as night fell, but asleep before the first stars appeared in the sky, sheltered from the wind under a bush, his back warmed by the fire's dying embers.

The jackals and the mocking call of the hyenas woke him up as they gathered round to claim the dead antelope, so he stoked up the fire until they withdrew back into the shadows. Then he lay there, looking at the sky, listening to the wind as it picked up and meditating on the fact that he had killed a man that day - the first time he had killed a human being in his life - which he knew meant that his own life would never be the same again.

He did not feel guilty about it because he considered his cause to be a just one, but he was concerned that it might unleash a war between the tribes, of the kind that he had heard so much about from his forefathers. A war that could spiral into a senseless massacre, where nobody knew why anyone was killing anyone or indeed what had started it all in the first place. The Tuareg, the few Imohags that remained wandering through the desert's confines, still faithful to their traditions and laws, were simply not in a position to defend themselves from this type of warfare, struggling as they were to protect themselves from the advances of civilisation alone.

He remembered the strange sensation that had passed through his body as the sword had softly entered Mubarrak's stomach and he could still hear the hoarse death rattle that had escaped from the back of his throat at that very same moment. As he had brought his arm back out, it was as if he had been carrying the life of his enemy on the end of his tabuka and he was already scared of having to use his sword against anyone again. He hurriedly reminded himself of the dry crack of the shot that had killed his sleeping guest and consoled himself with the fact that those men had committed an unpardonable crime.

It dawned on him that while injustice was bitter, it was an equally bitter experience having to right that wrong, because he had not taken any pleasure in killing Mubarrak. In fact, it had simply left him with a deeply unpleasant feeling of emptiness afterwards and just as Suilem had warned, his act of revenge had not brought back the dead.

Why, he wondered, was this unwritten law of hospitality that the Tuaregs put before all other laws so important - more important even than the laws of the Koran. He tried to imagine what kind of a place the desert would be if the traveller could not rely on their hospitality, on the help and respect that would be given to them whilst in their care.

According to legend, there were once two men who hated each other so much that one day the weakest of the two turned up at his enemy's jaima, asking for hospitality. In respect of their deep tradition, the Targui accepted his guest and offered him protection until finally, after some months, he tired of looking after him and giving him food and promised him that if he went on his way he would never try to kill him again. That was many years ago, but the Tuaregs have used this same method ever since to resolve their differences and put an end to their quarrels.

How would he have reacted if Mubarrak had come to his settlement to ask for his hospitality and to beg forgiveness?

He would never know the answer to that, but he would probably have behaved as the Targui did in the legend, otherwise he would only have ended up committing a crime in order to punish someone for having committed that very same crime.

As the jet planes roared through the high desert skies and the lorries hurtled along its well-trodden tracks, pushing his people back into the remotest corners of the plains, it was hard to say for how much longer they would manage to resist their relentless advances. What he could say with confidence, however, was that while one of them remained on those sands, even if the rest of the infinite and stony plains were devoid of life and the hamada devoid of its horizons, the laws of hospitality would remain sacred, otherwise no traveller would ever dare to cross the desert again.

Mubarrak's crime was unforgivable and he Gazel Sayah would take it upon himself to make those men that were not of the Tuareg people, aware that in the Sahara the rules of his race must continue to be respected. Those laws and customs had been created to suit an environment that had to be respected. They were intrinsic modes of behaviour that had been created to ensure their survival.

The wind picked up as dawn broke. The hyenas and jackals, having lost all hope of getting even the smallest morsel of the dead antelope, skulked off to their dark habitats, growling at their misfortune, joined by all the other creatures of the night: the long-eared fennecs, the desert rats, snakes, hares and foxes. As the sun started to heat up the land, these creatures would be asleep, conserving their energy until the shadows of the night returned to make their lives bearable once again. It was the law of nature that there, in that most desolate place on the planet, in contrast to the rest of the world, all activity was carried out by night, while the day was for sleeping.

Only man, despite the passage of time, had not managed to completely adapt to this nocturnal existence, and for that reason, at the first sign of light, Gazel found his camel, grazing about one kilometre away, took him by the halter and set off unhurriedly towards the east.

The Adoras military outpost was situated in a triangular oasis made up of about one hundred palm trees and three wells. It sat right in the very middle of a long line of dunes, which made its survival something of a miracle since it was constantly threatened by the shifting sand that surrounded it. But while the sea of dunes sheltered it from the wind, it also meant that, at around midday, it became a burning furnace with temperatures often soaring to sixty degrees.

The three dozen soldiers that made up the garrison spent half of their time under the shadow of the palm trees, cursing their bad luck, and the other half of it shovelling sand in a desperate effort to keep it at bay. They struggled on a daily basis to keep clear a small stretch of road that allowed them to communicate with the outside world and receive provisions and correspondence once every two months.

For the last thirty years, ever since a crazy colonel had become obsessed with the idea that the army should have control of those four wells, which were the only ones around for about one hundred kilometers, Adoras had become the "accursed destiny," both for the colonial troops then and for the natives there now. Of the tombs lined up on the edge of the palm grove, nine of them were due to "death by natural causes," while another six were due to suicides committed by men who simply could not bear the idea of living in that inferno for another day.

When a tribunal was unsure as to whether they should condemn an offender to the firing squad, life imprisonment or commute his sentence to fifteen years of compulsory service in Adoras, it was quite aware that all three punishments were of equal measure, even if the offender was under some illusion that by having his sentence commuted and being sent to Adoras, he was being let off lightly.

Captain Kaleb-el-Fasi was commander in chief of the garrison and supreme authority over a region that was as large as half of Italy, but where only a little over eight hundred people lived. He had been there for seven years as punishment for having killed a young lieutenant who had threatened to expose irregularities in the regiment's accounts at his previous posting. Condemned to death, his uncle, the famous General Obeid-el-Fasi, the independence hero who Kaleb had worked for as an assistant and confident during the War of Liberation, managed to get him a rehabilitation posting to a place that no other person in the military would ever have been sent, unless of course, their predicament had been similarly precarious.

Three years previously Capitain Kaleb, using only the files that had been made available to him, had worked out that in his regiment, twenty of the men were guilty of murder, fifteen of rape, sixty of armed robbery and countless others of theft, fraud, desertion and petty crime. These statistics, he had quickly realised, meant that he would have to draw on every drop of his experience and employ every ounce of shrewdness and brute force that he possessed in order to stay on top.

The respect he inspired was second only to the fear that the men there felt for his right-hand man, Sergeant Malik-el-Haideri. He was a thin, small man who looked weak and ill, but who was so cruel, shrewd and brave that he had managed to control that gang of beasts and survived five attempts on his life and two knife fights. Malik was, more often than not, behind the deaths labelled "natural causes," while two of the men who had committed suicide, had blown their brains out just to get away from him.

Now, seated on the peak of the highest dune that looked over the eastern side of the oasis, which was more than one hundred meters high and gilded with age, its core hard, the sand inside it having almost turned to stone, Sergeant Malik watched his men disinterestedly as they shovelled sand off the smaller dunes, which were threatening to engulf the furthest of the wells. Through his binoculars his eyes suddenly came to rest on a solitary rider who had just appeared on a white mehari and who seemed to be approaching the post, in no apparent hurry. He wondered what a Targui was doing in that godforsaken place since they had stopped using the Adoras wells about six years ago and had not made any contact with them since. The Bedouin caravans arrived less and less frequently and when they did, they would make a watering hole, rest for a few days on the furthest side of the oasis, keeping their women hidden and ensuring that they had absolutely no contact with the soldiers there. Then they would get on their way quickly, relieved that there had not been any trouble during their stay. But the Tuaregs were different. When the Tuaregs stopped to use the wells they would walk around with their heads held high, almost defiantly, allowing their woman to walk around freely, their faces uncovered and their legs and arms exposed to the air, despite the fact that the men living there had not enjoyed a woman for many years. They were also quick to reach for their rifles or sharp, curved daggers if anyone dared to cross them.

But after two warriors and three soldiers died once during a brawl, the sons of the wind had preferred to put a distance between themselves and the military post. But this solitary rider was coming resolutely towards them, approaching the last crest, silhouetted against the afternoon sun and his clothes billowing in the wind. Finally, he entered the palm grove and stopped next to the northern well, some one hundred meters from the first of the camp's huts.

He slid down the dune unhurriedly, crossed the camp and went over to the Targui who was giving water to his camel, this animal that was capable of drinking one hundred litres of water in one sitting alone.

'Aselam, aleikum!'

'Metulem, metulem,' Gazel replied.

'That is a fine beast you have there. And very thirsty.'

'We've come a long way.'

'Where from?'

'From the north.'

Sergeant Malik-el-Haideri hated the Targui veil because he took pride in being able to judge from a man's expression whether or not he was lying. This was never possible with a Targui as you could only see their eyes and they were only ever partially exposed and usually became smaller whenever they began to talk. Their voices were also distorted by it, which meant that he no choice but to believe him, since he had seen him arrive from the north and had no reason to suspect that Gazel would have made a huge diversion in order to make it appear that he was coming from any other direction.

'Where are you going?'

'South.'

He left his camel sprawled out, his belly full to bursting with water, satisfied and bloated, and started collecting wood with which to make himself a small fire.

'You can eat with the soldiers,' he told him.

Gazel pulled back a piece of cloth revealing the still succulent antelope, covered in dry blood.

'You can eat with me if you want. In exchange for your water.'

Sergeant Malik's stomach cried out. It had been more than fifteen days since the hunters had caught any prey. Over the years the animals had moved away from the surrounding area and there was not one true Bedouin among them, so their knowledge of the desert and its inhabitants was very limited.

'The water is for everyone,' he replied. 'But I would very much like to take you up on your offer. Where did you catch it?'

Gazel laughed inwardly at the clumsiness of his deception.

'In the north,' he replied.

He had gathered all the wood he now needed and taking a seat on the saddle blanket, he took out some flint and a wick, but Malik offered him some matches.

'Use these,' he said. 'They're easier.'

Once the fire was lit, he refused to take them back.

'Keep them. We've got lots more in the store.'

He sat down opposite him and watched as he hooked the antelope's legs over the ramrod of his rifle and prepared it for a slow roast over a gentle fire.

'Are you looking for work in the south?'

'I'm looking for a caravan.'

'Caravans don't pass by here much at this time of year. The last one came through about a month ago.'

'Mine awaits me,' came his enigmatic reply. The sergeant stared at him blankly.

'It has been waiting for me for over fifty years,' he added.

'The "great caravan?"' he finally exclaimed. 'You're in search of the legendary "great caravan?" Are you mad?'

'It's not a legend. My uncle was in it and I am not mad. But my cousin Suleiman, who spends his miserable days lugging bricks back and forth, he is, however, mad.'

'Nobody comes back alive when they go off in search of that caravan.'

Gazel gestured with his head to the stone graves that could just be made out between a few palm trees at the end of the oasis.

'They are no more dead than they are over there. And if they'd found it they'd be rich forever.'

'But these "lost lands" are unforgiving: there's no water or vegetation for your camel to eat, shade for shelter or any point of reference to help guide you. It's hell!'

'I know,' the Targui conceded. 'I've crossed one twice'

'You've crossed a "lost land?"' he repeated, aghast.

'Twice.'

Sergeant Malik did not need to see his face to realise that he was telling the truth and this piece of news suddenly roused his interest. He had spent long enough in the Sahara to know the value of a man who had been to a "lost land" and returned. He could count on his hands how many he had met, from Morocco to Egypt, and even Mubarrak-ben-Sad, the outpost's official guide, whom he regarded as one of the greatest masters of the desert and the stony plains, had once admitted that he would not dare to go there.

'But I do know of one man. I met him during a long expedition we went on to explore the Huaila. An inmouchar of the Kel-Talgimus, who crossed one and returned. How do you feel when you are in there?'

Gazel looked at him for some time then shrugged his shoulders:

'You feel nothing. You have to leave sentiment behind you. You have to rid yourself of all ideas and live like a stone, careful not to make any movement that uses up water. Even at night you have to move slowly, like a chameleon and then, once you have become desensitized to the heat and thirst and above all once you have overcome panic and found calm, only then do you have the remotest chance of survival.'

'Why did you do it? Were you in search of the "great caravan?"'

'No. I was looking to find something of my ancestors within me. They conquered the "lost lands."'

The other man shook his head in disbelief.

'Nobody has conquered the "lost lands,"' he said, shaking his head emphatically. 'Proof of which lies in the fact that all of your descendents are dead and those areas remains as hostile as when

Allah first created them.' He paused and shook his head again and then asked, more to himself than to his listener: 'Why would you do that? Why did He, who was so capable of creating such wonderful things, also create the desert?'

His reply was not arrogant, even though it might have been interpreted that way.

'In order to create the Imohag.'

Malik smiled in amusement.

'Is that right,' he said.

He pointed to the antelope's leg.

'I don't like my meat too well cooked,' he said. 'It's fine like that.'

Moving the ramrod away, Gazel took two pieces of meat, offered him a piece and then, using his very sharp dagger, began to shave thick slices of meat off of the other piece.

'If ever you are in difficulty,' he pointed out, 'don't cook the meat. Eat it raw. Eat any animal you can find and drink its blood. But don't move, above all don't ever move.'

'I'll bear that in mind,' the sergeant said. 'I'll bear that in mind but pray to Allah that I never find myself in that predicament.'

They finished their meal in silence then drank some fresh water from the well. Malik got up and stretched satisfactorily.

'I've got to go,' he said. 'I've got to take over from the captain and check that everything's in order. How long will you be staying for?'

Gazel shrugged his shoulders.

'I understand. Stay as long as you like, but don't come anywhere near the huts. The guards are under instruction to shoot to kill.'

'Why?'

Sergeant Malik-el-Haideri smiled enigmatically and nodded his head towards the wooden shack that was furthest away.

'The captain does not have many friends,' he said matter-of-factly. 'Neither of us do, but I know how to look out for myself.'

He got up and left just as the night began to descend on the oasis, slowly enveloping the palm grove. He could hear the sound of the soldiers' voices as they returned. The came straggling in with their spades over their shoulders, tired, sweaty and desperate for food and a straw bed that would carry them away for a few hours to a world of dreams and away from the living hell that was Adoras.

Twilight made a brief appearance as the sky turned seamlessly from red to black and the carbide lights in the cabins started to flicker in the darkness.

Only the captain's living quarters had shutters on the windows to stop anyone from seeing inside and as darkness descended, a sentry turned up to stand guard, some twenty metres from his door, gun at the ready.

Half an hour later the door opened and he could make out the silhouette of a tall, strong man. Gazel did not need to see the stars on his uniform to know that he was the man who had killed his guest. He watched him as he stood there for a few minutes, breathing in the night air deeply and then as he lit a cigarette. The match lit up the man's features and Gazel was reminded of the steely, contemptuous look he had given him, whilst insisting that he represented the law. He was tempted to finish him off with just one shot, there and then. From such a short distance, so clearly silhouetted against the light coming from the shack, he could have put a bullet in his head and put out the cigarette at the same time, but he decided not to. He just remained there watching him, some one hundred meters away, trying to imagine what the man would do if he knew that the Targui, whom he had offended and spurned, was sitting there in front of him. That he was there, leaning against a palm tree next to the dying embers of a fire, contemplating whether to kill him there and then, or at a later date.

These men who had been plucked out of the city and transplanted to the desert would never learn to love it, in fact they would always loathe it and long to escape from it, whatever the price. The Tuaregs were to them just another part of that hostile landscape and they were incapable of telling one man from another, as incapable as they were of differentiating between one long saber crest, sif dune and another, even if there was half a day's walk between the two of them.

They had no concept of time and space there, no notion of the desert's smells and colours and no ability to distinguish between a warrior of the veil people, or an Imohag of the spear people, an inmouchar from a servant, or a true Targui woman, strong and free, from a poor Bedouin harem slave.

He could have gone up to him and chatted for half an hour about the night and the stars, the winds and the gazelles and the captain would not have recognised that "accursed, stinking man, dressed in rags" who had tried to block his path only five days ago. The French had tried for years, in vain, to get the Tuaregs people to remove their veils. After realising that they would never abandon their veils and that it was impossible to tell one from the other by the sound of their voice and their gestures alone, they had given up on trying to distinguish between them at all.

Neither Malik, nor the officer, nor the men shovelling sand were French, but they still resembled them in their ignorance and contempt for the desert and its inhabitants.

When the captain had finished his cigarette he threw the butt in the sand, half-heartedly saluted his sentry, then closed his door, sliding a heavy bolt across it from the inside. The lights went off one after the other and silence hung over the camp and the oasis; a silence broken only occasionally by the rustle of the palm trees in the light breeze or the call of a hungry jackal.

Gazel wrapped himself up in his blanket, rested his head on his saddle, looked around him one last time at the huts and the line of vehicles parked up underneath a canvas make-shift garage, then fell asleep.

Dawn found him at the top of the highest and most heavily laden palm tree, throwing down heavy bunches of mature dates. He stuffed his sack with them, filled up his gerbas with water and then saddled up his mehari, who protested loudly, preferring to remain in the shade, near the well.

The soldiers had started to appear, urinating against the dunes and washing their faces in a water trough next to the biggest of the wells. Sergeant Malik-el-Haideri came out of his quarters and walked over towards him, his stride quick and confident.

'Are you going?' he asked, even though his question was, to all intents and purposes, pointless. 'I thought you wanted to rest for a few days.'

'I am not tired.'

'I can see that. And I'm sorry that is the case. It's good to talk with a stranger, this bunch of losers don't think about anything other than stealing or women.'

Gazel did not reply, being too busy securing the saddlebags so that they would not fall off with the swinging motion of the camel some five hundred meters into their journey and Malik gave him a hand on the other side of the animal, as he asked:

'If the captain gave me permission, would you take me with you in your search for the "great caravan?"'

The Targui shook his head:

'The "lost lands" are no place for a man like you. Only the Imohag can go there.'

'I could bring three camels with me. We would be able to take more water and provisions with us. There's enough money in that caravan. I could give some to the captain and with the rest I'd buy my transfer out of here and I'd still have enough to survive on for the rest of my life. Take me with you!'

'No.'

Sergeant Malik did not insist but looked over at the palm trees, the huts and the sand dunes, that enclosed them on all four sides. The dunes that imprisoned the outpost were like the bars on a cell, forever threatening to bury them alive.

'Eleven years more of this!' he grumbled to himself. 'If I manage to survive that long, I'll be an old man, and they'll still have taken away my right to retirement and a pension. Where will I go?'

He turned to the Targui once again. 'Would it not be better to die with some dignity in the desert, in the belief that a bit of luck might change everything?'

'Maybe.'

'It's what you're trying to do isn't it? You'd rather risk your life than spend the rest of it lugging bricks back and forth?'

'I am a Targui, you are not...'

'Oh go to hell with your stupid racial pride!' he protested angrily. 'You think you are superior just because you've put up with the heat and the thirst since you were a child. I've had to put up with this bunch of wasters here but I'm not sure who is worse. Go then! When I want to look for the "great caravan" I'll do so alone. I don't need you.'

Gazel smiled behind his veil, but not so the other man could see, encouraged his camel to stand up and went off slowly, leading him by the halter.

Sergeant Malik-el-Haideri watched him disappear into the labyrinth of narrow passages that wound through the dunes, south of their make-shift road, then turned away and, pensive, headed over to the biggest of the huts.

Captain Kaleb-el-Fasi always slept in until the sun began to scorch the tin roof of his cabin which, having been built it in the shadiest part of the palm grove, was usually around nine-o'clock in the morning. Unless that was, he had already been woken up by the clattering noise of dates falling onto the roof's metal slats.

He would say his prayers then plunge into the trough of the largest well, which was about two metres away from his door. It was there that Sergeant Malik usually briefed him on the day ahead and informed him of what was going on at the outpost, which was invariably very little.

But that morning his subordinate was a little chattier than usual, buoyed by an enthusiasm that was quite unlike him.

'That Targui is going in search of the "great caravan,"' he said.

The captain looked at him as if he was waiting for him to say something else, then asked:

'And...?'

'I asked him to take me with him, but he didn't want to.'

'He's not as crazy as I thought then. Since when have you been interested in the "great caravan" anyway?'

'Ever since I heard about it. They say that it carried merchandise worth about ten million francs in those days. These days the ivory and jewels it was rumoured to be carrying would be worth triple that.'

'A lot of people have died going in search of it.'

'They were just a bunch of opportunists who failed to take a scientific approach to the organisation of an expedition of this kind and simply did not have the appropriate equipment or the logistical back up to make it.'

Capitain Kaleb-el-Fasi looked at him long and hard as if he were about to severely reprimand him.

'Are you trying to suggest that we should use army equipment and our men to search for this caravan?' he asked in mock surprise.

'Why not?' came his sincere reply. 'They're always sending us on senseless expeditions in search of new wells, worthless stones or to study the tribes. On one occasion a bunch of engineers had us wandering around in search of petrol for six months.'

'And you found it.'

'Yes, but how did it benefit us? It was exhausting and exasperating; the troops suffered from ill-health and three men were blown to pieces in a jeep loaded with dynamite.'

'They were orders from the top.'

'I know but you have the authority to send me on any mission you want; survival exercises, for example, in the "lost lands." Imagine if we came back with a fortune! Half for the army, half for us and the troops. Don't you think that if it was well distributed, it might even soften up a few generals?'

His superior did not respond for a moment, ducking his head underwater where he remained for a few seconds, as if reflecting on the proposal, then came up and said, without looking at him:

'We could be locked up for what you're proposing.'

'And what difference would that make? Being banged up here or inside a cell. It's just a bit hotter here that's all. But less so than the in "lost lands" maybe.'

'Are you that desperate?'

'No more than you are. If we don't do something we'll never get out of here and you know it. One of these days these bastards will get the "cafard" and turn on us.'

'We haven't done a bad job at keeping them under control so far.'

'Yeah, with a lot of luck,' the well-built man admitted. 'But when is our luck going to start running out? We'll be old men soon, we won't have the energy any more and they'll just walk all over us.'

Captain Kaleb-el-Fasi, commander-in-chief of the lost military outpost at Adoras, or the "Devil's Ass", as they called it in the army, tilted his head back and contemplated the palm trees that were completely still in the absence of any breeze and the blue, almost white sky that hurt his eyes just to look at it.

He thought of his family; of his wife who had petitioned for divorce and got it because of his conviction; of his sons who had never written to him; of his friends and companions who had erased him from their memory, despite having sung his praises for many years. Then his thoughts drifted to the circle of robbers, murderers and drug addicts who all hated him to death and who would gladly stick a bayonet in his back or a grenade under his bed

'What do you need?' he said without turning round, trying to make his voice sound completely uninterested.

'A lorry, a jeep and five men. I'll take Mubarrak-ben-Sad as well, the Targui guide and I'll need camels.'

'How long will it take?'

'Four months. But we'll be in radio contact every week.'

This time he turned to look at him.

'You cannot force anyone to go with you. If you don't come back they'll have my head.'

'I know who'll come with me willingly and who won't blabber. It's best that the ones that stay behind don't know anything.'

The captain got slowly out of the water, slipped into some short, wide-legged trousers, put on his nails and let the hot air dry his body, shaking his head sceptically:

'I think you're as mad as that Targui,' he said. 'But maybe it's preferable to sticking around here and waiting to die.'

He paused then said: 'We'll have to come up with a reasonable argument for such a long trip,' he said smiling, then added: 'In case you don't come back.'

Malik grinned triumphantly, although he had always known that he would win him over. Ever since the Targui had disappeared from view, very early that morning amongst the dunes, he had been working out how best he could present his plan and the more he had thought about it, the more convinced he had become that he would get permission to do it.

They walked off together towards the orderly room, then with a slight smile, he said:

'I'd already thought about that.' The other man stopped to look at him.

'Slaves.'

'Slaves?'

'The Targui that left this morning might easily have brought us news of the slave trade and a caravan heading our way and in to our territory. Slave trafficking is increasing at an alarming rate again.'

'I know, but they are mainly headed for the Red Sea or to countries where they are still allowed in.'

'That's true,' Malik replied. 'But what's to stop us from trying to verify a report that we can later claim was just a false alarm?' his said, breaking into an ironic smile. 'Surely they'd just commend us for our conscientious nature and spirit of sacrifice.'

They walked over to the office, which was just a wide room with two tables in it and already stiflingly hot, even though it was still early. The captain went straight over to a large-scale map of the area that covered the entire back wall.

'I always wondered how you got yourself sent to this hole in the first place, you being as smart as you are. Where will you start the search?'

Malik pointed straight to a huge yellow patch with a white space in the middle of it that was devoid of any paths, camel tracks, wells, or settlements.

'Here, right in the middle of Tikdabra. The caravan should logically have avoided Tikdabra by going north and bypassing it. But if they took a wrong turn, and went into the dunes they would have found themselves in this bit of the "lost lands," and it would already have been too late by then to turn back. They would have had no choice other than to try and reach the Muley-el-Akbar wells, but they never made it.'

'That's just one theory. It could have been there as much as anywhere else.'

'Maybe. But they aren't in any other part,' he pointed out. 'The whole of the Tikdabra area has been thoroughly searched. To the east and west of it. But no one has ever dared to search Tikdabra itself. Or at least those who've tried, never came back.'

The captain estimated the size in a glance:

"Over fifteen hundred square kilometers of dunes and stony ground. You'd have as much chance of finding a white flea in a herd of meharis.'

His reply was concise:

'I've got eleven years to look for it.'

The captain sat down on an old chair made out of gazelle leather, rummaged around for a cigarette and then lit it slowly, concentrating his attention on the map that had been hanging there since he had first arrived at Adoras and that he knew like the back of his hand. He knew the desert well and what it meant to go into an erg like Tikdabra, which consisted of an uninterrupted line of very high dunes that went on and on like a sea of giant waves. It was a lethal trap full of quick sand where men and camels could suddenly find themselves buried chest deep. The dunes were like towers that appeared to surround, by way of protection, an immense plain without horizons. This terrain was as flat as the flattest of tables, onto which the sun beat down relentlessly, making it difficult to see or breathe and boiling the blood of men and animals alike.

'Not even a lizard could survive there,' he said eventually. 'Whoever decides to go with you is already restless enough, so you'll be doing me a favour by getting them off my back.' He opened the small safe that was fixed to the floor, hidden under some floorboards under the table. He counted the money in there and shook his head. 'You'll have to requisition some camels from the Bedouin people,' he said. 'I haven't got enough money to buy any more and you can't take ours with you.'

'Mubarrak will help me get hold of some.' He walked towards the door. 'With your permission, I'll go and talk to my men.'

He nodded in response to his salute, closed the box up again and sat there very still, his feet on the table, contemplating the map. He smiled, pleased that he had decided to accept the proposal. If it all went to worms, he would lose six men, a Targui guide and two vehicles. But nobody was going to give him a hard time for something that in those latitudes was, up to a point, fairly normal behaviour. There were a lot of patrols that just disappeared, maybe due to a guide's mistake, a vehicle breaking down or an axle snapping, which turned routine journeys into unavoidable tragedies. This fact was actually taken into account when the dregs of the country's prisons and camps were sent over to Adoras, the truth being that these men were not expected to return to civilization, because Society itself did not want them in its midst any longer. Once they were out there, nobody really cared if they stabbed each other to death, died of fevers, or got lost on routine patrols, or indeed, disappeared in search of a mythical treasure.

"The great caravan" was out there somewhere towards the south, everyone was agreed on that and it could not have just disappeared completely. The most valuable part of the merchandise was also sure to be intact still, despite the years gone by, or centuries even. With just a tiny piece of that cargo,

Captain Kaleb-el-Fasi could leave Adoras for good and move back to France, to Cannes and to the 'Hotel Majestic' where he had spent some of the best times of his life. A place where he had enjoyed the company of a beautiful shop assistant who worked in a boutique on Rue Antibes and who he had promised to return to one day, although that was many years ago now.

In the afternoons they would open up the huge windows that overlooked the swimming pool at La Croisette and the beach and make love facing the sea until it got dark. Then they would amble down to have supper at Le Moulin de Mougens, El Oasis, or Chez Félix, ending up in the casino to risk everything they had on a number eight.

He was paying a high price now for those days, too high, he thought. It was not the desert that really got to him, or the heat and the monotony, but the memories that haunted him and the painful knowledge that if one day he did get out of Adoras, he would be too old to enjoy all those things again - the hotels, the restaurants or the girls in Cannes.

He stayed there for a while lost in his memories, letting the sweat run off his body as the intense heat turned the camp into a raging inferno. He was waiting for his batman to arrive with the tray of greasy and repulsive couscous that he ate every day without ever feeling hungry. This was his daily diet, along with a few gulps of warm, slightly salty, cloudy water that still gave him diarrhoea, despite the fact he had been drinking it for many years.

Then, when the sun's rays started to pound down relentlessly and became so suffocating that not even a mosquito dared take to the air, he crossed the empty palm grove slowly and sought refuge once again in his hut, leaving the doors and windows wide open to ensure that he did not miss out on even the slightest whisper of a breeze outside.

It was the gaila hour, the sacred siesta hour in the desert, when for four hours during the day's most intense heat, man and beast alike would lie still in the shade so as not to become dehydrated or knocked out by sunstroke.

The soldiers were already asleep in their huts and only the sentry remained standing upright, protected by the shade of a lean-to. He struggled, as he squinted into the glaring light, often unsuccessfully, to keep his eyes open just enough to stop him from falling asleep.

An hour later and the Adoras military post was deadly quiet, as if it had been deserted. The hand on the thermometer in the shade (since it would have probably exploded in the sun), was dangerously close to fifty degrees centigrade and the plumes at the top of the palm trees were so still in the absence of any wind that you might not think they were real at all, but paintings, pencilled into the sky.

Their mouths wide open and their faces covered in sweat, exhausted and broken, like lifeless dolls, the men snored in their beds, crushed by the heat, incapable of even brushing off the mosquitoes that landed on their tongues in search of moisture. Somebody shouted in his sleep, or rather cried out as if in pain. One of the corporals woke up with a start, his eyes dilated with fear, having dreamt that he was suffocating.

A skeletal black man who was wide awake in the corner of the room watched him until he calmed down and went back to sleep again. His mind was racing with thoughts, as it had done since the moment the sergeant had told him in confidence that they would be setting off, in a few days time, on a crazy adventure to the most inhospitable place on earth in search of a lost caravan.

They would probably not come back alive, but that was surely better than shovelling sand day in and day out, until eventually they were shovelling sand over his dead body.

Captain Kaleb-el-Fasi was also asleep and snoring gently in his hut, dreaming of the lost caravan and its treasures. So deep was his sleep that he did not stir when a tall shadow crossed the threshold. A man slipped into the room without a sound, went over to his bed, leaned an old, heavy rifle up against the wall - a souvenir from when the Senussi had risen up against the French and the Italians - and placed a long, sharp dagger very carefully just under his chin.

Gazel Sayah sat down on the edge of the straw mattress and pressing the weapon against him, clapped his hand firmly across the mouth of the sleeping man.

The captain's right hand shot out automatically towards the revolver that he always kept on the floor next to the bed head, but the Targui pushed it gently away with his foot, whilst leaning still closer into him.

He whispered hoarsely:

'You make a sound and I'll slit your throat.'

He waited until he could tell from the man's eyes that he had understood and then very slowly he allowed him some air, without taking any pressure off the knife. A trickle of blood ran down the terrified captain's neck, mixing with the sweat that was dripping off his chest.

'Do you know who I am?'

He nodded.

'Why did you kill my guest?'

He swallowed, finally managing to whisper an answer:

'They were orders. Very strict orders. The young boy had to die. But not the other one.'

'Why?'

'I don't know.'

He pushed the tip of the knife in further.

'Why?' the Targui asked again.

'I don't know, I promise you,' he almost sobbed. 'I get an order and I have to obey. I have no choice.'

'Who gave you that order?'

'The governor of the province.'

'What's his name?'

'Hassan-ben-Koufra.'

'Where does he live?'

'In El-Akab.'

'And the other one... the older man? Where is he?'

'How should I know? They took him away, that's all I know.'

'Why?'

Captain Kaleb-el-Fasi did not answer. Maybe he realised that he had already said too much; maybe he was tired of the game; maybe he really did not know the answer. He was also desperately trying to work out how he could get away from the intruder, who clearly meant business and what the hell, he wondered, were his men doing and why were they not coming to his rescue.

The Targui was getting impatient. He pressed down harder on the knife and with his left hand he gripped his throat tightly, stopping a cry of pain that was trying to escape.

'Who is that old man?' he insisted. 'Why did they take him away?'

'He is Abdul-el-Kebir,'

he said in a tone of voice that insinuated that was all he should need to know. Then he realised that the name meant nothing to the intruder, who was still waiting for further clarification.

'You don't know who Abdul-el-Kebir is?'

'I've never heard of him.'

'He's a murderer. A filthy murderer and you're risking your life for him.'

'He was my guest.'

'That doesn't stop him from being a murderer.'

'Him being a murderer does not stop him from being my guest. Only I had the right to judge that.'

Then with a flick of his wrist he slashed the captain's jugular with one clean movement.

He observed the brief agony of his victim, cleaned his hands on the dirty sheet, picked up the revolver and the rifle and made his way to the door.

The sentry was asleep, in exactly the same position as before and there was still no sign of life or any breeze that might disturb the stillness of the deserted palm grove. He slipped away, moving deftly from tree to tree, then climbed up on to one of the dunes with practised agility and disappeared, as if he had been swallowed up by the sand.

It was late afternoon when the captain's batman found the body.

His shouts, verging on the hysterical, rang through the oasis, prompting the men to drop their shovels and go running over to the small shack, but the sergeant major shoved them all firmly back as they all tried to crowd into the hut.

When he was finally alone with the body, lying now in a fly-infested pool of blood, he sat down on the stool and cursed his bad luck. The son of a bitch could have waited four more days.

He was not at all sorry; nor did he feel the slightest bit of compassion for that son of a bitch, the biggest bastard of them all, lying in front of him, despite the fact that they had shared many years in that hellish place together. He also had been the only one with whom he could ever have a vaguely intelligible conversation with from time to time. Still, he did not doubt that Captain Kaleb-el-Fasi deserved to die, be it there or anywhere else, but he wished to hell that the timing had been better.

Now they would send in a new commandant, who would be neither better nor worse, just different. It would be years before he would know him well enough to take advantage of his weak points and learn to manage him in the same way that he had managed the one that now lay dead in front of him.

He was also worried about the complex process they would have to go through with the investigating commission, because even he did not have the remotest idea who, out of the bunch of murderers that stood some five meters from the door outside, talking excitedly to each other, was guilty this time.

They would all be suspects, including him, he quickly realised, since he would have much the same motives as any of the others: to get rid of the man that had made the lives of anyone under his command unbearable.

He had to find out who the murderer was before anyone turned up and hand it over as a closed case in order to avoid any further trouble.

He closed his eyes and mentally went through the faces of all his men, in search of a suspect, but finished the exercise totally disheartened.

He could dismiss about a dozen of them as possibly innocent. The rest of them, he realised, would all have taken great pleasure in slitting his commandant's throat.

'Mulay!' he screeched.

A broad, very tall, sour-faced man came in immediately and stood there, pale and shaken, almost trembling, in the doorway.

'At your orders sergeant,' he stuttered.

'You were on duty weren't you?'

'Yes, sergeant.'

'And you didn't see anyone?'

'I think I must have fallen asleep at some point, sergeant,' the giant of a man said, almost sobbing. 'Who would think such a thing could happen in broad daylight...?'

'Obviously not you. You'll probably be up before the firing squad for this. Even if you're not guilty of it, you're responsible for it.'

The other man gulped and his breathing became laboured as he put his hands out in front of him beseechingly:

'But it wasn't me sergeant. Why would I do it? In four days time we were off in search of that caravan.'

'If you mention that caravan again I'll personally arrange for you to be shot. I'll deny ever having spoken to you about it. It'll be your word against mine.'

'I understand sergeant,' Mulay said apologetically. 'I'll never mention it again.'

'I just wanted you to know that I was one of the few people that wanted him alive.'

Sergeant Major Malik-el-Haideri got up, took the dead man's packet of cigarettes from the table and lit one with his heavy silver lighter that he then slid nonchalantly into his own pocket.

'I understand,' he admitted. 'I understand very well, but you were also on guard and that means that it was your job to shoot at anyone who came near this hut. Bastard! Whoever did this I'll skin him alive!'

He glanced back at the body, went outside and stopped in the shade of the porch where he scanned all the faces of those present. Everyone was there.

'Listen to me and listen well!' he growled. 'We have to sort this out between us, unless we want a load of officials coming in to make our lives even more unbearable. Mulay was on guard, but I don't think it was him.'

'The rest of you, I suppose, were all asleep. Who wasn't in the hut and why?'

The soldiers looked at each other suspiciously, aware that the situation was pretty serious and that it might lead to an investigating commission being called in. Finally a petty officer spoke up timidly:

'I don't remember anyone being missing, sergeant. The heat was unbearable. It would have been very odd if anyone had stayed outside.'

There was a murmur of mutual agreement.

The sergeant meditated for a few moments.

'Who went to the bathroom?'

Three men put their hands up.

'I wasn't even two minutes,' one of them protested. 'He saw me and I saw him.'

He turned to look at the third man.

'And you, who saw you?'

The skinny black man came up from the back.

'Me. He went over to the dunes and then came straight back. I also saw the other two... I couldn't sleep and I can tell you for sure, sergeant, that nobody left the hut for longer than three minutes. The only one that wasn't here was Mulay,' he paused for a minute and then added casually: 'And you of course.'

The sergeant major shifted about uncomfortably and for a split second seemed to lose his composure as a cold trickle of sweat ran down his back. He turned to Mulay, who was standing quietly next to the door and gave him a withering look.

'So if it wasn't any of you lot and there's nobody around for at least a one hundred kilometre radius, it looks like you're going to have to...' He stopped suddenly, then starting praising the skies jubilantly as a thought suddenly flashed across his mind:

'The Targui! Well I'll be damned...! The Targui! Officer!'

'Yes, sergeant,'

'What was that you were telling me about something to do with a Targui not wanting you to enter his settlement? Can you remember what he was like?'

The officer shrugged his shoulders doubtfully:

'All the Tuareg people look the same when they wear that veil, sergeant.'

'But could it have been the one that stayed here yesterday?'

It was the skeletal black man that answered.

'It could have been him sergeant. I was also there. He was tall, thin with a blue, sleeveless djelabba over a white one and a small bag or charm made of red leather round his neck.'

The sergeant gestured for him to stop right there as he breathed a huge sigh of relief.

'It's him, without a doubt,' he said. That son of a bitch had the balls to come in here and slit the captain's throat right under our very noses. Officer! Lock Mulay up! If he escapes I'll have you shot. Then radio through to the capital. Ali!'

'At your orders, sergeant!' the black man replied.

'Get all the vehicles ready to go... We'll need maximum supplies of water, petrol and provisions. We'll catch that bastard even if he's hiding in that hellhole out there.'

Half an hour later, the Adoras military posting was buzzing with activity, the likes of which had not been seen since its first opened or at least not since the large caravans from the south had stopped going there.

He did not stop walking for the entire night, guiding his mount by the reins to the light of a half moon and thousands of stars that meant he could just make out the profile of the dunes and the sinuous contours of the paths that wound between them. He followed the gassis, tracks formed by capricious winds, which often, without warning, would suddenly disappear, forcing them to struggle back up on to the soft sand of a dune. As they climbed back up they would stumble and fall in the loose sand, the mehari snorting and pulling at the reins, in protest of their uncomfortable journey at a time when, by rights, it should have been resting or grazing peacefully on the plains.

They would only rest for a few minutes at a time, until they finally reached the erg, which suddenly opened up before them, infinite and flat, without horizon. The empty terrain was made up of black stones, cracked by the sun and a coarse sand, almost like gravel that the winds did not disturb apart from when they blew furiously during one of the big storms.

Gazel knew that from that point on he would no longer see any bushes, or grara, not even a dried up river bed, all the things you would see so frequently in the hamada. The monotonous terrain would be broken up only by the odd depression in the ground, caused by a salt pan with deep sides, in a landscape where a rider and his mount would stand out like a sore thumb.

But Gazel also knew that no other camel could compete with

his mehari on that terrain, with its thousands of pointy, sharp rocks, some of which were as high as half a meter, making it impossible for any type of motorized vehicle to drive through it.

And unless he was very much mistaken, the soldiers, when they came in search of him, would come in jeeps and vans and not being desert people they were neither used to long journeys, nor to swaying from side to side on a camel for days on end.

By dawn he was already far away from the dunes, which were now just a vague and winding line on the horizon and he guessed that the soldiers would just be setting off. It would take them at least two hours on the road that they had opened through the sand before they would reach the plains, some way to the west from his current position and even if one of the vehicles went straight for the erg, it would still not reach the edges of it until late morning, when the sun would already be high in the sky.

This, he calculated, gave him some breathing space, so he got down from the camel, lit a small fire and cooked the scant remains of the antelope that had already started to rot and said his morning prayers, his face to Mecca, towards the east, the direction from which his enemies would arrive. After having eaten heartily, he covered up the remains of the fire and grabbing the reins of his mount, started off on his journey once again, the sun already beating down on his back.

He headed due west, moving further away from Adoras and the land he was familiar with. His destination was El-Akab, which was north, but Gazel was a Targui, a man of the desert, so time, the hours, the days, even the months, were of little importance to him. He knew where El-Akab was and that it had been there for hundreds of years and would still be there long after he and even his grandchildren had been forgotten. He would have time to retrace his steps once the impatient soldiers got tired of looking for him.

'Right now they are furious,' he said out loud.

'But in a month they will have forgotten that I ever even existed.'

As midday approached he stopped and made the mehari kneel down into a small dip. He surrounded it with stones, stuck his rifle and sword into it and stretched a blanket over them to create some shade that was so essential at that time of day. Then he curled up underneath it and a minute later was fast asleep and invisible to anyone that was more than two hundred meters away.

He woke up with the sun hitting his face at an angle as it disappeared beneath the horizon. He peered out between the rocks and saw a small column of dust rising into the sky. It was coming from a vehicle that was making its way slowly to the edges of the plain, crawling along tentatively, as if afraid to lose the protection of the dunes and enter into the inhospitable immensity of the erg.

Sergeant Major Malik stopped the vehicle, switched off his radio and took in the never-ending plain before him slowly. It was as if some giant hand had planted thousands of sharp, black, pointed rocks all over it. Rocks that were capable of ripping a tyre to shreds or even blowing up a crankshaft if one was careless enough.

'I bet that son of a bitch is out there somewhere,' he said, lighting a cigarette nonchalantly. He then held out his hand without looking round and Ali, the black man gave him the microphone.

'Officer!' he called. 'Can you hear me?'

A very distant voice answered: 'I can hear you sergeant. Have you found anything?'

'Nothing. And you?'

'Not a trace.'

'Have you made contact with Almarik?'

'A while ago sergeant. He hasn't seen anything either. I've sent him in search of Mubarrak. He should hopefully arrive at his settlement tonight. He's going to call me at seven.'

'Alright,' he replied. 'Call me once you've made contact with him. Over and out.'

He put the microphone back, stood up on his seat, picked up his binoculars and searched the stony plains once again. He then jumped out of his car bad-temperedly and urinated with his back to the men, who took the opportunity to do the same.

'I'd have gone into that hell hole if I were him,' he muttered out loud. 'It's much quicker in there and he can travel through the night as well, while our vehicles would just fall apart.' He zipped up his fly, picked up his cigarette that he had left on the bonnet of the jeep and dragged hard. 'If we just had some idea where he was headed...'

'Maybe he's headed home,' Ali suggested. 'But that's the opposite direction, towards the southeast.'

'Home!' he growled sarcastically. 'Since when have these bastard sons of the wind ever had a home? The first thing they do at the remotest sign of danger is move their settlement and relocate their families to an even more remote spot, thousands of miles away.'

'No,' he shook his head resolutely. 'This Targui's home is wherever his camel is, which could be anywhere from the Atlantic coast to the Red Sea. That is the advantage he has over us: he doesn't need anything, or anybody.'

'What are we going to do then?'

He looked at the sinking sun and the sky that was stained with red and shook his head despondently.

'We won't do anything right now,' he said.

'Set up camp and make the evening meal. A man on guard at all times and if he falls asleep I'll shoot him there and then. Is that clear?'

He did not wait for a reply. He took a map out of the glove compartment, spread it out on the car and studied it carefully. He knew he could not trust it. The dunes shifted constantly, paths disappeared underneath the sand, the wells closed up and he also knew, from his own experience, that whoever had drawn up the map had never actually been into the erg itself, but drawn the lines using a bit of guess work and could easily have been a few hundred kilometers out. At the time of reckoning those one hundred kilometers could mean the difference between life and death, especially if your jeep had broken down and you were forced to continue on foot.

For a fleeting moment he was tempted to pack it all in and order a return to the outpost, because at the end of the day the captain had deserved his end. Had he not met the Targui he might have done just that and sent in a report, case closed. But he had been personally offended by the Targui, ridiculed even. He had been used by a shabby son of the wind who had purposefully deceived him and who must have been laughing under his filthy djelabba all the while they had spoken together about that crazy lost caravan and its treasures.

He had even helped him tie up the camel's load, ensuring he had sufficient water and that he was well set up for a long journey, when in reality all he was planning to do was hide behind a dune for a while and return that very same day. He peered over at the endless plains once again, which had become a grey smudge, stretching out before him. 'If I catch you,' he muttered to himself, 'I'll skin you alive, I swear.'

He said his afternoon prayers, threw a small leather bag that contained a handful of dates over his shoulder and munching on them slowly, took off once again. He continued to head west, accompanied only by the shadows that emerged as night fell, well aware that if he were to walk all night, at an average speed, he could put a crucial distance in between his pursuers and him.

The camel, having drunk enough water and rested sufficiently, was full and strong, his hump rounded and shiny, which meant that he had enough reserves to keep going for a week at that pace. A beast like that could lose up to one hundred kilos in weight before it would start to feel uncomfortable.

Gazel was used to going out on long hunting treks, so this journey was not unlike any other outing for him, when he would go in search of a wounded animal or a beautiful herd of animals on the move. He liked it out there, alone in the desert, it was the life he truly loved and although he would think of his family from time to time and at night, or when heat of the afternoon pressed down on him and he would miss Laila. He also knew that he could overcome that emotion for as long as it was necessary or for as long as it took to fulfil the task he had set himself, which in this case was to avenge the insult that had been laid upon him.

He was happy when the moon came out later to light the way and at midnight he could make out in the distance the silver reflection of a sebhka, a huge saltpan that, as he got closer, opened up before him like a petrified sea, without end.

He started to head north, edging round it and making sure to keep a certain distance because on the marshy, muddy shores of those lakes, billions of mosquitoes would gather in large clouds during the afternoons or at dawn, blocking out the sun and making it impossible for man or beast to get anywhere near the saltpan. Gazel had seen camels go crazy with pain from the mosquitoes as they attacked their eyes and mouths and he had watched as they ran off, shaking off their load and their riders, never to be seen again.

You could only approach the sebhkas during the day, when the sun was high enough to fry the wings of any mosquito that dared take to the air. At this time of day they just disappeared, as if they had never existed, as if this terrible punishment that Allah had sent down to the desert people, who had already been punished a thousand times over, had simply been a figment of their imagination.

Gazel had not been to that particular salt lake, but he had

heard other travellers talk about it and he could see nothing remarkable about it, except perhaps in terms of its size, from all the others that he had come across in his lifetime.

Many, many years ago when the sea, that is now the Sahara, withdrew, it left behind it pools like this one, which later dried up, slowly creating layers of salt, sometimes several meters thick in their centre. When it rained, an underground stream of saltpetrous water would feed into them, turning the banks into damp, spongy, sand mounds that the sun's harsh rays would dry into a hard crust, like a piece of bread, fresh from the oven. These crusts were treacherous and could cave in at any time underfoot, throwing the victim into a quagmire that looked like half-melted butter, then slowly swallowing him up. They were even more dangerous than the "fesh-hesh" sand, a type of quicksand that rider and camel could fall into and disappear, in a matter of seconds

The unpredictable "fesh-fesh" scared Gazel because there was never any warning, although at least, Gazel reflected, they finished off their victims quickly. By contrast, the moving sand found at the edges of the saltpans would ensnare its prisoners like flies in honey, drowning them slowly, with no means of escape, in the most agonising way imaginable.

Bearing these dangers in mind, he advanced slowly north, circling the white and seemingly edgeless area, conscious that this was another barrier between him and his pursuers that nature had provided them with, as the lake would be sure to swallow up any vehicle that dared to enter it.

'Mubarrak is dead. That bastard killed him with his sword. Almarik said it was a clean duel and that the Sal would not initiate a tribal war because of it. They consider it a closed chapter.'

'Unfortunately we cannot do the same. Keep your eyes peeled until you receive further orders.'

'Roger, sergeant. Over and out.'

Malik turned to the black man.

'We need to speak with the Tidiken outpost. Get me Lieutenant Razman. Tell me when you get through.'

He walked off into the night, contemplating the stars and the moon and the high dunes that threw out long, golden shadows behind them. He realised that despite the fact that the days ahead of him would be incredibly tough, he was happy to be there, on the edge of the erg, in pursuit of a man who knew the desert intimately and who would play a hard game of cat and mouse with them. But he was on the trail of someone and this alone made him feel alive again. He felt active and young, just as he had been in the days when he would lie in wait at the edges of the Kasbah for French officials to pass by, only to stick a knife in their belly and run away, back into the quarter's myriad of windy alleyways; or when he had thrown a bomb into a café in the European quarter, on the day that they had declared open warfare, certain that victory was within their grasp.

That had been a wonderful life, full and exciting, so different from the monotony of life in the barracks after independence, and so different to the horror of his exile in Adoras and his useless, eternal struggle against the invading sands.

'I want to catch that dirty Targui,' he said. 'And I want him alive so that I can rip off his veil and see his face and make him realise that I'll be the one to have the last laugh.'

He had spent a whole night tossing and turning on the hard straw mattress, dreaming about accompanying him to the "Lost Land" in search of the "great caravan," imagining the adventures they would have together. He had been excited by the prospect of spending time with a Targui and by the things he could have taught a man like him, a Targui who had crossed the "lost land" not once, but twice. In that one night the Targui had become his friend, he had given him hope of a future once again and then in the space of just a few hours, that very same man had dashed his dreams twice over, refusing to take him with him, then slitting the throat of his captain who he had just convinced to let him go.

No. That son of wind was going to pay for it with his life.

'Sergeant! The lieutenant's on the line.'

He ran over.

'Lieutenant Razman?'

'Yes, sergeant. Have you caught the Targui yet?'

'Not yet, lieutenant. But I think he's crossing the erg south of Tidiken... If you send in your men they could cut him short before he gets to the Sidi-el-Madia mountains..."

There was a silence. Then the lieutenant's voice finally came through, his tone cautious.

'But that's about two hundred kilometers from here, sergeant...'

'I know,' he admitted. 'But if he gets into the Sidi-el-Madia then we've lost him for sure. Not all the armies in the world could catch him there. It's a labyrinth.'

Lieutenant Razman thought for a minute before replying. He despised Sergeant Malik as much as he had despised Captain Kaleb-el-Fasi, whose death he had celebrated. In fact he disliked anyone who ended up at Adoras, they were the dregs of an army that he wanted to be an honourable and upstanding unit and that scumbag Malik had no place in it, not even to keep that godforsaken outpost up and running.

If a Targui had been brave enough to go into that hellhole, kill a captain and disappear into thin air, then deep down he was on his side, whatever the reason behind his actions. But he also realised that the honour of the army was at stake and if he refused to help and the Targui escaped, the sergeant would make sure in his report that he was the one that took the blame for it before his superiors.

In two years time he would be promoted to captain making him the highest authority in the region. If he managed to capture the murderer of an official –however much of a scumbag he might have been in real life- his promotion might well be fast-tracked. He sighed and nodded his head as if the other man could see him.

'Alright, sergeant,' he said finally. 'We'll leave at dawn. Over and out.'

He put the microphone down onto the table, switched it off and sat there very still, contemplating the transmitter as if it might provide him with the answer to his questions.

Souad's voice brought him back to reality.

'You don't like this mission do you?' she asked from the kitchen, barely lifting her head up.

'No, not really,' he admitted. 'I didn't set out to be a policeman, or to pursue a man through the desert just because he did something that, according to his laws, was the right thing to do.'

'That is no longer the law and you know it,' she said pointedly, sitting down at the other end of the long table. 'We are a modern and independent country and we are all now equal. What would become of us if we all went about according to our own rules? The country would be ungovernable. How can you reconcile the customs of the people from the coast or from the mountains with those of the Bedouins or the Tuareg from the desert? You have to start with a clean slate in order for a common legislation to be set down or we go to the dogs. Do you not see that?'

'Yes, if you've studied in a military academy like I did or in a French university as you did.' He paused to take down a curved pipe from the dozen or so that were hanging from a wooden shelf and started to fill it up calmly. 'But I doubt that someone who has spent their entire life in the furthest confines of the desert would understand that, unless we'd bothered to go and tell him that the situation had changed. Do we have the right to make him accept, overnight, that his way of life, the lives of his parents and their ancestors for over two thousand years are no longer valid? And why? What have we given them in exchange?'

'Freedom.'

'Is freedom the right to force your way into someone's house, kill their guest and take the other one away?' he said in a tone of astonishment. 'You're talking about the kind of freedom you might hear a student on campus discussing in a bar, not the kind a man who has always considered himself to be free anyway might think about it. He doesn't care whether it's the French in government, the fascists or the communists in power... Even Colonel Duperey, who despite being a "colonist" would have had much more respect for the Targui's traditions than that pig Captain Kaleb has, despite everything he did during the fight for independence.'

'You can't use Kaleb as an example. He was a loser.'

'But it's these types of wasters that they send in to deal with the purest people of our race, people who we should be protecting as living proof of the best examples of our history and our people. Now it's the likes of Kaleb and Malik and the governor Ben-Koufra that rule the desert, compared with the French, who always put their best officials in charge here.'

'Not everyone was like Colonel Duperey and you know that. Have you forgotten the Foreign Legion and its murderers? They also wreaked havoc with the tribes, decimating many of them, stealing their wells and their pastures and pushing them out onto the stony plains.'

Lieutenant Razman lit his pipe, glanced over to the kitchen and remarked:

'You're burning the meat. No...' he said and then added: 'I haven't forgotten the brutality of the Legion. But it seems to me that they were only behaving like that because they were locked in a war with the rebel tribes and wouldn't stop until they dominated them. It was their mission and they achieved it in the same way that tomorrow I will do my job and catch that Targui because he has rebelled against the established authority, whatever that might mean.' He paused and watched her as she took the meat out of the oven and put it on to two plates, which she brought over to the table. 'What's the difference then? During the war we behaved like the colonists, but in peaceful times we are incapable of imitating their behaviour.'

'You do though,' Souad said gently, her voice brimming with love. 'You make an effort to help them and to understand the Bedouins. You worry about their problems, you even give them your own money.' She shook her head incredulously. 'How much do they owe you and when will they pay it back? I haven't seen any of your pay for months, even though we thought we'd be able to save some while we were here.' He went to say something, but she stopped him short with her hand and continued: 'No. I'm not complaining. I am happy with what we have. I just want you to realise that it's not your job to figure out all of these problems. You're only the lieutenant of an outpost that doesn't even show up on the map. Relax and when you're governor of a territory like Colonel Duperey was and an intimate friend of the President of the Republic, then maybe you can do something.'

'I doubt there'll be anything left to protect by then,' he replied, chewing slowly on the meat, which was hard and leathery, having come from an old camel that had been sacrificed before it died naturally. 'And we will have annihilated, in just one generation of being an independent nation everything that has been around for centuries. How will history judge us then? What will our grandchildren say when they see how we used our freedom?' He went to say something else, but a discreet knock at the door interrupted him and he turned to face it. 'Come in!' he called out. Silhouetted in the doorway was the imposing figure of Sergeant Ajamuk, who stood to attention, his hand on his turban. 'At your command lieutenant!' he saluted. 'Good evening ma'am,' he added respectfully.

'Nothing to report from the post. Did you have an order?'

'Yes, but come in please,' the lieutenant said.

'We leave at dawn for the south. Nine men, in three vehicles. I'll go in front and you remain in charge here. Get everything ready please.'

'How long will you be away for?'

'Five days, a week at the most. Sergeant Malik thinks that the Targui is crossing the erg and heading towards Sidi-el-Madia.' He noticed that the other man's expression had changed into a grimace. 'I don't like it either, but it's our job.'

Sergeant Ajamuk knew his place but he also knew Lieutenant Razman well and that his opinion would be heard. 'With all due respect, sir,' he said. 'We really shouldn't get involved with that riffraff from Adoras or for that matter, their problems.'

'They are part of the army, Ajamuk,' he pointed out, 'whether we like it or not. Please sit down! Won't you have a sweet?'

'Thank you, but I don't want to put you out...'

Souad had already gone into the kitchen with the plates, their food only half-finished since the meat had been virtually inedible and returned with a tray of homemade sweetmeats that made the eyes of their guest widen in appreciation.

'Go for it sergeant!' she laughed. 'Try them. They only came out of the oven two hours ago.'

His hand shot out towards them as if they had a life of their own.

'Please forgive me ma'am,' Ajamuk said. 'My wife never manages to get them quite like this, however much she tries.' He dug his enormous and incredibly white teeth into the almond paste and munched on it, savouring it carefully. With his mouth still full he added: 'With your permission lieutenant, I think you should let me come with you. I know the area better than anyone else.'

'Someone's got to remain in charge here.'

'Mohamed can be trusted with that. And his wife can work with the radio.' He paused to swallow. 'Nothing much is going to happen here.'

The lieutenant thought about it while Souad served them some hot, sweet aromatic tea. He liked the sergeant, he enjoyed his company and he knew that of all his men he was probably the only one who would be able to catch the fugitive. Maybe that was why, almost unconsciously, he had wanted to leave him behind, because deep down he was still on the Targui's side. They looked at each other over the rims of their teacups and it was as if they had read each other's thoughts.

'If anyone has to catch him then it's much better that it's us rather than Malik. As soon as he's got him he'll shoot him there and then to settle the issue and make sure no one else gets involved.'

'Do you think so too? That's what I was afraid of.'

'Do you think he has a brighter future then if we hand him over to the governor?

He did not receive a reply, so continued: 'Captain Kaleb would not have dared to kill that man unless he'd had Ben-Koufra's backing. What I find strange is that orders weren't given to kill Abdul-el Kebir as well.' He turned to his wife who was giving him a stern, worried look from the kitchen and he sighed as if the subject matter suddenly tired him.

'Ok!' he muttered. 'It's not our problem. Alright...' he finally said. 'You come with me. Wake me up at four o'clock.'

Sergeant Ajamuk sprang up from his chair, stood to attention barely managing to hide his glee and walked towards the door. 'Thank you lieutenant! Goodnight ma'am and thank you for the sweetmeats.'

He went out closing the door behind him. Lieutenant Razman followed him out a few minutes later and sat on the porch staring into the night and the infinite desert that stretched out before him, as far as the eye could see.

Souad came out to see him and they remained there together, in silence, enjoying the clean, fresh air after the insufferable heat of the day.

She spoke finally:

'I don't think you should worry. The desert is a big place. It's quite unlikely that you'll find him.'

'If I do find him, maybe they'll promote me,' Razman said, without looking at her. 'Did that cross your mind?'

'Yes, it crossed my mind,' she admitted casually.

'And?'

'Sooner or later you'll get a promotion and it's better that you achieve that for something you're proud of rather than by playing the police dog. I'm not in a hurry, are you?'

'I'd like to give you a better life.'

'What's the point of an extra star and an increase in salary when you never wear a uniform and you give most of your salary away? You'll just end up lending more money.'

'They might send me elsewhere. We could go back to the city. To our world.'

She chuckled as if amused by his comment.

'Oh come on Razman. Who are you trying to kid. This is your world and you know it. You'd stay here whatever level they promote you to. And I'll stay here with you.'

He turned round to look at her and smiled.

'You know what?' he said. 'I'd like to make love like we did the other day...in the dunes.'

She disappeared into the house and reappeared with a rug in her arms.

The sun was already high in the sky by the time he had reached the edge of the salt lake and the ground was getting hotter, forcing the mosquitoes to seek refuge under the stones and bushes.

He stopped and looked across at the white expanse that glistened like a mirror some twenty meters below his feet. The white of the salt threw the harsh light back aggressively and even though he was accustomed to the blinding light of the desert sands, this was a different kind of glare that hurt his eyes and forced him to squint as it almost burnt his pupils.

He looked for a big stone and threw it in using both hands and waited as it sunk to the bottom. As he had expected the stone broke up the crust that had been dried by the sun on impact and almost immediately afterwards a creamy, brown liquid filled up the hole.

He carried on throwing stones onto it, each time a little further away, until they started to bounce off the surface without piercing it. He then leaned over the bank carefully and looked for areas that might be damp. He stayed there studying the edge of the saltpan meticulously for some time, trying to work out which bit would be the safest to climb down on to.

Once he was totally sure that he had chosen the correct spot, he made the camel get down on to its knees, put three handfuls of barley in front of him, set up camp and went straight to sleep.

Four hours later, as the sun began its timid descent, he opened his eyes as if an alarm clock had gone off suddenly at his side.

A few minutes later he was up and standing firmly on the camel's back, surveying the desert behind him. This time he did not make out any column of smoke rising into the air, but he knew that the heavy gravel in the erg would remain undisturbed as the vehicles struggled slowly through that rocky terrain.

He stayed there watching patiently and his patience was rewarded as soon enough he saw a sun's ray reflected off a metal object that was, he calculated, still very far away. He guessed it would take them about six hours to reach his current location.

He jumped down and took the animal's halter, despite his grunts of protest and led him to the edge of the saltpan, where they climbed down very carefully, step by step, paying attention so as not to fall, but also watching every stone and slab of rock with caution, because he knew that hidden underneath them were thousands of scorpion nests.

He let out a sigh of relief as he reached the bottom, then stopped and studied the crust that was some four meters away from him. He went over to it and tested it with his foot. It seemed hard enough so he let the halter out as much as possible, tying the end of it round his wrist, aware that if he were to sink, the camel would pull him to safety.

He felt the first mosquito bite his ankle. The heat was diminishing with the setting sun and soon the place would become unbearable.

He started to walk on it and the salt crust creaked under his weight as bits and pieces sunk beneath him, but it held from giving way completely.

The mehari followed him obediently, but after four meters it smelt danger and stopped indecisively, bellowing angrily, clearly reluctant to cross the never-ending expanse of salt that lay before them, with not a bush in sight.

'Come on you stupid creature!' he growled.

'Don't stop here!'

The animal bellowed once more, but a sharp tug and a few curses soon had it moving again. They walked for another ten meters and the animal seemed to calm down as the crust hardened and they were firm of foot once again.

They carried on walking slowly, always towards the setting sun. When night fell he mounted the camel, aware that he would not stray from their route now. He fell asleep there, curled up on the high seat, swaying around like a ship on a stormy sea, but as safe and happy as he would have been were he asleep under the ceiling of his jaima, next to Laila.

It was the quietest of nights. The wind did not howl, the camel's padded feet made no sound as they stepped across the salt flat and there were no hyenas or jackals howling for their prey to break the silence out there in the middle of the sebhka. The moon rose, full, bright and clean, making the endless plain sparkle with a million silvery mirrors, as the mehari and its rider glided over it, like an unreal and ghostly apparition that would appear out of nowhere only to disappear back into the night again. There was surely not another human being more alone in the world at that moment than the Targui, whose image, crossing the saltpan in the thick of night, was one of utter solitude.

'There he is!'

He held out his binoculars to Sergeant Ajamuk who lifted them in the direction that he was pointing and adjusted their vision in order to make out the rider, who was advancing slowly under a strong morning sun.

'Yes,' he admitted. 'He's there alright, but I think he's seen us. He's stopped and he's looking over here.'

Lieutenant Razman took the binoculars and peered through the shimmering haze of the saltpan at Gazel Sayah, who was looking across at them on the edge of the sebkha. He was aware that the falcon eyes of a Targui, accustomed to taking in long distances, could see as a far as a normal man could with the help of binoculars.

They looked at each other and even though he could only make out the silhouette of the beast and its rider, shimmering in the haze, he would have loved to have known what he was thinking at that moment, as it dawned on him that he had been caught in the middle of a salt trap from which there was no escape.

'This was much easier than we'd expected,' he commented.

'We haven't got him yet…' Ajamuk pointed out.

He turned round to face him.

'What do you mean?'

'Exactly what I said,' the sergeant replied casually. 'We can't take our vehicles down onto the saltpan. Even if we found a way to get down, we'd sink into the salt. And we'll never catch him on foot.'

Lieutenant Razman realised he had a point, stretched out his hand and grabbed the radiotelephone's microphone.

'Sergeant!' he shouted. 'Sergeant Malik! Can you hear me?' The apparatus crackled and screeched until finally the voice of Malik-el-Haideri came through loud and clear.

'I can hear you, lieutenant.'

'We're on the west side of the sebkha and we've located the fugitive. He's coming towards us, but unfortunately I think he's seen us.'

He could almost hear the sergeant cursing the news silently and after a pause he said:

'I can't go on any further. I've found a way to get down but the saltpan won't take the weight of the jeep.'

'I don't think there's anything we can do but wait at the edge until he's dying of thirst and is forced to give himself up.'

'Give himself up…?' his voice was a mixture of surprise and disbelief. 'A Targui who has killed two men will never give himself up.' Ajamuk nodded his head in agreement. 'He might stay there and die but he'll never hand himself in.'

'Maybe...' he admitted. 'But we clearly can't go after him. We'll wait.'

'You're in charge, lieutenant!'

'Stay in radio contact. Over and out!'

He flicked the switched off and turned to Ajamuk

'What's wrong with you?' he muttered. 'Do you suggest we just go down there and run after a Targui just so he can play games with us and take a few pot shots...?' He paused and then turned to one of his soldiers.

'Make me a white flag,' he said.

'You're not going to try and negotiate with him?' said Ajamuk in a tone of surprise. 'What will you achieve by doing that?' He shrugged his shoulders: 'I don't know. But I'm going to do everything in my power to avoid any further bloodshed.'

'Let me go,' the sergeant begged. 'I'm not a Targui, but I was born here and I know the area well.'

He shook his head decisively. 'I'm the highest authority south of Sidi-el-Madia,' he said. 'Maybe he'll listen to me.'

He picked up the spade by the handle, to which the soldier had attached a dirty handkerchief, removed his gun and started to climb carefully down the dangerous bank.

'If anything happens to me, you're in charge,' he stressed. 'Malik must not assume that position under any circumstances. Is that clear?'

'Don't worry.'

Lurching forward unsteadily, the lieutenant stumbled down the bank precariously, almost throwing himself into the abyss at one point, before finally reaching the bottom. He looked across nervously at the thin, salt crust and aware that his men were watching him, took a deep breath and started walking towards the distant silhouette of the rider, praying to the heavens that the ground would not open up beneath him.

Once he felt a bit safer he held up the rather pitiful flag in

front of him as he walked. The sun started to beat down relentlessly and he soon realised that within the confines of the saltpan,
where there was not even a hint of a breeze, the temperature was
probably another five degrees higher and it started to scorch his
lungs with each new breath.

He watched as the Targui made his camel kneel down and
how he remained upright at its side with his rifle at the ready.
Half way there he suddenly regretted his decision as the sweat
ran off every part of his body, soaking through his uniform and
his legs threatened to give way beneath him.

That last kilometre was without doubt the longest kilometre of
his life and when he had got within ten meters of Gazel, he
stopped in order to regain his strength and composure before
asking:

'Have you got any water?' The other man shook his head, his
rifle still pointing directly at Razman's chest:

'I need it. You can drink when you go back.'

He nodded his head and ran his tongue over his lips that only
tasted of the salt from his sweat

'You're right,' he admitted. 'I'm an idiot for not bringing my
water bottle. How do you cope with this heat?'

'I'm used to it... Have you come here to talk about the
weather?'

'No, I've come to ask you to give yourself up. You cannot
escape!'

'Only Allah will decide that. The desert is a big place.'

'But the saltpan isn't. My men have you surrounded.' He
looked over at the nearly empty gerba hanging around the
animal's neck. 'You haven't much water left. You won't last long
in here...' He paused. 'If you come with me I promise you a fair
trial.'

'Why should I be put on trial,' Gazel said casually. 'I killed
Mubarrak in a duel, in accordance with the rules of our race and
I killed the military man because he was a murderer who had

failed to respect the sacred rules of hospitality. According to the Tuareg laws I have not committed any crime.'

'Why are you running away then...?'

'Because I know that neither the Rumi infidels or yourselves, who have adopted their absurd rules, will respect mine, despite the fact that we meet in the desert. To you I'm just a dirty son of the wind who has killed one of your own men, not an inmouchar of the Kel-Talgimus, who only acted according to a law that has been in place for thousands of years; many years before you even dreamed of setting foot in these lands.'

The lieutenant lowered himself down carefully and sat down on the hard salt crust, shaking his head:

'You're not a dirty son of the wind to me. You are an Imohag, noble and brave and I understand your reasons.' He paused. 'I share them. I would probably have reacted in the same way had someone done that to me.' He sighed deeply. 'But I am obliged to hand you over to the authorities and avoid any further bloodshed. Please,' he begged, 'don't make things any more difficult than they already are.'

He could have sworn that the other man was laughing at him under his veil as he replied sarcastically:

'Difficult for whom?' He shook his head. 'For a Targui things only start to get really difficult from the moment he loses his freedom. Our lives are hard, but our freedom compensates for this. If we lose our freedom we lose our will to live.' He paused. 'What will they do to me? Condemn me to twenty years?'

'There's no reason it should be for so long.'

"How many then...five...eight! I have seen your prisons, they have told me how they live there and I know that I would not last a single day.' He waved his hand aggressively, in a gesture that seemed to dismiss his visitor. 'If you want to catch me, come and get me...'

Razman stood up clumsily, horrified by the idea that he had to retrace his steps under a sun that beat down more furiously by the minute.

'I won't come looking for you. Of that you can be sure,' he said, before turning his back to him.

Gazel watched him as he moved away slowly, holding himself up with the spade that he had previously used as a flag, unsure of whether he would reach the edge of the sebkha, before dying of exposure.

The Targui stuck his tabuka and his rifle into the hard salt, set up some shade and crawled underneath it, ready to sit out the day's harshest hours.

He did not sleep and his eyes remained fixed on the vehicles that reflected the sun from their metallic bonnets. He felt the heat of the saltpan getting thicker by the minute as it rose up from the ground and threatened to boil his blood. It was a heat so dense, suffocating and heavy that even his mehari, who was accustomed to the highest of temperatures, had started to complain.

He would not survive for too long out there, in the heart of the saltpan and he knew it. He had enough water left for one day.

Soon delirium would overtake him and then death; the most horrific of all deaths and a way of dying that every Tuareg feared most of all, from the moment he was born: to die of thirst.

Ajamuk looked up at the sun to check its height then turned round to look at the banks of the saltpan.

'In half an hour the mosquitoes will eat us alive,' he said.

'We have to get away from here.'

'We could light some fires.'

The sergeant shook his head. 'No, not a fire nor anything else for that matter will protect you from this plague,' he insisted.

'As soon as they start to attack, the soldiers will run off and I won't be able to stop them,' he smiled, 'because I'll be running too.'

He went to say something else, but one of the soldiers interrupted him, pointing towards the saltpan.

'Look,' he shouted. 'He's leaving.'

It was true; the Targui had taken down his ridiculous camp and was heading off, leading his animal by the halter.

He turned around to his assistant pensively:

'Where will he go?'

Ajamuk shrugged his shoulders:

'Who knows how a Targui's mind works. But I don't like it.'

'Neither do I.'

The lieutenant meditated for a few moments, visibly worried.

'Maybe he'll try and get out at night,' he ventured. 'You go north with three men. Saud, south... I'll cover this area and Malik and his people the west...'

He shook his head. 'If we keep our eyes peeled he won't get past us.'

The sergeant did not reply and it was clear that he did not share his superior's optimism. He was a Bedouin and knew the Tuareg well; he also knew his soldiers well, who were mountain people forced to carry out their national service in a desert they did not understand, nor wanted to.

He admired Lieutenant Razman for the efforts he had made to adapt to the desert lands and his stoic determination to become an expert on them, but he also knew that he still had a lot to learn. You could not expect to understand the Sahara and its people in just one year, not even ten and you would never really understand the minds of the people who lived in it; the sons of the wind who appeared to live a simple life but who were, in reality, profoundly complicated people.

He picked up the binoculars that were on the seat and focused them on the man who was getting smaller by the minute, followed by his swaying mount.

He could not fathom what on earth he was doing by going back into that abominable oven, but he knew for certain that he was up to something. If a Targui with only a little water left was on the move and his mount too, then there would have to be a very good reason why.

There was a sudden whizzing noise in his ear and he gave a start.

'Lets go!' he shouted. 'The mosquitoes!'

They jumped into their vehicles, already swiping the insects away from their faces with their hands and sped away as fast as they were able to on the rocky terrain, putting as much distance between themselves and that godforsaken place as was physically possible. Then they split up, each going a different direction.

Lieutenant Razman ordered the men that he had with him to set up camp and prepare the supper, then he got in touch with

Sergeant Malik-el-Haideri to inform him of the fugitive's movements.

'I'm not sure what he's up to either,' admitted Malik. 'But he's smart, that's for sure.'

He paused. 'Maybe it would be better to go in and look for him...'

'That's probably what he's hoping for,' he replied. 'But remember that he's famous for his marksmanship. With a camel and a rifle in there we'd be at his mercy.'

'We'll wait!'

And so they waited all night, thankful of a bright moon, their guns at the ready, alert and prepared to respond to the slightest sound or movement.

But nothing happened and when the sun came up above the horizon they went back to the edge of the saltpan and there, in the middle of the saltpan, they could make out the kneeling camel and a man sleeping peacefully under his shade.

Equidistant from each other and positioned at the four compass points, four pairs of binoculars watched him throughout the day, but the rider and his mount made no perceptible movement whatsoever.

As afternoon fell once again and just before the mosquitoes started up, Lieutenant Razman opened a contact line with all his men.

'He hasn't moved,' he told them.

'What do you think?'

Sergeant Malik remembered his words: 'You must live like a stone and not make any movement that uses up water... Even at night you have to move slowly like a chameleon and only then do you become resistant to the heat and the thirst; above all you must overcome any panic and remain calm. Only then will you have the remotest chance of survival.'

'He's saving his strength,' he said.

'He's about four hours away from the edge of the sebkha,'

Ajamuk interjected. 'And it'll take him another hour to get up in the dark and get to where we are,' he calculated mentally. 'We'll have to be on our guard at around midnight. If he waits any longer he won't have enough time to get much beyond us, although he may be able to reach us.'

'The camel will bolt if they try and get out here,' Saud said, from the extreme south. 'The mosquitoes form a cloud here. There's a water opening and if they come near it they'll drown immediately.'

Lieutenant Razman was quite convinced that the Targui would rather drown in the sands than be caught alive, but he kept his thoughts to himself and continued to give out orders.

'Four hours of rest,' he said, 'but after that everybody must be fully alert.'

They passed another long, tense night under a strong moon that lit up the plains, and by dawn they were all ravaged with tiredness, their eyes red from staring into the darkness and their nerves destroyed.

When they returned to the saltpan that morning he was still there, in the same place and in the same position, as if he had not moved a muscle all night.

The lieutenant's voice came across the microphone nervously.

'What do you think is going on...? Is he mad,' Malik asked bad-temperedly. 'He can't have any water left... How is he going to stand another day in that oven?'

Nobody had an answer. Even for them, outside of the basin and with plenty of water in the huge water drums, the idea of staying there under that relentless sun was too much to bear. The Targui, however, seemed quite predisposed to spending another day in there, without moving.

'It's suicide...' the lieutenant muttered to himself. 'I never thought a Targui would be capable of suicide. He will be condemned for eternity.'

There was never a longer day.

Nor a hotter one.

The salt reflected back the sun's rays, multiplying its strength, making his small shelter virtually useless, rendering both him and his mehari speechless. The camel was unable to move as he had tied his legs together once he had got the animal to kneel down. He could not bear to hurt him, it was the last thing this beast, who had carried him so loyally across the sands for so many years, deserved.

He said his prayers between dreams and when he was not asleep he remained stock still. He would not even have moved to brush off a fly, had there been any that is, since the insufferable heat meant that there was not one to be seen. He struggled to become a stone, to forget about his body and its needs, aware that there was not even a drop of water left in his gerba. He felt his skin dry up and the strange sensation of his blood thickening in his veins as it began to move more slowly through them.

After midday he lost consciousness and remained there, supported only by the body of the beast, his mouth open, unable to breathe in the air which had become so dense that it almost refused to go down into his lungs.

He was delirious, but made no sound because his mouth and purple tongue were so dry. Then, a movement made by his mehari and a cry that came from the very depths of his being brought him back to the living and he opened his eyes, only to close them immediately as they were dazzled by the brilliant, white light of the saltpan.

Never had a day seemed so long to him, not even when compared with the day that his firstborn had started spitting blood, throwing it up from his lungs as he was devoured by tuberculosis.

Nor one so hot.

Night fell and the earth started to get colder gradually. Finally he began to breathe more easily and was able to open his eyes without feeling as if his retinas were being drilled through. His mehari also emerged out of his stupor and shuffled about anxiously, moaning quietly.

He loved that beast and he lamented its inevitable death. He had seen him born and known from that very first moment that he would be a lively, noble and resilient animal. He had looked after him carefully and taught him to obey his voice and the contact of his heel with his neck - a language that only the two of them understood. He had never, not in all those years, had to hit him. The animal had never tried to attack him or bite him, not even during the rutting season in spring, when the other males would become hysterical and unmanageable, rebelling against their masters, throwing off their loads and the riders from their backs, time and time again. That beast was truly a blessing from Allah, but his time had come and he knew it.

He waited until the moon had appeared on the horizon and its light, reflected on the saltpan turned the night almost back into day, then he took out his sharp dagger and with one strong and deep slash, slit the animal's white throat.

He said the ritual prayers and collected the blood that was gushing out into his gerba. When they were full, he drank the still warm, almost palpitating liquid slowly and felt himself gradually coming back to life. He waited a few minutes, regained his composure, then gently felt the stomach of the animal, who, having been tied up, had not moved at all when he had died, apart from its head that had flopped down to one side. Once he was sure that he had found the right spot, he cleaned his dagger on the striped rug that hung from his saddle then dug it in hard, deeply, twisting it around again and again in an attempt to make the wound as wide as possible. When he withdrew the weapon, a small spurt of blood escaped, followed by a gush of green, smelly water, which he filled his second gerba with. Then, pinching his nose with one hand and closing his eyes, he put his lips around the wound and drank the repulsive liquid from it directly, knowing that his life depended on it.

He continued drinking until there was nothing left, even though his thirst had long been satisfied and his stomach was full to bursting.

He started to wretch but forced himself to think of something else and forget the smell and the taste of water that had been in the camel's stomach for five days and it took all his will as a Targui fighting for his life to manage it.

Finally, he fell asleep.

'He's dead,' muttered Lieutenant Razman. 'He's got to be dead. He hasn't moved for four days now, he must have just turned into a pillar of salt.'

'Do you want me to go and check,' one of the soldiers offered, thinking that he might be given stripes for such an act.

The heat was starting to ease off.

He shook his head over and over again as he lit his pipe with a sailor's lighter – the only lighter that really worked out there in the sand and wind.

'I don't trust that Targui…' he said. 'I don't want him to kill us at night.'

'But we can't spend the rest of our lives here,' the other one pointed out. 'We've only got enough water for four days.'

'I know…' he admitted. 'Tomorrow I'll send in a man from each point. I'm not going to take any stupid risks.'

Once he was alone, however, he wondered if the greatest risk of all might be just that: waiting there for him and playing the Targui's game. He was unable to work out what his plans were and still did not believe that he would have let himself die of heat and thirst without having first put up a fight. From what he knew of Gazel Sayah, he was one of the last, truly free Tuareg, a noble inmouchar, almost a prince among his people, capable of crossing the "lost land" and taking on an army in order to avenge a wrongdoing. It just did not make sense that a man like that would let himself die as soon as he felt trapped. Suicide did not figure in the minds of the Tuareg, nor did it in the minds of Muslims, who knew that if they tried to kill themselves they would be barred from eternal paradise. Maybe the fugitive, like many of his people, was not in reality a fervent believer, but preferred to follow their more ancient traditions. But still, he could not bring himself to believe that he would shoot himself, cut his wrists or allow himself to be consumed by the sun and thirst.

He had a plan, of that he was sure. The plan would be Machiavellian but simple. There was also no doubt that the elements around them would play a key role in that plan – a landscape that the Targui had learned, even before he was born, to use to his advantage. But try as he may, the lieutenant could not work out what that plan might be.

The Targui seemed to be gambling on his men's fatigue and indeed his own and on the fact that no one would believe that a man could survive for so long without water in that raging furnace. He was trying to get them to believe, almost subconsciously, that they were actually keeping watch over a dead body so that without even realising it, they would drop their guard, at which point he would just slip away into the immense desert.

It was a reasonable assumption, but every time he remembered the insufferable heat that he had endured down there in the saltpan and calculated how much water a human being would need to survive in there, Targui or not, he changed his mind and became convinced that there was no way on earth that the fugitive could still be alive.

'He's dead...' he repeated once again, furious with himself and his impotence. 'The son of a bitch has to be dead.'

But Gazel Sayah was not dead.

He was there, as still as he had been for the last four days and almost four nights, watching the sun sink below the horizon, heralding the arrival of the darkness that would fall without warning and he knew that on this night he would finally have to act.

It was as if his mind had emerged from a strange kind of stupor that he had consciously forced himself into in order to convert himself into an inanimate object. He had managed to transform himself into a desert shrub, a rock from the erg, or one of the millions of grains of salt in the sebkha, overcoming his need to drink, sweat or even urinate.

It was as if the very pores of his skin had closed up and like his bladder was no longer connected with his exterior. His blood had seemed to thicken into a soupy mass, pushed around his body by his heart that had slowed to a minimum of beats per minute.

He had to rid himself of every thought and every memory and close down his imagination, because he knew that the body and mind were inexorably linked. Even a simple memory of Laila, the idea of a well, full of clear water, or a dream that he had escaped from that inferno, would make his heart beat faster, undermining his efforts to become a "man of stone."

But he had managed it and now he awoke from his long trance to contemplate the remains of the day. He worked to get his mind out of its stupor and awaken his body, to get the blood flowing and his muscles moving in order to recover the strength and flexibility that would soon be required of them.

Then, in the shadows, once he was totally sure that nobody could see him, he started to move. First an arm, then the other, then finally his legs and his head as he eased himself out of his refuge and stood up, still using the camel's body, which had started to rot, to support himself with.

He looked for his gerba and summoning up all his will and strength once again, he swallowed the greenish, repugnant, thick liquid, which had started to congeal and was now more like egg white mixed with bile, than water.

He then got out his dagger and moving the saddle off the

animal, he cut through the skin of the camel's hump in order to extract a white fat that was already on the point of turning putrid and began to chew on it immediately, aware that it was the only thing that would give him back his strength.

Even in death, his faithful mount had given him a final offering: the blood from his veins and water from his stomach in order to fight off his thirst, as well as his precious fat reserves that would bring him back to life.

An hour later, now in the thick of night, he looked back at the beast thankfully one last time, gathered up his water gerbas, his weapons and started off, unhurriedly, towards the west.

He had taken off his blue djelabba so that he was even less visible now and was just a white smudge, moving silently across the plain. Even when the moon came out and he cast a faint shadow, he was still invisible to anyone more than twenty meters away from him.

He saw the bank just as the mosquitoes were starting to emerge, so he wrapped himself up in his turban, covering his eyes with his litham and letting the hems of his robes drag on the ground to stop the insects from biting his ankles.

They emerged, threateningly, in their millions, not as many as there were at dawn or sunset, but an impressive amount all the same. They were ferocious and forced him to slap them off his arms and neck while some of them even managed to bite him through his clothes.

He could feel the salt crust thinning under foot as it became more dangerous with each step, but he knew that in the dark all he could do was place his trust in Allah and hope that He would guide his way. Finally and with some relief, he felt the first slab of rock underfoot, a piece that had come away from the top of the bank and he looked for bit of firm ground to step on to, ignoring the danger of scorpion nests this time in his hurry to get out of the sebkha.

He eventually found a good spot to climb up from, about

three hundred meters to his left and when he finally peered over into the immensity of the erg and a light gust of wind hit his face, he pulled himself out and let himself fall onto the sand, exhausted. He gave thanks to his creator that he had been allowed to escape from the salt trap, even though he had reached breaking point out there, his nerves so frayed that at one point he was not even sure he was going to make it through.

He slept for some time, trying to ignore the noise of the mosquitoes buzzing around him and then he dragged himself, meter by meter, with the patience of a chameleon stalking an insect, for about half a kilometre, away from the edge of the saltpan.

Not once did he lift his head higher than a hand's breadth above the level of the rocks, not even moving a muscle when a snake slithered in front of his eyes.

He turned his face to the sky and looked at the stars to work out how long it would be before dawn arrived. Then he looked around him and found his spot: three square meters of thick gravel, almost completely surrounded by small black rocks. He took out his dagger and started to dig silently, moving the sand away carefully, until he had made a grave the length of his body and two hands deep. It was just getting light as climbed into it and the first of the sun's rays slid over him. He finished covering himself with gravel, leaving only his eyes, nose and mouth free, which, during the hottest hours of the day would be protected by the shadow from the rocks.

Somebody could have urinated just three meters away without realising that a man was hiding right there, under his very feet.

Every morning, as his jeep approached the edge of the sebkha he was overcome with the same two conflicting fears: the fear that the motionless figure would be in the same place still and the fear that it might be gone.

Every morning Lieutenant Razman would experience first a feeling of fury and then one of impotency. He would start off by cursing the dirty son of the wind who was running rings around him, only to be overcome with a profound sense of satisfaction as he realised that he had not been wrong about the Targui.

'It would take great courage to let yourself die of thirst rather than be put into prison. A lot of courage. He must be dead.'

The frantic voice of Sergeant Malik came over the radio:

'He's gone, lieutenant,' he said furiously. 'Everything looks the same from here, but I am certain that he's escaped.'

'Where to?' he snapped. 'Where on earth can a man who hasn't got a camel or water go to? Or is that not a camel?'

'Yes, it is,' the other man replied. 'And it looks like there's a man at its side, but it could also be a dummy.'

He paused. 'With all due respect, lieutenant sir, I'd like to go in and look for him.'

'Alright...' he said reluctantly. 'Tonight.'

'Now!'

'Listen sergeant!' he replied, trying his hardest to sound authoritative. 'I'm in charge. You will go out as night falls and come back at dawn. Is that clear?'

'Very clear, sir.'

'That goes for you too Ajamuk.'

'Saud...?'

'I'll send a man in as the sun sets.'

'That's settled then,' he concluded.

'I want to return to Tidikem tomorrow. I've had enough of this Targui and this absurd situation. If he's not dead I can't even be bothered to hand him over, you can shoot him dead.'

He immediately regretted issuing those orders as he knew that Sergeant Malik would take them literally and do everything in his power to finish off the Targui once and for all, but he could not go back on his word.

Deep down he thought it was probably for the best anyway,

since the Targui had given the impression that he would rather die than be shut up in a dirty cell.

He tried to picture the tall man with his noble gestures and measured speech, who, in his own mind, was simply doing his duty according to the dictates of his ancient traditions and realised there was no way that this man would ever survive amongst the rabbles he would meet in jail.

Most of his compatriots were wild, primitive people and Razman knew that. For one hundred years they had lived under the rule of the French colonisers who had made sure that these people remained ignorant. Even now that they were free and independent, those years of independence had not actually created a more cultured and educated population. On the contrary, there were many people who had interpreted this new-found freedom as a means to do as they wished, which saw men rising to power through force, adopting only those legacies left behind by the French that suited their situation.

The result was anarchy, crisis and continued political unrest. Power, it transpired, was a way of getting rich fast, as opposed to a way of guiding a nation forward.

The prisons were full to overflowing with criminals and politicians from the opposition and there was certainly not enough room in them for a Targui, born to live in the desert, the land without limits.

When his face was no longer in the shadow of the rock and the sun had started to beat down directly on to his face and thick drops of sweat ran down his forehead, he opened his eyes and without moving, looked around him.

He had slept without moving a muscle or even a grain of the sand that covered him, quite indifferent to the heat, the flies and even a lizard that had run across his face. The reptile had then scampered off behind a rock and remained there, watching cautiously, its dark, beady, flitting eyes fixed on the strange creature, with only eyes, a nose and a mouth, that had invaded his territory.

He listened. He could not hear a trace of any human voice in the wind and the sun, now very high, beat down vertically, which meant that it was the gaila hour, a time when few men were able to resist the drowsiness brought on by the heat and the urge to sleep. He turned his head, without moving his body at all and looked around him beyond the rocks. A little more than a kilometre to the south, on the edge of the saltpan, he could make out a vehicle with a canvas tarpaulin stretched out from it, tied with two long bits of rope to some large stones and big enough to provide shelter for a least a dozen men.

He could only make out one sentry, from the back, who was watching the sebkha, but he could not work out how many men were taking a siesta under the tarpaulin.

He knew, having watched them on previous days, that the other vehicles and their crew were far away and he did not have to worry right then about them.

His prey was there, before him, and he would remain there until the afternoon, when the mosquitoes would force them back once again into the erg.

He smiled as he tried to imagine how they would react had they known that he had them all there at the end of his rifle; that he could quite easily slip over to them like a reptile between the rocks, approach the sentry from behind and slit his throat and then do the same to the sleeping men inside, with equal ease.

He did not do it, but just moved one of the rocks an inch, so that it protected him a little more from the sun. The heat was becoming more intense, but the layer of sand protected him and there was a light breeze that made it easier to breath and anyway it was nothing compared to the suffocating and unbearable heat of the saltpan. The erg was part of his world and he had spent an endless amount of time buried like that, near herds of gazelles. He would let them approach slowly, grazing on the grara until he could almost spit on their snouts and when they came within arm's reach he would grab them and shoot a bullet into their heart. An enormous cheetah that had been eating his goats had met a similar fate. The ferocious and blood thirsty animal, that had seemed to be protected by an evil force, would attack as an unarmed shepherd watched over his flock, and then disappear without trace as soon as Gazel appeared with his rifle. So he hid himself in the sand for three days, until his eldest son arrived, as planned, with his goats and waited patiently for the blood-thirsty beast to appear. He saw him arrive, slithering from bush to bush along the ground, so silently that neither his son nor the animals saw him coming and just as he was about to jump he shot him in the head, cutting him down before its feet had even left the ground. He was proud of the skin from that animal, which inspired admiration from those who visited his jaima and was the reason, once the story had spread, that he became know throughout his region as "the Hunter."

The four men set off in unison, one to each point of the compass, under strict instructions to move in on the Targui at midnight, to shoot him dead if he resisted arrest and to return by dawn.

Sergeant Major Malik-el-Haideri would not let anyone go in his place and left before the mosquitoes had started up. He followed the tracks that the fugitive had left at the edge of the sebkha and climbed down into it, his rifle over his shoulder, still convinced that the dirty son of the wind had vanished.

He was unable to work out exactly when he had disappeared or where he would have gone to and he wondered how the Targui could have possibly escaped on foot and without water from that enormous erg, when the nearest well was about one hundred kilometers away, near the foothills of the Sidi-el-Madia mountains.

'One of these days his body will just turn up, burnt to a cinder by the sun, if the hyenas and jackals didn't get to him first,' he said to himself. But deep down he was not convinced because the Imohag had told him that he had crossed the "lost land" twice and he was certain that he had not been lying. For the Targui, one hundred kilometers of erg would probably not pose too much of a challenge, although he did not know at that point that if Malik did not find him in the saltpan, he would be waiting for him at the nearest well.

The whole hunt had, for Sergeant Malik, turned into more of

a personal vendetta, than simply a case of catching the fugitive in order to avoid intervention from the authorities. The Targui had made fun of him at the oasis, slit the captain's throat under his very nose, had made him run from one end of the desert to another like an idiot and finally kept him waiting for five days, without knowing exactly what he was waiting for in the first place.

His men were muttering behind his back now as well, of that he was certain. On their return to Adoras they would comment on how the big, tough sergeant major had been taken for a ride by an illiterate Targui. It was not easy to control that bunch at the best of times and if they were no longer terrified of him, which until then they had been, they may well decide to make a run for it. If a captain could be murdered and the murderer get away with it, then there was no reason why they could not do the same to a sergeant and then just disappear. Looking at it from that perspective, his life there would not be worth a handful of dates any more, unless of course, he caught the Targui.

That afternoon Razman ordered his men to head inland, away from the plague of mosquitoes and while his men were taking the tarpaulin down that they had used as a refuge, he looked back one last time to the middle of the saltpan, focusing his binoculars on the officer who was striding determinedly over to the spot that he had become so obsessed with.

The soldiers that had stayed behind did not bother to ask whether the Targui had moved or not any more. The dead did not move and they were all quite convinced that he was.

Maybe the son of the wind had been courageous enough to let the sun fry him alive and over time the salt would cover his body and mummify him along with his camel. They might be discovered in the course of the next one hundred years, completely preserved and people would wonder why on earth a man had gone with his camel to die in such a remote and lonely spot.

Lieutenant Razman smiled to himself at the idea that he may well become a symbol of the Tuareg spirit for centuries to come, long after they had disappeared as a race from the face of the earth.

A proud inmouchar, waiting passively for death in the shadow of his mehari, hunted down by his enemies but secure in the knowledge that it was far more noble and dignified to die in that way, than to surrender and be imprisoned.

'He'll become a legend,' he said. 'A legend like Omar Muktar or Hamodu... A legend that will make his race proud and he will serve as a reminder to his people that at one time all of the Imohags were like him.'

One of the men's voices brought him back down to earth.

'When you're ready, lieutenant.'

He looked back at the saltpan one last time, started up the vehicle and drove away from the mosquito-plagued area to set up camp in the same place that they had done so on every other night.

While one of the soldiers started to prepare a frugal supper on a small paraffin stove, he switched on the radio and called back to base.

Souad answered almost immediately.

'Have you got him?' she asked anxiously.

'No, not yet?'

There was a long silence and then finally she said quite sincerely.

'I'd be lying if I said I was sorry... Are you coming back tomorrow?'

'We haven't got any choice. The water's running out.'

'Take care!'

'Any news from the camp?'

'A camel gave birth last night... a girl.'

'That's great. See you tomorrow!'

He hung up, but remained there, the microphone still in his

hand, lost in thought as he contemplated the grey shroud that had started to envelop the plains.

A camel had been born and he was off in pursuit of a fugitive Targui. It was turning into to an exceptionally busy week at the military post of Tidikem, where months would often go by when nothing happened at all.

He wondered to himself once again if this was how he had imagined it would be when he had enrolled with the military academy; if this was what he had dreamed of when he read Colonel Duperey's biography - of emulating the man's heroic deeds and of becoming the new saviour of the Nomadic tribes. In reality there were no longer any Nomadic tribes around Tidikem, since they avoided the outpost and all contact with the military now at all costs, having had such bad experiences at Adoras.

It was a sad fact that these military men had no idea how to communicate with these natives, who in turn regarded them as shameless foreigners who requisitioned their camels, occupied their wells and hassled their women.

Night had fallen on the stony plains, the first hyena cackled in the distance and a splattering of stars blinked timidly in a sky that would very soon be awash with them, in a blazing and resplendent display that one could never tire of admiring. It was the stars on these calm nights that had kept him going through those long, tedious and desperate days. "The Tuareg prick the stars with their spears to light up their way..." It was a beautiful desert saying; just a phrase, but coined by somebody who knew the desert and those stars well; who knew what it meant to sit in contemplation of them, so close to hand, for hours on end. He had been fascinated by three things, since he was a child: fire; the sea crashing on the rocks at the bottom of a cliff and stars in a cloudless sky. Looking into a fire made him forget even to think, looking at the sea sparked off memories of his childhood and contemplating the night made him feel at peace with himself, with the past, the present and almost at peace with his own future.

And then suddenly, from out of the shadows, came the dead man walking and the first thing he saw was the metallic glisten of his rifle.

They stared at him, hardly daring to believe their eyes. This was no salt statue in the centre of the sebkha, but the Targui, there, right in front of them, his weapon pointing directly at them and a regulation revolver hanging at his waist. From the expression in his eyes, the only part of his face that was exposed, they could tell that he was ready to pull the trigger at the first sign of danger.

'Water!' he demanded.

He nodded and one of the soldiers held out his water bottle to him, his hand trembling. The Targui took a few steps back, lifted up his veil a little and without taking his eyes off them and with one hand on his rifle, he drank thirstily.

The lieutenant started to edge towards his holster that was on the driver's seat of the car, but the rifle swung round towards him and he saw how his finger tensed on the trigger simultaneously. He remained very still, regretting his move as it dawned on him that it was not worth risking his life simply to avenge Captain Kaleb.

'I thought you were dead,' he said.

'I know,' the Targui said, once he had finished drinking. 'I thought so too at one point...' He stretched out his hand, grabbed one of the soldier's plates and started to eat, lifting up his litham only slightly with his fingers. 'But I am an Imohag,' he pointed out. 'The desert respects me.'

'I can see that. Anyone else would have died. What are you going to do now?'

Gazel looked over to the jeep.

'Take me to the Sidi-el-Madia Mountains. No one will find me there.'

'And if I refuse?'

'I'll kill you and get one of them to take me.'

'Nobody will do that unless I order it.'

He looked at him as if unable to process the stupidity of what he had just said.

'They won't listen to you if you are dead,' he pointed out. 'I've got nothing against them... or you.'

He paused before saying calmly: 'It is wise to recognise when you have won and when you have lost. And you have lost.'

Lieutenant Razman nodded in agreement:

'You are right,' he admitted. 'I have lost. As soon as it's dawn I'll take you to the Sidi-el-Madia.'

'At dawn? No. Now!'

'Now,' he said in a surprised tone. 'It's bad enough navigating through the erg during the day. The stones slash the tyres and smash the axles, we won't even make a kilometre at night.'

The Targui took some time to reply. He had snatched a second plate from one of the soldiers and sat on the floor with his legs crossed and his weapon leaning against his knees, barely chewing and eating so fast that he almost choked. 'Listen,' he warned. 'If we get to the Sidi-el-Madia, you will live. If we don't get there I will kill you, even if none of this is your fault.' He let him think about what he had said and then added: 'And remember I am an inmouchar and I will always keep my word.'

One of the soldiers, who was barely more than a boy, spoke up:

'Watch it lieutenant. He's mad and looks like he'll do what he says.'

The Targui said nothing, but just looked at him hard and finally, pointing his weapon at him said:

'Undress!'

'What did you say?' the boy asked, aghast.

'Get undressed...' Then he pointed to another of the men. 'You too.'

They hesitated in protest but the Targui's voice held such authority that they realised they had no option and started to slowly remove their uniforms.

'Your boots too...'

They left them all in front of Gazel, who picked them up with one hand and threw them into the back of the vehicle. He got into it and nodded to Razman.

'The moon is out,' he said. 'Lets go!'

The lieutenant looked over at his men, who were completely naked and he was overcome with a sudden urge to rebel. For a few seconds he felt inclined to challenge him and even exchanged a conspiratorial look with his soldiers, but they shook their heads and the youngest one said despondently:

'Don't worry about us, lieutenant. Ajamuk will come and get us.'

'But you'll die of exposure before dawn.' He turned to Gazel. 'Leave them a blanket or something.'

The Targui looked as if he might concede, but then appeared to change his mind and said jokingly:

'Tell them to bury themselves in the sand. It'll keep them warm and it's good for their figures.'

Razman saluted them reluctantly, started up the engine and put his headlights on. He felt the end of the gun poking into his ribs.

'Without lights!'

He turned them off, but shook his head despairingly:

'You're mad...!' he muttered. 'Completely mad.'

He waited until his eyes had become used to the darkness again and then set off slowly, leaning forward as much as he could to try and see any obstacles along the way. It was a slow and difficult journey for the first three hours, until Gazel gave him permission to turn on the headlights, which meant that they were able to pick up a bit of speed, at which point one of the tyres burst.

The lieutenant sweated and cursed as he changed it, watched over all the while by the barrel of a gun and it took everything in his power not to take advantage of the situation; to chuck his spanner away and get into a bare-fisted fight that might put an end, once and for all, to the embarrassing situation.

But he knew that the Targui was bigger and stronger than he was and even if he had managed to get hold of his rifle, the enemy still had a revolver, a sword and a dagger.

All he could do was wave goodbye to any kind of promotion and pray that things would not get any more complicated. To be killed at twenty-eight by somebody whose ideas he fundamentally agreed with would be astoundingly stupid and he knew it.

On the dot of midnight the four men converged on the dead camel and it was of no surprise to anyone that their prey had fled. Sergeant Malik-el-Haideri took advantage of the occasion to start cursing loudly. He cursed the Targui and somewhat more emphatically the 'stupid lieutenant' who had let himself be fooled like a bare-faced beginner.

'What are we going to do now?' one of the soldiers said, disconcertedly.

'I don't know what the lieutenant will do, but with or without his consent I'm going to drive over to the Sidi-el-Madia well. That son of a bitch might be a Targui, but he can't possibly carry on without having drunk any water for so many days.'

A veteran that had been studying the mehari's body to the light of his lantern, pointed to the gash in his stomach.

'He's got water,' he said. 'A repellent water that would kill most people, but the Tuareg are able to survive on this. He also drank its blood.' He paused and then added in an assured tone: 'We'll never find him...'

Sergeant Major Malik-el-Haideri did not respond, looked back at the dead animal then turned around and started walking back towards his vehicle. From the level of decomposition, he calculated that the camel must have been dead for about forty-eight hours, which meant that the Targui would have sacrificed it two nights ago. If he had got on his way immediately, which he doubted, then he would have quite an advantage over them. If he had stayed for one more day there, just so they relaxed their watch a little more, then he could not have got very far, which meant that there may still have been time to catch up with him.

He knew that they were unlikely to catch him in the erg, because without his mount he could bury himself in the sand as soon as he saw a vehicle approaching. Even so, the water from the camel's stomach would not last another day before turning putrid and the fugitive would be in urgent need of fresh supplies.

In the gullies and mountain valleys of the massif you might scoop out a few drops of earthy, salty liquid, which would be enough to help a traveller who had wandered into its labyrinth of endless rocky slopes on his way, but would never be enough to survive from.

If they took over the well then it would force the Targui to hand himself over or otherwise condemn himself to a certain death. Unconsciously he started walking faster and to his surprise found himself almost running to the jeep, so great was his desire to catch him. The moon had sunk below the horizon, but his sense of direction was almost as good as a nomad, having lived for so many years in the desert, so that by the time he had reached the bank and scrambled up it, he still had a good hour before dawn. He ran over to his men, cursing the mosquitoes that were already flying towards him furiously.

Startled by the sudden commotion, his men surrounded him.

'What happened?' asked the black man, Ali.

'What do you think's happened? He's gone.'

'So what are we going to do now?'

The sergeant did not answer. He had taken out his radio apparatus and was calling it insistently.

'Lieutenant! Can you hear me lieutenant?' After he had tried getting through five times unsuccessfully, he swore loudly then started up the car:

'He's that stupid that I think he's actually fallen sleep... Let's go!'

He sped off, bouncing along the edge of the saltpan, heading straight for the northeast, his men hanging onto the sides of the vehicle for dear life.

At dawn, Lieutenant Razman stopped to fill up with petrol. He put what was left in the petrol can into the car and then turned it upside down to show Gazel that he had not been lying.

'It was almost finished,' he pointed out.

The Targui did not reply. He was sitting in the back of the vehicle watching as the horizon came into view and then as an uneven jagged black line emerged - the Sidi-el-Madia massif. The massif rose up suddenly from the plains, red and ochre, the fruit of an immense cataclysm that must have occurred around the same time that man first appeared on earth, as if some monstrous hand had pushed it up from the very centre of the earth and placed it there by magic.

The relentless winds that blew through the desert had, over millions of years, stripped its summit bare, removing all the earth, sand and vegetation, turning it into an endless stretch of naked, polished rock, scorched by the sun, cracked and broken up by the extreme changes in temperature between night and day. Travellers who had crossed those mountains often spoke of the wailing, moaning voices they had heard at dawn, but which were in fact nothing more than the cracking of the hot stones as the temperature dropped sharply and suddenly.

It was a truly inhospitable place in the heart of an even more inhospitable land. It was as if the Creator himself had used it as a dumping ground for all the bits and pieces left over from his other fine works, leaving behind a muddle of rocky outcrops, saltpans, sands and "lost lands."

But to Gazel, the Sidi-el Madia was not some godforsaken hellhole but a labyrinth, inside which an entire army could hide without ever being found.

'How much petrol is there left...?' he finally asked.

'Enough for two hours, three at the most. At this speed and on this terrain it consumes a lot...' He paused and then added in a worried tone: 'I don't think we'll make it to the well.'

Gazel shook his head.

'We're not going to the well.'

'But you said...!'

The Targui nodded:

'I know what I said,' he admitted. 'You heard it and your men heard it and they will tell the others.'

There was a pause. 'During those days I spent alone on the saltpan I asked myself how you could have possibly overtaken me when I had such an advantage on you, but yesterday I saw you speaking on that apparatus and I understood. What's it called...a radio? Yes that's what it is. My cousin Suleiman bought one. Two months of shifting bricks from one place to the next just to buy something that screeches out loud at you! That's how you found me, am I right?'

Lieutenant Razman nodded silently.

Gazel reached out, grabbed the earpiece and threw it away. Then with the butt of his gun he destroyed the rest of the apparatus.

'It's not fair,' he said. 'I am alone and you are many. It's not fair that you are also using French methods.'

The lieutenant had taken down his trousers and was squatting some three meters away from the jeep.

'Sometimes I don't think you quite realise what's happening here,' he said casually. 'It's not about a struggle between you and us. It's about the fact that you have committed a crime and you have to pay for that. You can't just murder someone and go unpunished.'

Gazel had also left the vehicle to do the same thing and was squatting down, still carrying his weapon.

'That's what I told the captain,' he replied. 'He shouldn't have murdered my guest.' He paused. 'But nobody punished him. I had to do it myself.'

'The captain was carrying out his orders.'

'Whose orders? From his superiors I suppose.'

'From the governor.'

'And who is the governor and what right has he to give out these orders? What authority has he over me, my family, my settlement and my guests…?'

'The authority given to him by the regional government.'

'What government?'

'The Government of the Republic.'

'What is a Republic?'

The lieutenant snorted then looked around for the right kind of stone to clean himself with. He got up and buttoned up his trousers calmly.

'You don't really want me to explain the ways of the world to you right now do you?'

The Targui searched for a stone and cleaned himself with it, then threw sand at his bottom several times, remained in the same position for a few seconds and got up.

'Why not…?' he asked. 'It's all very well for you to tell me that I have committed a crime, but then you won't explain to me why that is. It all seems a bit absurd.'

Razman had taken the water can and poured some of it into a small saucepan that was hanging on a chain from the back of the vehicle and started to wash out his mouth and hands with it.

'Don't waste it,' the Targui snapped. 'I'm going to need it.'

He obeyed him then turned around to face him.

'I think maybe you are right,' he admitted. 'I should probably explain to you that we are no longer a colony and that just as things changed for the Tuareg people when the French arrived, things have changed again now they have gone.'

'If they have gone it seems logical that we return to our ancient traditions.'

'No. No, it's not logical. The last one hundred years have not passed by in vain. Many things have happened. The world, the whole world, has been transformed.'

Gazel took in his surroundings with a sweep of his hands.

'Nothing has changed here. The desert has remained the same and will do for another one hundred years more. Nobody has come to me and said: "Here, take water, food or ammunition and medicine because the French have now left. We can no longer respect your customs, laws and traditions, that your ancestors and their ancestors followed, but we are going to give you some better ones in exchange, in order to make your lives in the Sahara easier, so easy that you will no longer need to follow your ancient traditions..."'

The lieutenant meditated for a few moments, his head lowered, staring at his boots as if deep down he felt somehow responsible and then shrugging his shoulders and sitting down on the running board, he replied:

'It's true. You should have been informed, but we are a young country that has just gained independence and it'll take some years before we adapt to this new situation.'

'In that case...' Gazel continued, his logical train of thought something quite remarkable, 'while you are not ready to adapt to that, it would be better to respect what already exists. It is stupid to destroy something before anything has been built to replace it with.'

Razman realised that there was very little he could say in response. The truth was that he had not found the answer either. He was often overwhelmed with similar questions that raced around his head as he contemplated, with some dismay, the deterioration of the society into which he had been born.

'It's best we leave this subject now,' he said. 'We'll never agree on it. Would you like something to eat?'

Gazel nodded and he looked for the large wooden box that had the provisions in it. He opened up a can of meat that they shared, with some biscuits and hard dry, goat's cheese. The sun came up, heating up the earth and reflecting off the black rocks of the Sidi-el-Madia, which stood out against the horizon more sharply by the minute.

'Where are we going?' the lieutenant finally asked.

Gazel pointed over to their right: 'There's the well. We'll head to the other peak over to the left.'

'I drove under it once. You can't climb it.'

'I can. The Huaila mountains are similar. Even worse perhaps! I used to hunt mufflon there. I killed five once. We had dried meat for a year and my children slept on their skins.'

'Gazel "the Hunter,"' the lieutenant exclaimed, smiling a little. 'You feel proud of who you are; of being a Targui, don't you?'

'If I wasn't, I would change who I was. Are you not proud of who you are?' he said, tilting his head to one side.

'Not really...' he admitted. 'At the moment I would rather be on your side than the side I'm on. But we cannot build a country by doing that.'

'If things are built too quickly then they will soon go bad,' the Targui said pointedly.

'We should set off. We've been talking too much.'

They started off again, but a wheel burst and then two hours later the car engine backfired then broke down completely, about five kilometers away from the high, vertical cliff that they were headed for and where the great erg of Tidiken finally came to rest.

'This is as far as we can go,' Razman said as he looked up at the smooth, black, gleaming wall, which looked like the walls of a castle belonging to a Cyclops.

'Are you really going up there?'

Gazel nodded his head silently, jumped out of the car and started putting food and ammunition into the soldiers' rucksacks. He unloaded the weapons, checked that none of them had any bullets left in them and studied the regulatory guns, choosing the best one and leaving his on the backseat: 'My father gave me it when I was young,' he said. 'I have never used another. But it's old now and hard to get ammunition for that calibre.'

'I'll keep it as a museum piece,' the lieutenant replied. 'I'll put a plaque on it: "This belonged to the bandit-hunter Gazel Sayah."'

'I am not a bandit.'

He smiled gently:

'I was only joking.'

'Jokes are fine when told at night time, by the light of a fire and amongst friends.' He paused. 'Now I must tell you something. Do not follow me, because if I see you again I will kill you.'

'If they order me to find you I will have to try and catch you,' he reminded him.

The Targui stopped cleaning out his old gerba with clean water and stared at him incredulously: 'How can you live like this, always waiting for the next set of orders. How can you feel like a man and free if you are always dependent on the requirements of others? If they told you to catch an innocent man would you go ahead and catch him? If they told you to leave a murderer like the captain in peace, would you leave him in peace? I do not understand...!'

'Life is clearly not as simple as it seems to be here in the desert.'

'Then do not bring that way of life into the desert. The distinction between good and evil, justice and injustice is clear here.' He finished filling up his gerbas and then checked that the soldiers' water bottles were also full. The water drum was almost empty and the lieutenant pointed it out: 'Are you going to leave me without any water?' he said in a worried tone. 'At least give me a water bottle.'

He shook his head resolutely:

'A little thirst will help you to understand how I felt out there in the saltpan,' he replied. 'It is a good thing to learn how to cope with thirst in the desert.'

'But I'm not a Targui,' he protested. 'I can't walk back to my settlement. It's too far and I'd get lost. Please.' He shook his head again. 'You must not move from here,' he advised. 'Once I've reached the mountains you should make a fire with your soldiers' mats and clothes. They'll see the smoke and come and get you.'

He paused. 'Do you give me your word that you will wait until I have reached the top?' He nodded silently and watched without moving out of his seat, as the Targui loaded himself with rucksacks, water bottles, the gerba and his weapons. He did not seem to notice their weight as he walked off with a firm, fast and resolute stride, seemingly impervious to the heat.

He was a little over one hundred meters away when Razman hooted the horn insistently, forcing him to turn around:

'Good luck,' he shouted.

The other man lifted his hand in response, turned around and continued on his way.

There's an old saying that "palm trees love to have their heads in the fire and their feet in the water," proof of which lay before his very eyes. More than twenty thousand palm trees stretched out before him and into the distance, their plumes reaching up to the sky, impervious to the scorching heat, with their roots firmly entrenched in the fresh clear water that flowed into the earth from the hundreds of underground springs and innumerable wells in the area.

It was a truly beautiful spectacle, even though the sun beat down mercilessly, defiantly and unashamedly, because from inside his huge dark office, protected from the outside by thick windows and white net curtains, the air conditioning remained at the same temperature, day in and day out and throughout the seasons, just above freezing and just as the governor, Hassan-ben-Koufra liked to have it.

Once he was settled in his office, a glass of tea in his hand and a smouldering "DavidoffAmbassatrice" in the other, the desert seemed almost bearable. He would even go as far to say that at sunset, when the sun seemed to stop and rest for a while in the tops of the palm trees, providing the only break to El-Akab's horizon before disappearing completely behind the mosque's minaret, it felt surprisingly close to paradise.

The balconies of the building overlooked a secluded garden that, according to legend had been designed by Colonel Duperey himself, who had ordered the palace to be built. There, the rose and carnation beds wrestled for space and lemon and apple trees stood nestled amongst the tall cypresses from where the coos of a thousand turtledoves could be heard and where, at the end of their long migratory flights, the swifts would settle in huge groups.

El-Akab was, without doubt a beautiful place; the most beautiful oasis in the Sahara, from Marrakech to the shores of the Nile, which is why it had been chosen as the capital of a province that was, all told, much bigger than many other European countries.

And from his icy palace office, his Excellency, the governor Hassan-ben-Koufra, ruled over his empire with the absolute power of a viceroy, well known for his firm hand, restrained manner and cutting tongue.

'You are useless, lieutenant,' he said, turning to look at him with a smile on his face that made it look like he had just congratulated him rather than insulted him. 'Aren't a dozen men enough to catch a fugitive armed with an old rifle? What more did you need, an entire division?'

'I didn't want to risk their lives, your Excellency. I've told you that already. He would have shot us down one after the other with that old rifle. He is a great and legendary marksman and our men have not fired more than forty bullets in their entire lives...'

He paused.

'We are under orders not to waste ammunition.'

'I know,' the governor admitted, moving away from the balcony and returning to his enormous desk. 'I gave that order. If there's no war in sight, I consider it a waste of money to spend time training up a bunch of recruits into first class marksmen, when they'll only be going home after one year. As long as they know how to pull the trigger, that'll do.'

'But that's not enough, your Excellency. Excuse my impertinence, but in the desert a man's life is often entirely dependent on his marksmanship.' He swallowed. 'This was one of those situations.'

'Listen lieutnenant,' Hassan-ben-Koufra replied, without losing his composure - something it might be said that no-one had ever seen him lose. 'And bear in mind that I can say this freely since I am not a military man. To respect the life of your soldiers does seem to be a very admirable notion, but there are times and this was one of them,' he paused intentionally, 'when the soldiers had to accomplish their mission above all else, because the honour of the army, to which you belong, was at stake. To have allowed a Bedouin to kill a captain and one of our guides, to strip two of our soldiers naked and make a lieutenant drive across the desert constitutes a discredit to you, the armed forces and to me as the highest authority in this province.'

Lieutenant Razman nodded silently as he tried to stop himself from shivering, his uniform being far too thin for the icy temperature of the office.

'They asked for my help to catch a man who would be brought to trial your Excellency,' he replied, trying to speak with a tone of calm authority. 'Not to kill him like a dog.' He paused. 'If I was expected to act as a policeman, then I should have received those orders loud and clear. I wanted to help and I realise that the end result was unfortunate, but I sincerely believe that it was better than returning home with five bodies.'

The governor shook his head and leant back in his chair as if to conclude the conversation.

'That was for me to decide and from the reports that I have received it would have been better if we'd had five corpses. We inherited the respect that the nomads held for the French and now, for the first time and thanks to that Bedouin and your ineptitude, it's been shattered. It won't do...' he muttered. 'It just won't do.'

'I am sorry.'

'You will be sorry, lieutenant I can assure you. From today you are posted to Adoras where you will replace Kaleb-el-Fasi.'

Lieutenant Razman immediately broke out into a cold sweat that had nothing to do with the air conditioning and he noticed that his knees were trembling so much they were virtually knocking each other.

'Adoras!' he repeated incredulously. 'That is not fair your Excellency. I may have made a mistake but I am not a criminal.'

'Adoras is not a prison,' the governor replied calmly. 'It is simply a frontier post. I have the power to send anyone there that I consider good for the job.'

'But everybody knows that only the scum of the earth are sent there...! The very dregs of the army!' The governor Hassan-ben-Koufra shrugged his shoulders indifferently and turned to look at a report that was lying on the table with exaggerated interest. Then, without looking up he said:

'That is only an opinion, not an officially accepted fact. You have one month to arrange your things and organise the transfer...'

Lieutenant Razman went to say something, but then realising it was pointless, saluted him stiffly and walked towards the door, praying that his legs would not give way and give the bastard the satisfaction of seeing him collapse.

When he got outside he leaned his forehead against one of the marble columns and remained there for a few seconds, trying to regain his composure and steady his legs. He certainly did not want to go flying down the majestic, marble staircase and into the flowerbeds below, in front of some twenty or so busy workers.

One of the workers slipped past his back silently, knocked three times on the office door, went in and closed it behind him.

The governor who had stopped pretending to study the report and was contemplating the mosque through the windows from his chair, leaned in towards the recent arrival, who was standing respectfully at the edge of the carpet and asked:

'What is it Anuhar?'

'No news of the Targui, your Excellency. He's disappeared.'

'I'm not surprised,' he admitted. 'These sons of the wind can cross a desert from one end to the other in a month. He will have gone back to his own people. Do we know who he is exactly?'

'Gazel Sayah of the Kel-Talgimus. He wanders through a large territory near the Huaila mountains.'

The governor Hassan-ben-Koufra glanced over at the map of the region hanging on the wall and shook his head pessimistically.

'The Huaila mountains!' he repeated. 'They are right on the border.'

'The borders barely exist in that zone, sir. They have yet to be determined exactly.'

'Nothing there is "determined exactly,"' he said, standing up and pacing the length of his immense office. 'To go in search of a Targui on the run in those lonely places would be like looking for a needle in a haystack.' He turned round to face him. 'File it Mojkri.'

Anuhar-el-Mojkri, the governor's efficient secretary of eight years allowed himself the luxury of a deep frown:

'The military won't like that, your Excellency. He murdered a captain.'

'They despised Captain Kaleb-el-Fasi,' he reminded him. 'He was a nasty piece of work.' He looked for a "Davidoff" again and lit it slowly. 'Just like El-Haideri...'

'It's only those kind of people who can take charge of that rabble at Adoras.'

'Lieutenant Razman will be in charge of that from now on.'

'Razman...?' El Mojkri said in a tone of astonishment. 'You've posted Razman to Adoras...? He won't last three months there.'

He smiled as if something had suddenly amused him. 'That's why he was about to faint out there. They'll rape him before they slit his throat.'

The governor fell back into a wide, black, leather chair in the corner of the room, exhaled a column of smoke and shook his head:

'Maybe not,' he said slowly. 'Maybe he'll actually get his act together. He'll have to fight for his life and that'll wake him up to the fact that he didn't come here to read 'Beau Geste' or follow on from Duperey.' He paused for a while.

'I was entrusted with a mission to clear out the vestiges of old-fashioned, decadent romanticism and unhealthy paternalism and to get this province and its people working towards a common good. There's petrol, iron, copper and wood here and a thousand more riches that we need to exploit if we are to become a powerful, progressive and modern nation.'

He nodded to himself, lost in his own rhetoric. 'And it's not with people like Razman that we'll achieve that, but with the likes of Malik and Captain Kaleb. It's a sad fact, but the Tuaregs don't really belong to the twentieth century and neither do the Amazon Indians or the American Redskins. Can you imagine a bunch of Sioux Indians running around the prairies in the mid West, chasing herds of buffalos in between oil wells and nuclear power stations? There are some life forms whose historical cycle reach a natural conclusion and they are condemned to extinction and whether we like it or not, that is the case with our nomads. They have to adapt or be exterminated.'

'That's a tough line to take.'

'It was also tough getting rid of the French – of the people we'd lived with for a hundred years - many of them were my friends, we'd been at school together, we knew each other's names and hobbies. But the time had come to finish with all that, without being sentimental and so we did. Some things are above Bourgeois morals and this is one of them.' He paused again and meditated. 'The President was very clear when he said to me: "Hassan… The nomads are a minority on their way to a logical extinction. Turn them into useful workers or encourage their extinction in order to avoid suffering or complications."'

'But what about his last speech?' he ventured timidly.

'Oh, come on Anuhar!' he said, reprimanding him like a child. 'Those aren't things you can say in public, especially while some of those nomads are listening and the world is watching our newly independent country. The North Americans for example, became staunch advocates of human rights issues overnight, but only once they'd completely annihilated all of the Indians' rights.'

'They were different times.'

'But identical circumstances. A nation that has just gained independence that needs to exploit all its riches and rid itself of the heavy weight of a people that cannot move forward. We will give them the chance to integrate with our people. We won't annihilate them by shooting them, nor will we herd them up into "reserves"…'

'And what about those ones who don't want to integrate? Those who believe, just as Gazel does, that their ancient laws should still apply in the desert? What will we do with them? Hunt them down with guns like they did with the Redskins?'

'No, of course not. We will just expel them. You said yourself that the desert's borders remain undefined and they don't respect them any way. Let them cross them and join up with their brothers from the other countries.' He held his hands up in the air. 'But if they stay, then they must adapt to our way of life or be prepared to pay the consequences.'

'They won't adapt,' Anuhar-el-Mojkri replied. 'I've got to know some of them recently and although a few of them might renounce their past, most of them remain quite rigidly attached to the sands and their customs.' He pointed outside, towards the far away tower as its muezzin called the faithful to prayer.

'Are you going to the mosque?' The governor nodded silently, went over to the table, stubbed out his cigar in the heavy crystal ashtray and leafed through the document that he had been looking at beforehand.

'We'll come back here afterwards,' he said. 'One secretary must remain here as this has to be sent off to the capital tomorrow.'

'Will you be eating at home?'

'No. Please let my wife know.'

They left the room. Anuhar stayed behind to give out some instructions and then ran down the stairs to catch up with the governor, who had got into the black limousine that was waiting for him. The chauffeur, who had already put the air conditioning on to maximum strength, drove the men to the mosque in silence, where they prayed side by side, surrounded by the Bedouin, who left a clear space, respectfully around them. As they left, the governor looked around admiringly at the shadows cast by the palm trees in the grove.

He liked that time of day. It was without doubt the most beautiful time of day in the oasis, just as dawn was the most beautiful time in the desert. He liked to wander slowly through the gardens and wells, watching the hundreds of birds flying in from afar to spend the night in the treetops.

He used to say that this was the time of day when the smells would come to life, having been crushed by a suffocating sun during the heat-induced lethargy of the day. The governor, Hassan-ben–Koufra, was in fact quite convinced that there was no where else on earth that could match the strength of the perfume that the roses, the jasmine and the carnations, born out of that rich, warm soil, gave off at that hour of the day.

He dismissed his chauffeur with a wave of the hand and walked slowly up the path, forgetting for a minute the thousands of problems he, as governor of that desolate region and a handful of semi-savages, had to deal with.

The ever-faithful Anuhar followed him like a shadow, aware that he liked to spend those precious moments in silence and familiar with all the places he usually stopped; where he would light his cigar and from which flower bed he would pluck a rose to put on Tamat's bedside table. This routine had become something of a daily ritual and he would only miss it if it was unusually hot, or he had a mountain of paperwork to wade through, since it constituted his only form of exercise and provided him with a brief respite from the day's duties.

Night fell as quickly as it always did in the tropics, as if it liked to place a curfew on the amount of time that man could spend enjoying the beauty and calmness of those sunsets. But they were not bothered by the darkness that would soon descend over the gardens and the palm grove, since they knew every path and every fountain by heart, and the lights from the palace up ahead would soon light their way.

On this occasion, however, just before darkness had completely descended, a new shadow emerged from one of the palm trees or maybe it just slipped out of the very ground itself. Even before they could make it out clearly, or see for certain that it was holding a heavy revolver, they knew at once who it was and that he had been waiting for them.

Anuhar wanted to shout, but the black barrel of the canon was already pointing between his eyes.

'Silence. I don't want to do you any harm.'

The governor Ben-Koufra did not even bat an eyelid.

'So, what do you want?'

'My guest. Do you know who I am? I'd imagine you do.' He paused.

'But I don't have your guest...'

Gazel Sayah looked at him for long enough to know that he was not lying.

'Where is he?' he asked.

'Far away.' He paused. 'It's no good. You'll never find him.' The Targui's dark eyes glowered above his veil for a few seconds. He pressed down more firmly on his gun: 'We shall see...' he said and then he pointed to Anuhar-el-Mojkri. 'You can go,' he ordered. 'If in one week's time Abdul-el-Kebir is not healthy, free and alone in the guelta, north of the Sidi-el-Madia mountains, I'll cut your master's head off. Do you understand?' Anuhar-el Mojkri was not able to reply, so Hassan-ben-Koufra answered for him:

'If you're looking for Abdul-el–Kebir, you may as well shoot me now so we can avoid any further bother,' he said confidently. 'They will never hand him over.'

'Why?'

'The President would not allow it.'

'What President?'

'Who else, other than the President of the Republic.'

'Not even in exchange for your life?'

'Not even in exchange for my life.'

Gazel shrugged his shoulders and turned round slowly to face Anuhar-el-Mojkri:

'Just deliver my message.'

He paused. 'And tell the President, whoever he is, that if he does not return my guest, I will kill him too.'

'You're mad!'

'No. I'm a Targui.' He waved his gun at him.

'Now go and remember: in one week in the guelta, north of the Sidi-el-Mahia mountains.' He dug the barrel of the gun into the governor's kidneys and pushed him in the other direction. 'This way!' he ordered.

Anuhar-el-Mojkri took a few steps then turned around, just in time to see them disappearing into the shadows of the palm grove.

Then he ran towards the lights of the palace.

'Abdul-el-Kebir was the architect of our independence, a national hero, the first president of the nation, as a nation. Do you really mean to say that you have never heard of him?'

'Never.'

'Where have you been hiding all these years?'

'In the desert. Nobody came to tell me what had happened.'

'Don't you get travellers passing through your settlements?'

'A few. But we have more important things to talk about. What happened to Abdul-el-Kebir?'

'The current president overthrew him. He removed him from power, but he respected him and didn't dare to kill him. They rose to power together and were locked up in a French prison for many years together.' He shook his head. 'No, he couldn't kill him... Neither his conscience nor his heart would have let him.'

'But he's in prison isn't he?'

'They deported him. To the desert.'

'Where?'

'To the desert. Like I said.'

'The desert is a big place.'

'But not so big that a fanatical supporters didn't manage to find him and help him to escape. That was why he turned up at your jaima.'

'Who was the young boy?'

'A fanatic.' He stared into the fire that was burning slowly and seemed momentarily lost in his own thoughts. When he did speak it was half to himself and he did not look at the Targui. 'A fanatic who wanted to start a civil war. If Abdul had been freed he would have organised the opposition whilst in exile and that would have sparked a blood bath. The French who were actually after his head for some time, now support him.' He paused. 'They prefer him to us.'

He lifted his head slowly, taking in the cave around him and finally resting his gaze on Gazel, who was leaning back against a crop of protruding rocks and said in a sincere tone of voice:

'Do you not understand that you are wasting your time? They will never exchange me for him and I forgive them for that. I'm just a simple governor; a loyal and useful worker, that does his work to the best of his capacity but for whom nobody would risk the possibility of a civil war. Many years will have to pass before Abdul-el-Kebir fades from the people's memories and his name loses its significance.'

He picked up his glass of tea with difficulty as his hands were tied together and lifted it to his mouth, testing it to make sure it did not burn him. 'And things haven't been going too well lately...' he continued. 'Mistakes have been made. The kind of mistakes any newly independent nation or new government might make, but a lot of people don't understand this and they are unhappy. Abdul was good at promising things. Promises that the people now want to see to fulfilled, but that we have not been able to, because they were Utopian ideals.'

He was silent again as he put his glass down on to the sand near to the fire, aware of the Targui staring at him; of his eyes glaring at him above his litham, almost piercing right through him.

'You are scared of him,' he finally said. 'You and your people are very scared of him. Am I not right?'

He nodded.

'We swore allegiance to him and even though I didn't take

part in the conspiracy and only got involved after it had happened, I did not dare to protest,' he smiled sadly. 'They bought my silence by making me the all-powerful governor of an immense territory and I accepted it thankfully. But you are right, deep down I still fear him. We all fear him because at the end of the day we know that he will be back to call us all to account. Abdul always returns.'

'Where is he now?'

'In the desert again.'

'Whereabouts?'

'I will never tell you.'

The Targui stared at him fixedly, his look stern and his voice full of conviction when he said:

'If I ask you to tell me then you will,' he said. 'My ancestors were famous for the way they tortured their prisoners and even though we no longer use those methods, the old ways have been passed on by word of mouth, as something of a curiosity.' He picked up the kettle and filled up the two glasses again. 'Listen!' he continued. 'Maybe you don't understand because you weren't born here, but I will not be able to sleep at night until I know that this man is free once again, as free as he was the day he appeared at the door of my jaima. If I have to kill to achieve that, or torture, I will do it, even though I don't like it. I cannot bring the man that you ordered to be killed back to life, but I can give the other man his freedom back.'

'You can't.'

His stare had a strange intensity about it.

'Are you sure?'

'Entirely. In El-Akab only I know where he is and as much as you torture me I will still not tell you where he is.'

'You are wrong,' Gazel said. 'Somebody else knows.'

'Who?'

'Your wife.'

He was pleased to see that he had been right, because Hassan-ben-Koufra's face suddenly changed and for the first time since they had met, he seemed to lose his composure. He tried to protest feebly but Gazel interrupted him with a swift gesture of his hand.

'Do not try to deceive me,' he snapped.

'I've been watching you for fifteen days and I've seen you with her. She is one of those women who men tell all their secrets to in absolute confidence. Or am I mistaken?'

He looked at him quizzically.

'Sometimes I wonder if you are a simple, ignorant Targui, born and bred in the backwater of all deserts, or if you're hiding someone else behind that veil.'

The Targui smirked:

'They say that our race even then, in the time of the pharaohs, was an intelligent, cultured and powerful one, back in the days when we inhabited the island of Crete. So intelligent and powerful were they that they tried to invade Egypt, but a woman betrayed them and they lost the great battle. Some of them fled to the east and settled by the sea, to become the so-called Phoenicians that went on to rule the oceans. Others fled west and settled in the sands, becoming rulers of the desert. Thousands of years later you arrived, the barbaric Arabs who Mohammad had just dragged out of the darkest ignorance…'

'Yes, I've heard of that legend that proclaims you to be descendents of the "garamants." But I don't believe it.'

'Believe what you will, but what is quite certain is that we were here long before you were and we were always more intelligent, just less ambitious. We are happy with our lives and do not aspire to anything else. We would rather leave you to think what you will of us. But when we are provoked we will react.' He hardened his voice: 'You will tell me where Abdul-el-Kebir is or I will have to ask your wife?'

The governor Hassan-ben-Koufra was reminded of the advice the Minister of the Interior had given him on the eve of his departure to El-Akab:

'Do not trust the Tuaregs,' he had said. 'Do not be fooled by their appearance, because I can tell you that they have the most analytical and cunning brains on the continent. They are a race apart. They could rule us with ease. A Targui would understand what the sea is without ever having seen it, or resolve a philosophical problem that neither you nor I would understand a word of. Their culture is an ancient one and even though as a social group they are in decline, their environment altered and their warrior spirits more subdued, they are still extremely notable individuals. Be wary of them...!'

'A Targui would never hurt a woman,' he said finally. 'I don't think you are an exception. Respect for women is almost as important for you as your laws of hospitality. Would you break one rule in order to enforce another?'

'Probably not,' Gazel admitted.

'But I would not do her any harm. If she knows that your life depended on it then she would tell me where to find Abdul-el-Kebir.'

Hassan-ben-Koufra thought of Tamat and their thirteen years of marriage and their two children and he knew that the Targui was right. He could not blame her, as he knew that he would do the same. At the end of the day even if he told him where Abdul-el-Kebir was, it did not mean that he would automatically be freed.

'He's in the Gerifies fortress,' he sighed.

Gazel felt confident that he was telling the truth and mentally calculated the distance.

'I'll need three days to get there and one more to get camels and provisions.' He thought for a while and then started to laugh:

'That means that by the time they've set up an ambush for me in the guelta of the Sidi-el-Madia I will already be in Gerifies.' He drank his tea very slowly, savouring it. 'They will wait for us for one day; two at most before learning the truth and sending out a message to wait for me there… I have time!' he said confidently. 'Yes. I think I have time.'

'What are you going to do with me,' the governor asked, his voice trembling slightly.

'I should kill you but I will leave you enough water and food for ten days. If you have told me the truth, I will send someone to get you. If you have lied and Abdul-el-Kebir is not there then you will die of hunger and thirst, because you will never be able to break free from these camel skin ties.'

'How do I know for sure that you will send someone to look for me?'

'You don't, but I will. Do you have any money?'

The governor Hassan-ben-Koufra pointed with his chin towards his wallet that was in the back pocket of his trousers and the Targui took it out. He removed the biggest notes and split them in half, took one half and left the rest in the wallet, which he put by the fire.'

'I will find a nomad and give him this money, then I will tell him where he might find the rest of it.' He smiled under his veil. 'A Bedouin would travel a month on camelback to get hold of that amount of money. Don't worry,' he said, trying to reassure him. 'They will come for you. Now take off your trousers.'

'Why?' he said in a tone of alarm.

'You'll be spending ten days in this cave with your feet and hands tied up. If you urinate and then you soil yourself on top, you'll only get sores.' He held up his hands. 'It's best if you keep your bottom bare.'

His Excellency, the governor Hassan-ben-Koufra, supreme and undisputed authority of an area that was bigger than France was about to protest but then seemed to think better of it, swallowed his pride and anger and started to undo, with difficulty, the belt of his trousers.

Gazel helped him take them off, tied him up carefully and then removed his watch and his ring, which had a large shiny stone set into it.

'This will pay for the camels and provisions,' he pointed out. 'I am poor and I had to kill my mount. He was a beautiful mehari. I will never find another like him.'

He gathered together his things, left his water gerba leaning against a wall and a sack of dried fruit and pointing to them said:

'Look after these. Above all, the water. And don't try to free yourself. It'll only make you sweat and you'll need to drink more and then you may not have enough water to last you. Try and sleep...that is the best way of saving your energy.' He left. Outside it was dark and the sky was black and moonless. The stars seemed closer than ever, almost brushing the tops of the peaks that rose above his head and he stood there thinking, maybe trying to orientate himself or mentally tracing the path he would take from there to the far away fortress. He needed above all, mounts, ample provisions and gerbas into which he could put as much water as possible as he was fairly sure that there were no wells around the Tikdabra erg and further south there was only the great "lost lands", which seemed to have no limits.

He walked all night long with a fast and bounding step, at a pace that would have exhausted most people, but that was normal for a Targui. Dawn crept up on him as the sun rose over the crest of a hill that overlooked a valley where once, many years ago, a river would have ran through. The nomads knew that all they had to do there was plunge an atankor half a meter in and they would get enough water for five camels, which made it an obligatory stop-over for the caravans that came from the south that were headed for the great El-Akab oasis.

He could make out a total of three encampments along the riverbed that, with the first light of day, were starting to revive the fires and gather in their animals from the slopes, as they got ready to set off again.

He watched them closely without being seen himself and once he was totally sure that there were no soldiers in any of them, he walked down to the biggest of the jaimas and stopped in front of it. Inside, four men were sipping their morning tea.

'Metulem, metulem!' 'Aselam aleikum' they replied in unison. 'Sit down and have some tea with us. Biscuits?'

He was pleased with the biscuits, the cheese, which was almost rancid, but strong and tasty and the juicy dates, accompanied by a greasy, sweet and sugary tea that warmed up his body and chased away the cold he felt from having spent a dawn in the desert.

The one who seemed to be in charge of the group, a Bedouin with a scraggy beard and sharp eyes, was watching him intently and eventually asked, without the slightest alteration in his tone of voice:

'Is it you Gazel? Gazel Sayah of the Kel-Talgimus?' As he nodded, he added: 'They're looking for you.'

'I know.'

'Have you killed the governor?'

'No.'

They were looking at him intently and had stopped chewing, probably in an attempt to work out whether he was telling the truth or not.

Finally the Bedouin said casually:

'Do you need anything?'

'Four meharis and some food and water.'

He took the watch and the ring out of his red leather bag that was hanging round his neck and showed them: 'I'll pay with these.'

A scrawny old man with the long, delicate, hands of a craftsman, took the ring and studied it with the scrutiny of someone who knows what they are doing, while the scraggy-bearded man looked at the heavy watch.

The craftsman eventually gave the piece of jewellery to his boss:

'It's worth at least ten camels,' he declared. 'It's a good stone.'

The other man nodded, holding out the watch to him.

'Take what you want in exchange for the ring,' he smiled. 'You might need this.'

'I don't know how to use it.'

'Neither do I, but when you need to sell it you'll get a good price for it. It's made of gold.'

'They are offering money for your head,' the craftsman said, almost in passing. 'A lot of money.'

'Do you know of anybody who would want it?'

'None of us do,' the youngest of the group, who had been transfixed by the Targui, a look of open admiration on his face, piped up. 'Do you need some help? I could accompany you.'

The chief, who was probably also the boy's father shook his head disapprovingly:

'He doesn't need any help. Your silence is enough,' he paused. 'And neither must we get mixed up in this. The military are furious and we've already had enough problems with them.'

He turned to Gazel. 'I am sorry, but I must protect my people.'

Gazel Sayah nodded.

'I understand. You are doing enough by selling me your camels.'

He looked over at the young boy sympathetically. 'And you are right, I don't need help, just silence.'

The boy lowered his head slightly, as if enjoying his deference, then got up.

'I will choose the best camels for you and whatever else you need. I will also fill up your gerbas.'

He went out quickly, followed by the watchful eye of the others and the chief, who was clearly proud of him.

'He is brave and spirited and he admires what you are doing,' he commented. 'You're fast becoming the most famous man in the desert.'

'That is not what I am after,' he replied, unwaveringly. 'All I want to do is live in peace with my family.' He paused. 'And for them to respect our laws.'

'You will never be able to live in peace with your family now,' the craftsman warned him. 'You will have to leave the country.'

'There is a border south of the "lost lands,"' the chief said. 'And another to the east, some three days from the Huaila mountains.' He shook his head. 'The ones in the west are too far, you would never get there. To the north you've got the sea and the cities. I have never been there either.'

'How will I know when I have crossed the border into safety?' he asked.

They looked at each other, unable to give him an answer. A black man, an Akli son of slaves, who had until that moment remained silent, spoke up:

'Nobody knows exactly. No one,' he said confidently.

'Last year I took a caravan down to the Niger, but we were never able to work out when we had crossed it into the other country, either on the way there or on our return.'

'How long did it take you to get to the river?'

The Akli thought about his answer for a while. Then, finally and not very convincingly he ventured:

'Maybe a month...' He tutted as if trying to get rid of some bad memories. 'Almost double, on our return. There was a drought and the wells had dried up so we had to go a long way round to avoid Tikdabra. When I was young you used to pass decent wells and grasslands before arriving at the river. But now the wells have been reclaimed by the sand, the last traces of grass have disappeared and the sand is threatening the banks of the river itself. These are grasslands where the Peuls used to graze their livestock but that now aren't fit for the hungriest of camels any more. There's not a trace left of the wells that were once populated in the area either, so there are no longer any places to rest.' He tutted again. 'And I am not that old.'

He reiterated his words: 'No, I am not old. The desert is advancing too quickly.'

'I do nor care whether the desert is advancing and swallowing up other lands or not,' Gazel remarked. 'I am happy here. I worry more about the desert not being big enough for us to be able to live in it peacefully. The more it grows, the better. Maybe one day they'll just forget about us.'

'They will never forget,' the craftsman interjected. 'They have found oil, which is what the Rumi are most interested in. I know, because I worked in the capital for two years and there, all of the conversations revolved, in one way or another, around oil.'

Gazel looked at the old man with renewed interest. The craftsman, like all artisans, whether they worked with silver or gold as he did, or with leather or stone, were considered by the Tuaregs as an inferior caste, half way between an Imohag and an ingad or serf and even sometimes between an ingad and an Akli slave. But despite this ranking, they also recognised that within their social system, these craftsmen were probably the most cultured of them all, with many of them able to read and write, while some of them had travelled beyond the desert's borders.

'I was in a town once.' he finally said. 'But it was very small and at that time governed by the French. Have things changed a lot?'

'A lot,' he conceded. 'In those times you had the French on one side and us on the other. Now our brothers are fighting each other, with one wanting one thing and the other another.'

He shook his head sadly. 'And when the French left, they divided up the territories putting borders in by just drawing a line on the map, which often split up the same tribe or put members of the same family into two different countries. So if the government was communist, they had to be communist; if the government was fascist, they had to be fascist; if the king ruled it was a monarchy...'

He stopped and looking at him questioningly asked:

'Do you know what it means to be a communist?'

Gazel shook his head.

'I've never heard of them. Are they our sector?'

'More or less. But not religious. Only political.'

'Political?' he replied, not understanding the term.

'They believe that all men should be equal, with the same rights and tasks and that wealth should be evenly distributed.'

'They believe that the clever man and the stupid man should be equal. That the Imohag and the slave, the worker and the layabout, the warrior and the coward are all the same?' he cried out in surprise. 'Are they mad? If Allah made us all different, why on earth should they try and claim that we are all equal?' he snorted. 'Being born a Targui would mean nothing then?'

'It's more complicated than that,' he admitted.

'Well it must be, because that kind of nonsense is not even worth discussion,' he said, then paused as if bringing the subject to an end, before asking:

'Have you heard of Abdul-el-Kebir?'

'We've all heard of him,' the Bedouin chief said, interrupting the craftsman. 'He was the one that got rid of the French and governed for the first few years.'

'What kind of a man is he?'

'A fair man,' the other conceded. 'Mistaken, but fair.'

'Why mistaken?'

'Whoever places all their trust in others, only to be overthrown by them and imprisoned, has to have been mistaken.'

Gazel turned round to the old man.

'Is he one of those men that believe that we should all be equal? What are they called?'

'Communists?' the craftsman said. 'No. I don't believe he was exactly a communist. They say he was a socialist.'

'And what's that?'

'Something else.'

'Similar?'

'I'm not sure.'

He searched the faces of the other men for an answer, but they just shrugged their shoulders, all as ignorant as each other. He sighed and left the subject behind, aware that he was not going to get very far with any more questions of that nature.

'I have to go' he said as he stood up to leave.

'Aselam aleikum.'

'Aselam aleikum.'

He walked over to where they were loading up his camels and checked them over with his expert eye, saw that everything was in order, got up onto the fastest of them and after making it stand up, took out a fistful of notes and handed them to the boy.

'You'll find the other half in the cave of the Tatalet gorge, half a day's walk from here. Do you know it?'

'I know it,' he confirmed. 'Is that where you have hidden the governor?'

'Next to the notes,' he replied. 'In one week, on your way back from El-Akab, set him free.'

'You can trust in me.'

'Thank you. And remember: in one week, not before.'

'Take care. May Allah be with you!' The Targui dug his heels into the mehari's neck and the animal turned go, followed by the others and they set off together, unhurriedly, disappearing from view behind a cluster of rocks.

The little boy returned alone and sat down at the door of his jaima. His father smiled gently.

'Don't worry about him,' he said.

'He's a Targui and there is no-one in the world that is capable of catching a lone Targui in the desert.'

The light and the silence woke him.

The sun flooded in through the latticed window in shafts, illuminating the rows of books and reflecting off the brass ashtray that was full of cigarette butts. But even though it was almost midday, there did not seem to be any noise coming from the patio and he was sure that he had not heard the wake up call that normally went off every morning.

The silence bothered him. Over the years he had become used to a strict military regime where everything he did was carried out to a rigid timetable. Any disruption to this routine, like not having been woken at six o'clock on the dot with half an hour to wash before breakfast, made him feel strangely uneasy.

And the silence.

The suffocating silence from the patio, which at that hour was usually full of the sound of the soldiers chatting away before the great heat descended, made him jump from his bed, pull on his trousers and run over to the window.

Not a soul to be seen. He could not see anybody next to the well or by the battlements on the west corner, which was the only bit of the wall he could see from his room.

'Hey!' he called out in a worried voice. 'What's happened? Where is everybody?'

There was no reply. He called out again, but still no response and the silence unnerved him.

'They've abandoned me...' was the first thought that crossed his mind. 'They've left me here to die of hunger and thirst.'

He ran to the door and was surprised to find it half open. He went out onto the patio and a violent sun scorched his eyes, as it bounced back off the white walls, painted a thousand times over by soldiers who had had nothing better to do for days and months on end.

But no one appeared. There was no one on guard at the sentry boxes in the corner or next to the gate, through which you could see the desert stretching out to eternity.

'Hey!' he shouted again. 'What's going on? What's happening?'

Only silence again. That accursed silence and not even a light breeze, carrying signs of life with it, blew to alter the quiet of the place. It was if it had been petrified, crushed and destroyed by a sun that was already starting to beat down mercilessly.

He went down the four steps in two jumps and walked over to the well, still calling out to the mess, the soldiers' quarters and the orderly room.

'Captain...! Captain...! What kind of a joke is this? Where are you all?'

A dark shadow slipped out of the kitchen. It was a tall, very thin Targui with a dark litham covering his face, a rifle in one hand and a long sword in the other.

He stopped under the porch.

'They are dead,' he said.

He looked at him incredulously.

'Dead?' he repeated, dumbfounded. 'All of them?'

'All of them.'

'Who killed them?'

'Me.'

He walked over to him, not quite able to believe his ears.

'You...?' he asked, shaking his head, as if trying to get rid of the idea.

'Are you trying to tell me that you, without anybody else's help have killed twelve soldiers, a sergeant and an official?'

He nodded calmly.

'They were asleep.'

Abdul-el-Kebir had seen thousands of people die, had in fact ordered the execution of many and even though he had loathed each and everyone of his jailers, he was overcome with an unbearable feeling of fear and an emptiness in the pit of his stomach. He leant against the wooden post that supported the doorway so as not to lose his balance.

'You killed them while they were sleeping?' he stammered. 'Why?'

'Because they killed my guest.' He paused. 'And because there were too many of them. If one of them had sounded the alarm you would have remained here forever, to die between these four walls.'

Abdul-el-Kebir watched him in silence and nodded his head as if it all made sense suddenly.

'Now I remember,' he admitted.

'You are the Targui that gave us hospitality. I saw you as they carried me away.'

'Yes,' he nodded. 'I am Gazel Sayah and you were my guest. It is my duty to take you across the border.'

'Why?'

He looked at him uncomprehendingly. Finally he answered:

'It is the custom. You asked for my protection and so I must protect you.'

'Killing fourteen men in order to protect me seems a little excessive, don't you think?'

The Targui did not respond and glanced towards the open door.

'I'll get the camels.' he said. 'Get ready for a long journey.'

He watched him as he walked away and disappeared from view behind the main gate that was slightly open and he suddenly felt oppressed, there alone in the abandoned fort. He felt oppressed and shocked, even more than he had been the day he had arrived there; when he had realised that he would never leave that place alive, that it would be both his prison and his grave.

He remained there for a few minutes, quite still, straining to hear something, although he knew it would only be the wind or the men that made a noise and on that day there was no wind and the men were all dead.

All fourteen of them!

He remembered their faces, one by one, from the incredibly pale and pointed face of the captain, who hated the sun and preferred to remain in the half-light of his study, to the sweaty, red-cheeked cook, to the dirty corporal with his long, cheeky moustache, who used to clean his cell and bring him food every day.

He knew every sentinel and every minion. He had played dice with them and written letters to their families and read novels to them during the interminable desert nights. He had often wondered who were the real prisoners up there, them or him, in that fortress set deep within the desert's confines.

He had known them all and now they were dead.

He wondered what type of a man it took to admit killing fourteen human beings as they slept, without altering the tone of his voice or expressing a trace of guilt or repent in his manner.

He was a Targui. At university they had learned that this race was quite unlike any other race and that their morals and customs were completely different to any other group in the world. They were a proud, indomitable and rebellious people who followed their own rules. Still, no one had told him that their customs allowed for the murder of sleeping men, in cold blood. 'Morality is a question of custom and we cannot judge them, therefore, according to our own criteria, since the way they behave is the result of ancient customs and their vision of life and its criteria are totally different to our own...'

The words of the old man came back to him as if it were just yesterday and he could see him sitting behind his enormous table, his hands and the sleeves of his black jacket, white with chalk. He remembered the efforts he would go to, to try and make his students understand that just because some of the ethnic groups in their country, which was at the time on the brink of independence, had not had much contact with the French, they should not be considered any more inferior.

'One of our continent's greatest problems,' he would say over and over again, 'is the undeniable fact that a lot of African people are even more racist than our very own colonisers were. Neighbouring tribes, almost brothers, hate and despise each other and as we become independent countries it is becoming increasingly apparent that the black man's worst enemy is another black man who speaks a different dialect. We must not make the same mistake. You will be in charge of this nation one day and you must be fully aware that the Bedouins, the Tuaregs and the mountain Cabilenos are not inferior, just very different.'

Different.

He had never thought twice about ordering an attack on one of the cafés where the French used to meet, even though he knew that many innocent people would be killed. He had never hesitated before firing off a machine gun at paratroopers or legionaries. Death had simply been a part of his adolescent life and remained that way well into the first few years of his rule, when he had sent dozens of collaborators to the gallows. There was no reason why he should have been so taken aback by the death of fourteen jailers. He had known those jailers though, each one of them, their names, their likes and dislikes and he also knew that their throats had been slit whilst they had been asleep.

He slowly crossed the patio and stopped at the large window of the barrack hut, cupped his hands against the window and peered inside.

All he could make out was a row of bulky shapes, the hard old beds lined up some two metres apart from each other, covered in dirty sheets with not even a spot of blood visible, most of it having already been absorbed by the thick, straw mattresses.

Not a sound could be heard. Nobody was snoring or snuffling, sleep talking, or scratching their sun-burned, sandy skin.

Just the silence and the noise of some flies banging against the window as if even they had had their fill of blood and were fighting to get out into the light and fresh air.

Ten meters further down he opened the door to the captain's quarters and the sun flooded into the cluttered, dusty room and on the large bed, he could just make out the contours of a small, thin body, covered with a very white sheet.

He closed the door again and walked around the rest of the fortress, but there were no other bodies to be found. The sentry boxes were empty and there was no one at the gate, as if the Targui, according to some strange ritual, had preferred to drag them back into their beds and cover them up there.

He went back into his prison cell and started getting together his letters, the photos of his sons and a well-thumbed copy of the Koran, which he had carried with him for as long as he could remember and put everything, including the few items of clothing he possessed, into a canvas bag.

Then he sat down in the shadow of the porch, near to the well, as the sun beat down, without mercy, gradually erasing every inch of shadow from the ground.

The suffocating heat made him sink into an uneasy slumber, from which he awoke intermittently with a jump, startled by the intense silence and the unsettling sensation of emptiness he felt. He started to sweat profusely, his ears almost hurting, as if he had drowned in a hollow universe and he muttered some words outloud just to remind himself that he had a voice and that sound still existed.

Was there anywhere in the world more silent than that great pantheon, which had been converted into an old fortress set deep within the Sahara, on that windless day?

Why on earth it had been built there nobody knew. It sat in the centre of the plain, far away from the well-known wells and caravan routes, far from the oasis and the borders, in the heart of absolutely nowhere.

The Gerifies fort, in itself, small and pointless and only useful in theory as a logistical back up and place of rest for any nomads patrolling the area, had been considered as good a spot as any other in that five hundred kilometre radius. So a well had been dug and battlement walls built and rickety old furniture brought in, probably from other barracks that had been dismantled. A handful of men were then condemned to keep watch there, sent to this corner of the desert, which was so remote that according to legend, not one traveller had ever passed by it.

Legend also had it that it took three months before a garrison of the French Foreign Legion based there, had realised that they were no longer part of the colonial armed forces but foreigners that had been overthrown.

There were six tombs lines up against the rear wall. They had each, at one time, had a wooden cross with a name written on them, but many years ago a cook had been forced to use them as firewood. Abdul-el-Kebir had often wondered to himself what on earth six Christians were doing there, so far from their homeland and why they had joined the Foreign Legion in the first place, only to end their days in the solitude of the endless Saharan plain.

'One day they'll dig me a grave next to those tombs?' he would say to himself. 'Then there'll be seven anonymous tombs and my guardians will be able to leave Gerifies...and the hero of national independence will rest for eternity next to six unknown mercenaries.'

But things had not worked out quite like that and now they

needed fourteen more tombs; tombs which no one would bother to mark since no one really cared about a bunch of useless jailers.

He turned round again instinctively to look back at the hut, still barely able to believe that there, inside, were all those bodies that had already started to rot in the dry, suffocating heat and that just the night before had filled the place with their voices and their presence.

He had often been tempted to strangle some of them with his bare hands. During his years as a prisoner he had generally been treated with respect but there were some who had subjected him to all manner of humiliations, especially after his latest escapade. His punishment for escaping had been extended to the whole garrison, who had been deprived of leave for one year, prompting many of them to plot his end once and for all so that they could be freed from that place, which had, to all extents and purposes, become their prison as well.

The idea of taking off again filled him with dread as he imagined the infinite journey across the sands and the stony plains, always under a relentless sun, without knowing where they were headed or whether the desolate plain they walked on would ever end.

He remembered with horror, the torment of thirst and the intolerable pain of his cramped muscles and wondered to himself what on earth he was doing sitting there in the shade with his bag in hand, waiting for a man, a murderer who was going to take him away across the sands and stony plains once again.

He appeared at his side out of nowhere, silently, despite the fact that he was accompanied by four camels. They followed him noiselessly, maybe in imitation of their master's stealth or aware, perhaps, that they had just walked into a mausoleum.

He pointed to the huts with his head:

'Why did you put the men in their beds? Did you think they would be better off in there, than where you killed them? Why did you bother?'

Gazel observed him for a moment, a look of incomprehension on his face.

Finally he shrugged his shoulders:

'A bird of prey will find a dead body left in the open air within two hours,' he replied. 'But it will take three days before the smell of them comes through those walls and by then we'll be well on our way towards the border.'

'What border?'

'Aren't all the borders good?'

'The ones to the south and the east are good. I'll be hung from the gallows if we cross the west one?'

Gazel did not respond, immersed as he was with the task of getting water from the well for his insatiably thirsty animals to drink. Once he had finished, he glanced over at the canvas bag.

'Is that all you have?' he asked.

'It's all I have.'

'That's not a lot for someone who used to be president of the country.' He looked back. 'Go into the kitchen and bring out provisions and any vessels you can find.' He shook his head. 'Water will be a problem on this journey.'

'Isn't water always a problem in the desert?'

'Yes, of course, but more so where we're going.'

'And where, might I ask, are we going?'

'To a place where no one can follow us: to the "lost land" of Tikdabra.'

'Where can they have got to?'

There was no answer as the Minister of the Interior, Ali Madani, a tall, strong man with slicked down hair and small eyes, that he tried to hide, alongside his intentions, behind a pair of thick, dark glasses, scanned the faces in front of him and when still no one answered, he insisted:

'Come on men! I haven't travelled one thousand five hundred kilometers just to sit here looking at you all. I imagined that you would all be experts on the Saharan desert and the Tuareg customs. I repeat: where could they have gone to?'

'Anywhere.' a colonel said sullenly, as if it were already a lost cause. 'He was headed north, but then his footprints disappeared once they got on to rocky terrain. From there on out the desert is all his.'

'Are you trying to tell me,' the minister spluttered, trying to hide his indignation, 'that a Bedouin, a simple Bedouin, could go into one of their fortresses, slit the throats of fourteen men, free the State's most dangerous man and disappear with him into the desert that to all intents and purposes is "his."' He shook his head incredulously. 'I thought that the desert was "ours," colonel. That the country was under jurisdiction of the army and the forces of law and order.'

'Ninety-five percent of this country is made up of desert, your Excellency,' the general and commander-in-chief of the area, said in an irritated tone of voice. 'But all of the country's wealth and resources are concentrated in just ten percent of it, along the coast. I have to control an area as big as half of Europe with the dregs of an army and minimum financing. That, proportionally, is one man for every one thousand kilometers, men who are posted to an oasis here and a fortress there, without any logic behind it all, whatsoever. In the light of those statistics, do you really think, your Excellency, that we can call the desert our own? Our penetration and influence is so minimal that a Targui would never know, not even in twenty years time, that we were an independent nation. He is the master of the desert,' he stressed. 'The only master that exists.'

The minister Madani appeared to accept his argument, or at least preferred not to reply and turned to face Lieutenant Razman who had remained standing up out of respect, in a corner next to Sergeant Major Malik-el-Haideri.

'What about you lieutenant, you've spent the most time with this Targui, what do you think?'

'That he's very cunning sir. One way or another he will do what we least expect him to do.'

'Describe him to me.'

'Tall and thin.'

The minister sat there expectantly, waiting for him to carry on with the description, but when he did not, said:

'And what else?'

'Nothing else, your Excellency. He's always completely covered up. You only ever see his eyes and his hands, which are strong...'

The minister snorted:

'For crying out loud!' he exclaimed banging his pen against the table. 'Are we up against a ghost here...? Tall, thin, dark eyes, strong hands... Is this all we know about a man that has the army at his mercy, keeps the President awake at night, has kidnapped the governor and taken away Abdul-el-Kebir? You're a bunch of half wits!'

'No, we're not,' the colonel retorted. 'Under the laws here the Tuaregs are allowed to cover their faces, in keeping with their tradition. The description is at least of a Targui, but there must be some three hundred thousand of them, a third of whom live on this side of the border, so we have to accept at this point that his description fits at least fifty thousand male adults.'

The minister said nothing. He removed his glasses, put them to one side and rubbed his eyes, his face creased into an expression of deep concern. He had hardly slept a wink in the last forty-eight hours and the long journey from El-Akab and the heat had exhausted him. But he knew he could not leave until he had found Abdul-el-Kebir or his days as Minister of the Interior were numbered and he would be demoted to the position of some obscure official with no future.

Abdul-el-Kebir was a time bomb that could, in less than one month, blow the government and its system sky high, if he managed to reach the border and get to Paris. Once Abdul got to France, the French would provide him with the support that they had previously denied him. With French money and strong support at home there would no stopping him and those that had betrayed him would have just enough time to pack their bags and go into hiding, to live in the eternal fear that one day or another they would be brought to justice.

He had to catch Abdul-el-Kebir and he had to finish him off once and for all, because he did not feel able to go through with all that anxiety a second time round. If the President had ordered for him to be shot dead the first time he had escaped then none of this would have happened and at least he would have finally finished off the problem once and for all, whoever it might have upset.

'We have to find him,' he said finally. 'Ask for whatever you need; men, planes, tanks. Whatever it takes! Just find him. That is an order!'

'Sir!'

He turned his face towards the voice.

'Yes, sergeant?'

'Sir,' Malik repeated in a voice that was barely audible. 'I am convinced that they've gone into the "lost land" of Tikdabra.'

'The "lost land?" They'd have to be mad... What on earth would they do that for?'

'I saw the tracks he left as they moved away from the Gerifies Fortress. Four heavily loaded camels. And there weren't any receptacles that could have carried water left in the fortress. If the Targui was keen to get away quickly he would not have done so with four camels, nor would they have been so laden down.'

'But his footprints were headed north and the "lost land" is towards the south if I'm not mistaken.'

'You are not mistaken sir. But that Targui has already deceived us quite a few times. He would think nothing of losing a day by heading north if it was enough to get us off his scent and then to turn around and head for Tikdabra. On the other side he will be safe.'

'No human being has ever crossed that region,' the colonel pointed out. 'That's why we chose it as a border, because it doesn't need protection.'

'No other human being could survive in the centre of a saltpan for five days, but I watched how that Targui survived, colonel,' Malik replied. 'With all due respect, I would like to point out that we are not dealing with a normal man. His powers of endurance are beyond belief.'

'But he is not alone. And Abdul-el-Kebir is an old man, considerably weakened by his last attempt to escape and from his years in prison. Do you really think he will be able to survive thirty days of thirst at a temperature of over sixty degrees? If they're stupid enough to try it in the first place, then we needn't bother looking for them.'

Sergeant Major Malik-el-Haideri did not dare to contradict a man who was so above his station, so the minister answered for him.

'It may well be a shot in the dark,' he conceded, 'but the sergeant and the lieutenant are here because they are the only ones that have had any contact with this savage and their opinion is especially important. What do you think lieutenant.'

'Gazel is capable of anything, sir. Including keeping an old man alive at the expense of his own life. For him, protecting his guest has become the sole reason for his existence, even more important to him than the protection of his own family. If he considers Tikdabra the safest place to hide in, then he will go there, to the "lost land."

'Alright. We'll look for him there then. Now,' he paused. 'You mentioned something about a family. What do you know about them? If we found them then maybe we could set up an exchange.'

'They've abandoned their grazing grounds,' the general said in a voice that revealed how disagreeable he found the entire matter. 'And it does not seem right to get women and children involved in this. What would people think of our army if we had to stoop to those levels in order to solve this issue?'

'The army doesn't have to get involved in that, general. My people can take care of it. Although...' he added with some deliberation, 'I don't think the army can come off any worse in this than it already has.'

The general disagreed with the minister ferociously, but managed to keep it to himself. He reminded himself that for the time being Ali Madani was the President's right-hand man and the second most influential man in the country, while he was just a simple military man, who had recently been promoted to the position of general. He believed that the current situation was more down to the ineptitude of political figures like him, rather than due to a lack of efficiency within the armed forces, but it was neither the time nor the place for such a discussion that would only get him into trouble. He bit down hard on his lip and sat there attentively. The minister would probably have disappeared from the political scene by the time he became brigadier anyway.

'How many helicopters have you got?' he heard the minister ask the colonel.

'One.'

'I'll send in three more. Planes?'

'Six. But we cannot spare any of them. Most of the outposts are dependent on air supplies.'

'I'll send in a squadron. I want the whole area around Gerifies searched.' He paused. 'And I want two regiments to position themselves at either side of the "lost land" of Tikdabra.'

'But that's outside of our borders,' the colonel protested. 'It'll be seen as an invasion of a neighbouring country.'

'Leave those issues to the Foreign Ministry and concern yourself more with my orders.'

His was interrupted by a sharp knock at the door. It opened and an orderly went in and whispered something into Anuhar-el-Mojkri's ear. The secretary had not said a word for the entire meeting, but on hearing the news his composure changed considerably.

He nodded, closed the door and said:

'Excuse me your Excellency, but I've been told that the governor has just arrived back.'

'Hassan-ben-Koufra?' Madani said in a tone of astonishment. 'Alive?'

'Yes sir. He's in a bad way, but he's alive. He's waiting for you in his office.'

The minister jumped up and without even saluting anyone present, left the room, crossed the high gallery, followed by Anuhar-el-Mojkri and the astounded stares of local officials. He strode into the governor's large, half-lit office, slamming the heavy door behind him and leaving the secretary, who had practically run straight into it, outside.

The governor Hassan-ben-Koufra, with a ten-day growth on his chin, dirty, haggard and wide-eyed, was a mere shadow of the proud, tall and arrogant man that had left that same office on that fatal afternoon on his way to prayers. Slumped into one of the heavy armchairs, he stared out, without seeing, at the palm grove through the heavy lace curtains and it was evident that his mind was elsewhere, probably still in the cave where he had suffered the most traumatic experience of his life. He did not even lift his eyes when Madani went in, who had to sit right in front of him in order to make his presence felt.

'I didn't expect to see you again.'

His looked up slowly, his eyes reddened with tiredness and dilated in terror, as he struggled to recognise his visitor. Eventually he muttered in a hoarse, barely audible voice:

'Me neither.' He lifted up his raw, wounded wrists. 'Look!'

'It's better than being dead. And you are now to blame for the death of fourteen men and for placing our country in grave danger.'

'I never thought he'd manage it. I was convinced that I was sending him into a trap and that at Gerifies they would kill him. We have our best men there...'

'Our best?' he exclaimed. 'He slit their throats like chickens, one by one... And now Abdul is free. Do you realise what this means?'

He nodded:

'We'll get them.'

'How? He's not with a young, inept fanatic any more but a Targui who knows this terrain better than any of us will ever know it.' He sat down opposite him on the sofa and ran his fingers through his hair mechanically. 'And to think it was me that put your name forward for this position and pushed for you to get it.'

'I'm sorry.'

'You're sorry?' He let out a bitter and derogatory cackle.

'At least if you were dead, we could say that you were tortured to inhumane limits. But you're here, alive and bragging about a few wounds that'll heal in less than fifteen days. A rebellious student would have resisted for longer against my men than you did for that Targui. You were tougher once.'

'When I was young and the French paratroopers were torturing me, I believed the cause to be a good one. Maybe I'm not convinced that keeping Abdul imprisoned for life is a just cause.'

'It seemed fair to you at the time you were given this study and appointed governor,' he reminded him. 'And you appeared to be happy with our decision. It was "Abdul the enemy" then, the devil incarnate, who was bringing the country to its knees by keeping us intimates out of government. No Hassan,' he shook his head decidedly, 'don't try and pull the wool over my eyes, I know you too well. The truth of the matter is that over the years, power and comfort have made you soft and frightened. You could play the hero and fight when you had nothing to lose except for the hope of a better future. But now you've got your palace and your Swiss bank account you've lost it. Don't try and deny it,' he said viciously. 'Remember that my job is to keep myself informed and I know how much those oil companies pay you for your collaboration.'

'Less than they do to you probably.'

'Of course,' Ali Madani admitted, unashamedly. 'But for the time being you're the one in trouble, not me.' He walked over to the window to look at the muezzin who was calling the faithful to prayer from the mosque's minaret and said without looking at him:

'Pray that I can do something about this mess, otherwise you'll be losing more than your job as governor.'

'Are you telling me I'm dismissed?'

'Of course!' he replied. 'And I can assure you that if I don't get Abdul, I will have you tried for treason.'

The governor Hassan-ben-Koufra did not answer, but just continued to stare at the sores on his wrists, meditating on the fact that only some days beforehand he had been doing the same thing that Madani was doing right now: judging a man harshly for something that was actually the Targui's fault. The Targui who was fast becoming a national obsession.

His mind drifted back to the days he had spent in the cave. They were days that had been wracked with worry and anguish as he had wondered whether the Targui would actually send someone for him or leave him there to die like a dog, of terror and thirst.

He also thought about how clever the Targui had been to find his weak spot so easily and extract the information he needed, without so much as laying a finger on him.

He hated the Targui for all of that, but above all he hated him for having kept his promise to send someone in to save him.

'Why?' Ali Madani asked, turning to look at him again, as if he had been reading his thoughts. 'Why did this man who has killed in such cold blood, set you free?'

'He promised me he would.'

'Yes and a Targui always fulfils a promise, I know that. Still I find it hard to understand how he finds it lawful to slit the throats of I don't know how many sleeping men, but unlawful to break a promise made to the enemy.' He shook his head and went to sit down behind the large table, in the chair that used to belong to his subordinate. 'It makes me wonder how we can all be so different yet still live in the same country,' he continued, half talking to himself. 'This part of our heritage is what we have to thank the French for. They mixed us up like a great big pudding and then cut us up into tiny pieces, dividing us up as they saw fit. Now, twenty years later, we are sitting here still trying, without much success, to understand our own people.'

'We knew all that already,' Hassan-ben-Koufra said wearily.

'We all reached the same conclusion, but nobody thought to

renounce the part which didn't belong to us and be content with a smaller, more homogenous country.'

He opened and closed his hands slowly and painfully. 'We were blinded by ambition and the desire to conquer as much territory as we could, even though we knew we wouldn't ever be able to govern it. Then our politics decided that if the Bedouins were unable to adapt to our way of life we must destroy them. What would we have done if the French had tried to destroy us simply because we wouldn't adapt to their way of life?'

'What we ended up doing – becoming an independent nation. Maybe that is the future for the Tuaregs, perhaps they should become independent of us.'

'Can you imagine them being independent? The French probably thought the same of us, that is until we started throwing bombs and showing them that we really could be independent. This Gazel, or whatever you want to call him, has demonstrated that he can beat us. If they all joined forces, I can bet you that they would conquer the desert from us and half the world would be ready to lend them a hand in exchange for the petrol in their terrain. No,' he said with an air of finality. 'We won't so much as give them the opportunity to find out that they could swap their camels for gold Cadillacs.'

'Is that why you are here?'

'For that and to finish off Abdul-el-Kebir once and for all.'

The landscape was like a sea of naked women lying in the sun, their skin golden, sometimes bronzed, at times burned, and the tips of the oldest ladies tinged with red. They were enormous, their breasts often rising to over two hundred metres high, with buttocks that were sometimes over a kilometre wide. They had long, never-ending legs, inaccessible legs, through which the camels climbed, clumsily, and heavily, shrieking and biting with each step as they struggled not to fall back down to the bottom of the dune and be devoured by the sand once and for all.

The gassis, the paths that ran between the dunes, would often lead them into windy labyrinths that led them nowhere or right back to the beginning and it was only thanks to Gazel's incredible sense of direction and personal conviction that they managed to advance south, day by day, without once retracing their steps.

Abdul-el-Kebir, who prided himself on how well he knew the country that he had governed for a number of years and who had lived in the heart of the desert, would never have imagined, not even in his worst nightmares, that such a vast sea of dunes could actually have existed. It was like an erg that you could not see the end of, even from the highest of ghourds.

Sand and wind were the only things to exist out there, on the outskirts of the great "lost land" and he could not believe, as the Targui had told him, that there was something even worse out there than the petrified landscape he now found himself in.

They spent the days sheltering from the wind and sun in the shade of a roomy, wide, yellow-coloured tent that they shared with their camels, only resuming their journey in the early evening and continuing through the night to the light of the moon and the stars. Dawn would arrive suddenly and never failed to take their breath away, as the shadows scurried away across the sabre-shaped sifs, running from crest to crest, the grains of sand on those fine, blade-like tips, somehow defying the rules of gravity.

'How much longer?' he asked at dawn on the fifth day, as he realised with the first light that he still could not make out the start of the great plain.

'I don't know. Nobody has ever crossed this. Nobody has ever counted the days of travel across these sands or the time it takes to cross the "lost land."'

'So we are headed for a certain death then.'

'By saying nobody has done it, does not mean that it cannot be done.'

He shook his head incredulously.

'I am flabbergasted by the unerring faith you seem to have in yourself,' he said. 'I myself am starting to feel scared.'

'Fear is your main enemy in the desert,' came his reply. 'Fear leads to desperation and madness and madness leads to stupidity and death.'

'Are you ever afraid?'

'Of the desert? No. I was born here and spent my life in it. We have four camels and the females have enough milk for today and tomorrow and there are no signs of a harmatan coming. If the wind respects us, there is hope.'

'How many days of hope?' Abdul asked himself.

He went to sleep trying to calculate how many days of hope they had left, how much longer they would have to endure the suffering but was awoken at midday by a buzzing sound overhead. He opened his eyes and saw the silhouette of Gazel, kneeling at the corner of the tent and looking up at the sky.

'Aeroplanes,' he said without turning round.

Abdul crawled over to him and looked up to see a small reconnaissance plane circling overhead that was about five kilometers away and approaching them slowly.

'Can they see us?'

Gazel shook his head, but even so he went over to the camels and tied up their feet to stop them from getting up.

'The noise will startle them.' he said. 'And if they bolt they'll give us away.'

When he had finished, he waited patiently until the plane had disappeared behind the tip of the nearest dune on one of its circuits, then left the tent and covered up the most visible parts of it with sand.

The animals bayed nervously and one of the females tried to bite them several times, but after about fifteen minutes, having only flown directly over them once, the buzzing noise started to fade away and the plane became a small dot on the horizon.

Gazel, who was sitting half in the shade, leaning against one of his mounts, took out a handful of dates from a leather bag and started to eat them as if nothing out of the ordinary had happened and looking as relaxed as he might have been, were he sitting comfortably in his own jaima.

'Do you really think you can remove them from power if we manage to cross the border?' he asked, although it was clear that he was not actually that interested in the answer.

'That's what they think. Although, I'm not so sure. Most of my people have died or been imprisoned. Others betrayed me.' He took some dates that the Targui was offering him. 'It won't be easy,' he added. 'But if I manage it, you can have anything you ask for. I will owe it all to you.'

Gazel shook his head slowly:

'You will not owe me anything and I will still be in your debt for the death of your friend. Whatever I do and however many years pass, I will never be able to give him back the life that he entrusted me with.'

He looked at him for some time, trying to understand the man from the depths of his deep, dark eyes, which were still the only part of his face that he had seen up to that point.

'I keep wondering why some lives mean so much to you, while others mean so little. There was nothing you could have done that day, but your guilt has pursued and tormented you. But you seem completely indifferent to the deaths of the soldiers whose throats you slit.'

He did not receive an answer. The Targui just shrugged his shoulders and continued to put dates into his mouth, under his veil.

'Are you my friend?' Abdul suddenly asked out of the blue.

He looked at him in surprise:

'Yes. I suppose so.'

'The Tuareg usually show their faces when they are with family and friends, but you haven't done so with me.'

Gazel meditated for a few seconds and then slowly raised his hand and pulled down his veil, allowing him to study his thin, firm and deeply lined face, at leisure. He smiled:

'It's a face like any other face.'

'I imagined you to look different.'

'Different?'

'Older maybe. How old are you?'

'I don't know. I've never counted. My mother died when I was a child and that is the only thing that women seem concerned with. I'm not as strong as I was, but I have not started to tire yet either.'

'I can't imagine you ever getting tired. Do you have a family?'

'A wife and four children. My first wife died.'

'I have two children. My wife also died, although they won't tell me when.'

'How long have you been in prison?'

'Fourteen years.'

Gazel remained silent, trying to gauge what fourteen years meant in the life of a person, but try as he may he could not even vaguely imagine what it would be like to be locked up for that length of time.

'Were you always in the Gerifies fortress?'

'For that time, yes. But before then I spent eight years in French prisons.' He smiled bitterly. 'When I was younger I fought for freedom.'

'And in spite of everything, you still want to fight even though they might betray you and lock you up again?'

'I belong to a class of men that can only exist at the top of the pile or right at the bottom.'

'How long were you at the top for?'

'In power? Three and a half years.'

'That does not make sense,' the Targui replied, shaking his head repeatedly. 'However great it might be to be in power, three and a half years in charge cannot surely justify twenty-two years of imprisonment. No. Not even if it were the other way round. For us Tuaregs, liberty is the most important thing of all. That is why we do not build houses from stone, because we would feel hemmed in by the walls around us. I want to know that I can pull up any one of my walls in the jaima at any time, just to look at the immensity of the desert beyond it. And I like to watch the wind blowing through the canes of our sheribas.' He paused. 'Allah could not see us if we were hidden beneath a stone roof.'

'He sees us everywhere. Even from inside the deepest of dungeons. He weighs up our sufferings and compensates for them if they are for a just cause. My cause is a just one,' he concluded.

'Why?'

He looked at him disconcertedly.

'What do you mean, why?'

'Why is your cause any more just than theirs? You're all after power aren't you?'

'There are many different ways to exercise power. Some will use it to their own advantage. Others use it in order to benefit society, to achieve a better future for their people. That's what I was trying to do, which was why they could not find anything to accuse me of when they overthrew me and did not, therefore, dare to shoot me.'

'They must have had some reason to overthrow you?'

'I wouldn't let them steal,' he smiled. 'I wanted to build a government made up of honest men, without realising that there were not enough honest men in any one country to make up an entire government. Now they've all got yachts, palaces on the Riviera and Swiss bank accounts, despite the fact that when we were young we swore we would beat out corruption with the same spirit that we beat out the French. We could fight the French because, however hard they might have tried, we would never have become French. But it wasn't so straightforward when fighting against corruption, because people become corrupt all too easily.'

He looked at him intently: 'Do you understand what I am talking about?'

'I am a Targui, not an idiot. The difference between us lies in the fact that we the Tuaregs look across to your world, observe it, understand it and then distance ourselves from it. You do not come anywhere near our world and neither do you ever come anywhere near to understanding it. That is why we will always be a superior race.'

Abdul-el-Kebir smiled for the first time in a long time, truly amused by the Targui's words:

'Do the Tuaregs still really believe that they are a race that was hand-picked by the gods?'

Gazel pointed outside:

'Who else could have survived for two thousand years living on these sands? If the water ran out, I would still be living long after the worms had already devoured your body. Is that not proof enough that we were chosen by the gods?'

'Maybe...and if that is true, then now is the time to call on them for help, for what the desert has not managed to do in two thousand years, man will manage in twenty. They want to destroy you; wipe you off the face of the earth, even though they'll not be able to build anything on top of your tombs.'

Gazel closed his eyes, seemingly unperturbed by this threat or warning:

'Nobody can ever destroy the Tuaregs,' he said decidedly. 'Only the Tuaregs themselves and they no longer fight each other; they have been in peace for many years now.' He paused and without opening his eyes, added: 'Now it's better that you sleep. The night will be long.'

The night was indeed a long and tiring one. They walked from the minute the sun, red and trembling, started to disappear behind the clouds of dust that hovered over the crests of the dunes, until that very same sun, well rested and brilliant, re-emerged from the left to reveal once again, the same curved landscape of gigantic, sun-bathing women.

They said their prayers facing Mecca and studied the horizon once again.

'How long now?'

'Tomorrow we will reach the plain. And things will start to get more difficult.'

'How do you know?'

The Targui did not have an answer. It was a feeling; like knowing that a sand storm was on its way or that a heat wave was imminent; like being able to sense that a herd of antelope was just over the other side of a dune or like running down a forgotten path without getting lost.

'I just know.' was all he could utter in the end. 'By dawn we will reach the plain.'

'I'm happy then. I'm fed up with going up and down the

dunes and sinking into the sand.'

'No, you won't be happy,' he said with conviction. 'There's a breeze here. However light, it still refreshes you and helps you along. These rivers of sand are formed by wind streams. But the "lost lands," they are like dead valleys where everything is still and where the air is so hot and dense you can almost touch it. Your blood will almost boil and your lungs and head will feel as if they might burst, which is why no animals or plants could ever survive there. And nobody,' he stressed, pointing ahead with his finger, 'has ever managed to cross that plain.'

Abdul-el-Kebir did not reply, impressed not by what the Targui had said, but by the tone of his voice. He had got to know him and knew, from the moment they had set off together, that he was a competent force, with nothing or no one appearing to unsettle him, so sure was he of the ground beneath his feet and the world that surrounded him. He was a serene, hermetic and distant man who could anticipate danger and deal with it, but now, as he spoke about the "lost land" with such awe, a feeling of great dread descended upon him. For any other human being the erg that they were crossing would have meant the end of the road, a sure descent into madness and a hopeless death. For the Targui it was the more "comfortable" part of a journey that would soon start to become really difficult. The very idea of what constituted something "difficult" for a man like Gazel, filled Abdul with horror.

Gazel, for his part was struggling to work out whether or not he was overestimating his capabilities by ignoring the advice, or was it a law, that his people had passed on by word of mouth for generations, that warned: "Stay away from Tikdabra."

Rub-al-Jali, to the south of the Arabian Peninsula and Tikdabra in the heart of the Sahara were the two most inhospitable regions on the planet. They were places that the heavens were supposed to have put aside to house the spirits of the most hideous murderers, child killers and rapists and where the tormented souls who had fled the holy wars, were also said to wander.

Gazel Sayah had learned as a child not to be scared by stories of spirits, ghosts and apparitions, but he had been scared by the stories of other "lost lands" that were less famous and much less terrible than Tikdabra, so he was able to imagine with some accuracy what lay in store for them in the coming days.

He looked at his companion. He had in fact been studying him from the moment that he had noticed that flash of fear cross his face when he had told him that he had killed his guardians. But, he reasoned, if he had endured that long in captivity and still had hope and was ready to fight again, then he was clearly a courageous man with no ordinary spirit.

But the spirit to fight, Gazel knew well enough, was nothing like the spirit needed to take on the desert. You never fought with the desert, because you would never defeat it. You had to resist the desert, by lying and cheating and then finally by running away from it with your life, just as it thought it had you firmly in its grip. In the "lost lands" you could not be a hero in the flesh, only a bloodless stone, because the only things that survived in those landscapes were the stones. Gazel was worried that Abdul-el-Kebir, like any other human being who had not been born an Imohag and raised amongst the sand and stones, would not even begin to understand the concept of becoming a stone.

He looked at him again. He was definitely not afraid of other men, but he was also crushed by the solitude and silence of that quietly aggressive landscape, where everything was made up of curves and soft colours; but where no animals walked or snakes or scorpions dared to tread; where not even the mosquitoes would go, even at sunset. It was a place that stank of death, even though it smelt of nothing, since even smell, in that aseptic sea of dunes, had been erased many thousands of years previously.

Abdul had already started to show the first signs of anxiety, overwhelmed by the huge sea of sand that they were in, even though their problems had barely begun. His pulse was already racing as they scaled the highest dunes, the old ghourds that were reddened and as hard as basalt, from where all you could see was the endless, repetitive landscape both ahead of them and behind them. And he was already starting to curse the camels every time they threw their load to the ground, or fell down and threatened never to get up again.

And this was only the beginning.

They put up the tent and two planes returned half way through the morning.

Gazel was thankful of their presence and that they were flying directly over their heads, insistently but still without discovering them, because he realised that these planes were evidence of the danger they were in and would spur Abdul on. They acted as tangible reminders of the prison that awaited him; of the dirtier and more degrading death that he would suffer at the hands of his pursuers.

Both of them knew that if they disappeared in the "lost land" of Tikdabra that they would soon become legends; on the same scale as the "great caravan" or like all the other heroes of our time who never surrendered. One hundred years would have to pass before the people who had loved him, gave up hope that the mythical Abdul-el-Kebir would return from the desert, while his enemies would have no choice but to live with his ghost, because there would never be any physical or palpable proof that he had died.

The planes broke up the silence once again, leaving a smell of benzene in the air that stirred up old memories. Once they had gone away again he went out to look at them, watching as they circled the skies in search of their prey.

'They seem to know where we're headed. Wouldn't it be better to turn back and try and escape from the other side?'

The Targui shook his head slowly.

'Just because they suspect that's where we are going doesn't mean to say they will be able to find us. And even if they do find us they would still have to come and get us. And nobody will do that. The desert right now is our only enemy, but it is also our ally. Think about that and forget about everything else.'

But try as he might, Abdul-el-Kebir could not forget, because for the first time in his life he realised that he was well and truly terrified.

The light was different and there was nothing that might cast a shadow anywhere on that white, flat and limitless terrain.

The last few dunes died out gently, like thirsty tongues or waves from a weary sea that had crashed hopelessly onto a beach without end. It was as if nature had placed a natural frontier there on a whim, with no obvious explanation for why the sand should end right there and the plain suddenly begin.

The silence intensified to such an extent that Abdul could hear his own racing heartbeat and the blood throbbing in his temples.

As soon as he started to hear his own heart beat he closed his eyes, trying to get the image of that nightmarish landscape out of his mind, but the picture had stuck onto his retina and he was convinced that it was this image that would haunt him in his final, agonising moments.

There were no mountains, no rocks, no nothing, just a slight depression. It was a blank piece of paper, upon which all the books in the world could have been written. Insh. Allah!

What had God, with his limitless powers of imagination, been thinking of when he created this space that was so totally devoid of anything, so utterly empty?

Insh. Allah! It was a decision He had made and so it must be accepted. He had created a poem within a poem; a desert within a desert.

Gazel had been right and the wind had suddenly dropped at the edge of the dunes, giving way to a rarefied atmosphere and in less than one hundred meters the temperature had risen by fifteen degrees. It was like a buffet of hot air that made you want to recoil back towards the sweet protection of the dunes, which, only a short while back, had seemed unbearable.

They set off once the sun had sunk below the horizon, even though the air had not cooled down at all. It was as if the laws of nature did not apply to that accursed place, as if the mass of rarefied air that swirled through the "lost land" was trapped under a large glass bell that cut it off from the rest of the planet.

The camels brayed in terror as their instinct told them that the hard, hot ground beneath them would only take them to the end of all roads.

As darkness fell, the stars came out and Gazel fixed his route on one of them, which he would follow constantly. Later a pale moon appeared that projected, perhaps for the first time since time immemorial, shadows onto that ghostly plain.

The Targui walked on foot with a constant, mechanical step, while Abdul rode on the strongest of the camels - a young female who did not seem too affected by fatigue or the lack of water. As soon as the milky white of dawn began to erase the stars from the sky he stopped, made the animals kneel down and lifted a white, camel-hair awning over them.

An hour later Abdul-el-Kebir started to feel as if he was suffocating and that the air was not reaching his lungs.

'Water,' he called out.

Gazel only opened his eyes and shook his head very slightly.

'I'm going to die...!'

'No.'

'I am going to die...!'

'Stop moving. You have to remain still. Like the camels. Like me. Let your heart calm down and work slowly and your lungs breathe in the minimum of air necessary. Do not think of

Tuareg

anything.'

'Just a sip...' he begged again. 'A sip...!'

'It will make it worse. You can drink when evening falls.'

'In the evening!' he said in a horrified tone. 'That's not for another eight hours!'

He soon realised it was pointless to insist, so he closed his eyes, emptied his head and tried to relax all his muscles, to forget about water, about the desert thirst, or the terror that had settled, like a living being, in the pit of his stomach.

He tried to get his mind to abandon his body and leave it there, alone, resting on the camel, just as the Targui was doing and who, it seemed, had converted himself into a stone. And he contemplated himself, divided up like that, in two parts; one part witness, completely separated from the reality of thirst, the heat and the desert; the other just an empty shell, a human casing that could no longer feel or suffer at all.

Without falling asleep completely he drifted into far away spaces and past, happier times, when he had been with his boys, who he had last seen as children and who would now be grown men with children of their own.

Fantasy and reality came to blows as scenes of his real life crashed intensely into fictitious events that at the time seemed almost more vivid, but that were in fact just figments of an unhinged imagination.

He woke up twice in anguish, thinking that he was still in prison, an anguish that only increased with the realisation that he was free, but locked inside the biggest prison of them all.

The Targui remained where he was, in front of him, like a statue, unmoving and hardly breathing. He watched him as he tried to understand what he was made of and what kind of emotions he was going through.

He was scared of him, but respected him at the same time. He felt thankful to him for having freed him and was probably one of the most self-assured, upstanding and admirable human beings that he had ever met. But there was something, maybe fourteen bodies, that came between them both.

Or maybe it was just a question of race and culture. As Gazel had said, a man from the coast would never get to know a Targui, or accept his customs.

The Tuaregs were the only group, of all the Islamic people, that still remained faithful to the teachings of Mohammad. They believed in sexual equality and not only did the women never cover their faces – unlike the men - they also enjoyed total sexual liberty until they were married. Their women did not have to account for their actions, either to their parents or to their future husbands and their choice of husband was usually based on their own personal preference.

The Tuaregs were famous in the desert for their "lovemaking ceremonies," or the Ahal, when boys and girls would get together to have supper by the light of the fire, tell stories, play their one-stringed anzads and dance in groups until the early hours. Then the women would take the men's palms and trace patterns on them, patterns that only the Tuaregs knew the meaning of and which told of how the girl desired to make love that night.

Then every couple would disappear into the darkness, to the dunes and the soft sand, upon which white gandurahs had been laid, to fulfil the desires that the girls had expressed in their patterns.

For a traditional Arab, who would insist on his future wife's or daughter's virginity, such customs were beyond scandalous and Abdul knew of countries like Arabia and Libya, including regions in his own country, where you would be stoned to death or have your head cut off for a similar offense.

But the Imohag had always defended the right of their women to have sex and to dress as they pleased; to have a voice and to vote on family matters, ever since the old days of Muslim expansion when religious fanaticism was at its most rigid and demanding.

For as far back as people could remember they had been known as a race that would accept the best of what they were offered, but tended to reject anything that might curtail their liberty or sense of identity. Even though they were ungovernable, Abdul-el-Kebir still knew that he would be proud to be their ruler.

The Tuaregs would know how to accept and understand what he was trying to offer them and they would never try to betray him or condone the betrayal of him by anyone else, because once they had sworn allegiance to an amenokal then that allegiance lasted well beyond the grave.

But the men from the coast, who had celebrated his ascent to power almost fanatically once the French had been expelled and to whom he had given a homeland and a reason to feel proud of themselves, had not known how to cope with their sworn allegiance. At the first signs of danger had withdrawn back into the depths of their miserable huts.

'What does it mean to be a socialist?' Gazel had asked him on the first night, when he had still felt like talking as they lurched around on the backs of the swaying camels.

'It means that justice is the same for everyone.'

'Are you a socialist?'

'More or less.'

'Do you believe that everybody, like the Imohag and the servant, is equal?'

'In the eyes of the law? Yes.'

'I'm not referring to the law. I'm referring to whether servants and sirs are considered equals.'

'In one way...' he tried to find a way of explaining further, without compromising himself. 'The Tuaregs are the only people left on earth who still unashamedly have slaves. It is not just.'

'I don't have slaves, I have servants.'

'Really? And what would you do to them if they escaped or no longer wanted to work for you?'

'I would search for them, flog them and bring them back. He was born in my home, I gave him water, food and protection when he was unable to do so himself. What right does he have to just get up and go when he feels like it?'

'The right to his own freedom. Would you accept that you were a servant to somebody else, just because they fed you when you were a child? How long does it take for one to repay that debt?'

'That is not how it works. I was born an Imohag. And they were born Aklis.'

'And who says that an Imohag is superior to an Akli?'

'Allah. If that wasn't the case he would not have made them cowards, thieves and servants. He wouldn't have made us brave, honourable and proud.'

'My word!' he exclaimed. 'You are more fanatical than a fascist.'

'What is a fascist?'

'Somebody who claims that his race is superior to the rest.'

'Then I'm a fascist.'

'You really are,' he said with conviction. 'Although I'm sure that if you knew what it really meant, then you would renounce that label.'

'Why?'

'That's not something I can explain to you while we're lolloping around on a camel that seems half drunk. We'll leave that one for a more suitable occasion.'

But that occasion had not arisen again and seemed less likely to with each day that passed, as the fatigue, thirst and heat threatened to overwhelm Abdul and the simple task of saying even one word seemed to require a superhuman effort.

When he finally woke up, Gazel had taken down their camp and was loading up three of the animals once again.

He gestured to the fourth camel with his head:

'We'll have to kill it tonight.'

'Surely that will attract the vultures and the vultures will attract the planes. They'll track our route.'

'The vultures don't come into the "lost land."' He had taken a small ladle and filled it with water. He handed it to Abdul. 'The air is too hot.'

He drank urgently and held it out to him for more, but the Targui had already closed the gerba firmly.

'No more.'

'That's it?' said Abdul in astonishment. 'That hardly wet my throat.'

Gazel pointed over to the camel once again.

'Tonight you will drink its blood and eat its meat. Tomorrow is the start of Ramadan.'

'Ramadan?' he repeated in disbelief. 'Do you really think we are in a fit state to observe the fasting rules of Ramadan?'

He could have sworn that the Targui had smiled.

'Isn't this the perfect place to be in if we our to observe its rules? It'll be easy for us to respect its laws out here,' he said.

The animals had already stood up and he put out his hand to help Abdul up.

'Let's go,' he said. 'The road is long.'

'How long will this ordeal last?'

Gazel shook his head: 'I don't know. I give you my word that I really don't know. We must pray that Allah makes it as short as possible, but even he is not capable of making a desert smaller. That is all I know and that is all we have to go by.'

The sergeant shook his head once again: 'Nobody is taking water from this well, nor anyone else for five hundred kilometers around, until we find out where Gazel Sayah's family is hiding.'

The old man shrugged his shoulders, powerless to help them: 'They went. They took down their camp and left. How would we know where they went?'

'The Tauregs always know everything that goes on in the desert. They'll get to hear if a camel dies or a goat is sick. I've no idea how, but that's how it is. You must think I'm stupid if you think I'm going to believe that a whole family, with their jaimas, animals, children and slaves could just move from one end of an area to the other without anyone knowing where they'd gone to.'

'They just left.'

'Where to?'

'I don't know.'

'Then you'll just have to find out, that is if you want more water.'

'My animals will all die. My family too.'

'That is not my problem,' he said, pointing an accusatory finger at him and poking him in the chest, almost provoking the old man to pull out his dagger. 'One of your men,' he continued, 'a filthy murderer, has killed many soldiers. Soldiers who protected us from bandits; who looked for water and dug wells and kept areas free of sand; men who went in pursuit of caravans when they were lost, risking their lives in the desert.' He shook his head over and over again. 'No. You will not have access to this water until Gazel Sayah is found.'

'Gazel is not with his family.'

'How do you know?'

'Because otherwise you wouldn't have gone looking for him in the "lost land" of Tikdabra.'

'We could be wrong. And if we don't find him some time soon he's sure to go back to his own people.' His tone of voice suddenly softened as he tried to take a more conciliatory line: 'We don't want to hurt his family. We have nothing against his wife and children. We only want him and we will wait for him. Sooner or later he will turn up.'

The old man shook his head.

'He will never turn up. Not if you are anywhere near, because he knows the desert better than anyone else.' He paused. 'And neither is it honourable for warriors or soldiers to mix women and children up in men's battles. That is a rule of thumb as old as the universe.'

'Listen to me old man!' he said in a voice that had become clipped and threatening once again. 'I haven't come here for a lesson in morality. That bastard murdered a captain under my very nose, kidnapped the governor, slit the throat of a load of sleeping boys and I am quite certain, he thinks he can take our whole country for a merry ride. And that is simply not the case. So you have to choose.'

The old man got up and walked over to the edge of the well without saying anything. He had not taken more than five steps before Malik shouted: 'And don't forget that my men need to eat. We will sacrifice one of your camels every day and you can pass the bill onto our new governor in El-Akab!'

The old man stopped for a second, but did not turn around and then continued slowly back over to his children and his animals.

Malik looked over to the black soldier.

'Ali!'

The man who had been summoned, hurried over:

'Yes, sergeant?'

'You're black, like his stupid slaves. He won't tell me anything because he's a Targui and believes his honour will be stained forever, but the Aklis are more likely to talk. They like to tell you what they know and some of them will be open to a bit of money and that'll get their master off the hook.' He paused briefly. 'Take them some water and food tonight and act like you're one of them -solidarity between black brothers and all that - then try and get the information we need.'

'If they think I'm acting as a spy, those Tuaregs will slit my throat.'

'But if they don't, you'll be promoted to corporal.' He stuffed a bundle of crumpled notes into his hand. 'Win them over with these.'

Sergeant Malik-el-Haideri knew the Tuaregs well and he knew their slaves too. He had only just drifted off to sleep when he heard footsteps outside his tent.

'Sergeant!'

He poked his head out and was not surprised to see a smiling black face in front of him:

'In the guelta of the Huaila mountains. Next to Ahmed-el-Ainin's tomb, the marabout.'

'Do you know where that is?'

'Not exactly, but they told me how to get there.'

'Is it far?'

'A day and a half's journey.'

'Let the corporal know. We'll leave at dawn.'

The black man smiled proudly: 'I am the corporal now,' he reminded him. 'Lance corporal.'

Malik smiled back.

'You're right. You are now lance corporal. Make sure that

everything's set by the time the sun comes out…and bring me some tea fifteen minutes beforehand.'

The pilot shook his head again.

'Listen, lieutenant,' he repeated. 'We've flown over those dunes at less than one hundred metres. We could have made out a rat from that height, if there were any rats in that accursed place. But there was nothing. Nothing!' he insisted. 'Do you have any idea the kind of tracks that four camels leave in the sand? If they'd been there we'd have seen them.'

'Not if it's a Targui leading those camels,' Razman replied knowingly. 'Especially this particular Targui. He wouldn't let them march in single file, otherwise they'd leave a visible path. He'd make sure they walked four abreast so that their feet wouldn't sink down into the hard sand of the dunes. If the sand was soft, their tracks would be erased by the wind in under an hour.' He paused, while they all watched him expectantly. 'The Tuaregs travel at night and stop at dawn. You're never out before eight in the morning, which means you get there around midday. By that time all of their tracks have already been erased.'

'But what about them? Where could four camels and a man possibly hide?'

'Oh come on captain!' he exclaimed, gesticulating with open arms. 'You've flown over these dunes every day. Hundreds, thousands, maybe millions of dunes! Do you not think an entire army could camouflage themselves in that landscape? A small hollow, a clear, coloured piece of fabric covered with a bit of sand and you're laughing… '

'Alright,' the pilot who had spoken first, conceded. 'You may be right, but what are we going to do now? Go back and carry on wasting time and petrol? We'll never find him,' he insisted. 'We'll never find him!'

Lieutenant Razman shook his head and signalled with his hands for them to calm down as he went over to the large map of the region that was pasted on to the wall of the hanger.

'No.' he said. 'I don't want to go back to the erg but to the actual "lost land." If my calculations are correct they must have reached the plain already. Could you land there?' The two men looked at each other, clearly horrified with his proposal.

'Do you have any idea what the temperature on the plain is?'

'Yes,' he admitted. 'The sand can get as hot as eighty degrees centigrade at midday.'

'So do you know what that means for these old planes that are as badly maintained as ours? Motor cooling problems, turbulence, unseen pockets of uncontrollable air and above all ignition. We could land, of course, but we'd take the risk of not being able to take off again, or the possibility that it might just explode once we managed to make contact.' He made a gesture with his hand that indicated his decision was final. 'I won't do it.'

It was clear that his companion shared the same point of view. But Razman insisted:

'Even if the order came from higher up?' He lowered his voice instinctively. 'Do you know who we're looking for here?'

'Yes,' the more talkative of the two said. 'We've heard rumours, but these are political issues, things that we, the military, shouldn't get mixed up in.' He paused and pointed to the map with a wide sweep of his hand.

'If I was ordered to land somewhere in the desert because we were at war and the enemy had invaded us, we would land without question. But we won't do it just to hunt down Abdul-el-Kebir, because he would never have asked us to do the same.'

Lieutenant Razman stiffened and without being able to help it, looked over at the mechanics that were toiling away to put a plane together on the other side of the wide hanger. Then lowering his voice he warned:

'What you just said is dangerous.'

'I know,' the pilot replied. 'But I think that after so many years it's time we started to say what we really think. If you don't catch him in Tikdabra, and I can't imagine that you will, Abdul-el-Kebir will return very soon and the time will come when everyone will be forced to justify their positions.'

'So you're saying that you're pleased you didn't find him.'

'My mission was to look for him and I looked for him as hard as I could. It's not my fault that we didn't find him. Deep down it makes me scared to think of what might happen. With Abdul at large the country will be divided, there will be confrontations and maybe civil war. Nobody wants that for their own people.'

As he left the hanger to go back to his billet, Razman considered the pilot's words and for the first time realised that the most horrific outcome of all this could indeed be civil war. It would probably lead to a confrontation between two factions of the same people, divided by one man: Abdul-el-Kebir.

After more than a century of colonialism its people were not divided into very clearly determined social classes: the rich being very rich, the poor very poor. But the nation did not mirror the classic pattern of a developed country either, with capitalists on the one side and the proletariat on the other, both facing death in a hopeless struggle for the supremacy of their ideals. With an illiteracy rate of seventy percent and a long tradition of being oppressed, it was still only a man's charisma and his rousing words that would move the people to stand up and take action.

And on that level, Razman knew, Abdul-el-Kebir would win hands down thanks to his noble, open face that inspired confidence and his eloquent words that would make people follow him to the end of the earth if he told them to. After all, he had fulfilled his initial promise and freed them from colonialism.

Lying down on his bed, looking at the whirring blades of the old ventilator that did not, despite its grand efforts, manage to cool the air, he asked himself what side he would take when the time of reckoning came.

He remembered Abdul-el-Kebir from his childhood and when he had been his hero and the walls of his bedroom had been covered with posters of him. Then he thought back to the governor Hassan-ben-Koufra and all the others that made up that group and he realised that he had made a personal decision on that matter long ago.

Then he thought about the Targui; that strange man who had overcome thirst and death and who had blatantly laughed at him and he tried to imagine where he was now, what he was doing at that precise moment and what he talked about with Abdul, once they had stopped walking and laid down to rest, exhausted by their long journey.

'I don't know why I'm chasing them,' he said to himself. 'If deep down I would rather be on the run with them.'

They had drunk the camel's blood and eaten its meat. He felt strong and animated, full of energy and capable of taking on the "lost land" without trepidation. But he was worried about his companion's fears and how silent he had become. With the light of each new day, as the same landscape stretched out before them, he could read the increasing desperation in his eyes.

'It's not possible!' was the last thing he had heard him say. 'It's not possible!'

He had to help him get down from the camel now and carry him into the shade to give him water, whilst cradling his head as if he were a frightened boy. Gazel wondered where his strength had gone and what strange spell the plain had cast on him.

'He's an old man,' he repeated over and over again. 'A man who has aged before his time, having spent so many years imprisoned between four walls so now everything for him, other than thought, requires a superhuman effort.'

How could he tell him that their real difficulties had not yet even begun? They still had water and three camels to drink the blood of. It was still a while before those strange bright lights, like a thousand suns, would start to burn behind their eyes, the surest symptom that dehydration was setting in. The road was still a long one, a very long one and would demand enormous will power and an invincible spirit, without ever offering an ounce of hope or reward in return.

"Stay away from Tikdabra."

He could not remember when he had first heard that warning, probably while he was in the womb of his mother, but now he was there, somewhere in Tikdabra, carrying with him a man who was fast becoming a shadow. He was quite sure, moreover, that he, Gazel Sayah, "the Hunter," Imohag of the Kel-Talgimus, could have conquered Tikdabra alone, with the help of his four camels.

He would be the first man ever to have achieved it and his fame would have spread throughout the desert far and wide and his name passed on by word of mouth, as he became a legend. But he was carrying an unbearable weight with him, like the chains put on the ankles of rebel slaves by their masters and the weight, this man who had been destroyed and beaten down in less than a week, meant that neither him nor any other Targui in the desert would ever make it through that empty land.

He realised that the moment would come when he would either have to shoot the man in order to relieve him of his sufferings and save himself, or they would both of them end up suffering the most hideous of deaths.

'He will ask me to kill him,' he said to himself. 'When he cannot go on any more and I will have to do it.'

He could only hope that it was not already too late.

If his guest asked to die voluntarily, it was within his rights to do so and he would be free of all responsibility from that moment and free to try and save himself.

'Five days,' he calculated. 'In five days time he will still be in a condition to ask for it himself. If he lasts any longer then it will be too late for both of us.'

He was presented with a difficult dilemma, on the one hand he should try and keep his companion whole, feed his hope and try to save him in every humane way possible. On the other hand, he realised that for every hour and day that he managed to prolong his companion's life, the possibility of him surviving for another day or hour decreased.

Abdul-el-Kebir, because of his constitution and out of habit, drank three times as much as Gazel did. This meant that when the time came, the Targui would have four times more chance of surviving, if he were alone.

He watched him as he slept, restlessly, murmuring occasionally and with his mouth wide open, as if searching for air. He would be doing him a favour if he extended that sleep now to eternity, freeing him from the terrors of the punishing days that lay ahead of them. It would almost be kinder to ease him into an eternal sleep right then, at least while there was still a measure of hope in his heart; the hope that they might yet manage to cross the border.

What border? It had to be there, somewhere ahead of them or maybe it was already behind them. Nobody in the whole world would know to point them in the right direction since the Tikdabra "lost land" had never accepted a human presence in it before, let alone allowed the imposition of a border upon it.

Maybe "it" was the border; the final frontier between countries, between religion and life and death. "It" sat there like a barrier to man and Gazel realised that in one way he loved the "lost land." He loved the fact that he was there of his own free will and that he might be the first ever human being, since the beginning of time to know what it was like to take on the "desert of all deserts."

'I feel strong enough to beat you,' was the last thing he said, before falling into a deep sleep. 'I feel capable of defeating you and putting an end to the legend once and for all.'

But once he was asleep a voice came into his head that echoed repeatedly and monotonously: "Stay away from Tikdabra." Then the image of Laila emerged from out of the shadows and she stroked his forehead and gave him fresh water from the deepest of wells. She sang to him in the same way that she had sang to him on the night of the Ahal, at the festival of love-making, when she had drawn strange patterns on his hands, patterns that only his people knew how to interpret. Laila! Laila!

She stopped in her task of grinding maize and lifted up her dark eyes to look at Suilem's wrinkled face. He was staring up at a peak that overlooked the guelta.

'Soldiers,' was all he said.

And soldiers they were and they came from every angle, their weapons at the ready, as if attacking a dangerous enemy enclave instead of a miserable nomadic camp occupied by only women, old men and children.

She took one look at them and knew immediately what was happening, so she turned around and said to the Akli in no uncertain terms:

'Hide,' she ordered. 'Your master will need to know what's happened.'

The old man hesitated for a minute before obeying, then slipped off in between the jaimas and sheribas and disappeared into a bed of reeds by a small lake, as if he had been swallowed up by it.

Laila then called her husband's children and the women servants over, took the littlest into her arms and stood there, tall and strong in front of the man who appeared to be in charge of the group.

'What do you want from my camp?' she asked, even though she already knew.

'Gazel Sayah. Do you know him?'

'He is my husband. But he is not here.'

Sergeant Malik took in the tall and defiant Targui, without any veils covering her face or heavy drapes over her arms, breasts or strong legs, at leisure. He had not been close to a woman like that for years, not since he had been posted to the desert and had been forced to rid himself of all such thoughts and desires. He replied softly, a smile playing at his lips:

'I know he's not here. He's very far away, in Tikdabra.'

She shuddered with horror as he uttered that fearful word, but managed to hide the terror she felt. The Tuareg women were never supposed to reveal their fear.

'If you know where he is, then why have you come here?'

'To protect you. You will have to come with us because your husband has turned into a dangerous criminal and the authorities are afraid that an angry mob might attack you.'

Laila had to stop herself from laughing at the audacity of this man, as she gestured with a sweep of her hand around her and said:

'Mob?' she repeated. 'What mob? There isn't a soul around here for at least two days in either direction.'

Malik-el-Haideri smiled like the cat that had got the cream. He felt happy and vaguely amused for the first time in a long time.

'News travels fast in the desert,' he said. 'You know that. Word will soon spread and we have to try and prevent the start of any tribal warfare. You will come with us.'

'And if we refuse to?'

'You will come anyway. By force.' He looked at them all. 'Is everyone here?' They nodded silently as he pointed in the direction from which they had arrived. 'Right, off we go then!'

Laila pointed to the camp.

'We have to take the camp down.'

'The camp will stay where it is. My men will remain here and wait for your husband.'

For the first time Laila nearly lost her composure and her reply was almost beseeching.

'But it's all we have.'

Malik laughed contemptuously.

'It's not much then. But where we're going you won't need anything.' He paused. 'You must understand that I can't go wandering around the desert carrying blankets and carpets and

199

pots and pans like some kind of tinker.' He gestured to one of his men. 'Get them to start moving. Ali, stay here with four men and you know what to do if the Targui turns up!'

Fifteen minutes later Laila turned round to look down at the small valley where, by the water of the guelta she just could just make out her jaimas and sheribas, the goat pen and the corner of ground by the reed beds where the camels were grazing. That and a man were all she had ever had in her life, apart from the son she was carrying in her arms and she was overcome with fear that she would never see her home or her husband again. She turned to Malik who had stopped at her side.

'What do you really want from us?' she asked. 'I've never seen women and children get involved in a confrontation that is between men. Is your army so weak that you need us in your battle against Gazel?'

'He's got somebody that we want,' came his reply. 'Now we have something that he wants. We'll play him at his own game and you should be thankful that we didn't slit any of your throats while you slept. We will offer him an exchange. One man for all of his family.'

'If that man was his guest, then I cannot accept that. Our laws forbid it.'

'Your laws do not exist!'

Malik-el-Haideri had sat down on a stone and lit a cigarette as the line of soldiers and prisoners began their descent down the rocky mountainside towards the flat land, where their vehicles were parked. 'Your law, made by the Tuaregs for the convenience and exclusive use of the Tuaregs, is not recognised as valid by our national laws.'

He blew smoke into the woman's face. 'Your husband has failed to understand this, despite our best intentions, so now we're going to have to make him understand this in a less pleasant way. You cannot do whatever you want under the umbrella of your own tradition, somehow relying on the immensity of this desert to support it. He will come back one day and on that day he will be forced to take responsibility for his actions. If he wants to see his wife and children free again then he will have to hand him over and be tried.'

'He will never hand him over,' Laila said with conviction.

'Then get used to the fact that you'll never be free again.'

She did not answer, but looked back to the reed beds where she knew that Suilem the Akli was hiding and then, as if turning her back on her past forever, she turned around and started off down the hill after her family.

Malik-el-Haideri finished his cigarette, clearly flustered by the presence of this woman and he watched the gentle swaying of her hips as she walked away. Then stubbing his cigarette out angrily, he got up and followed her down slowly.

He saw it with the first light of day, although at first he thought that he was seeing things. On closer inspection, however, he realised that there really was "something," lying there on that flat, formless ground, but could not work out for the life of him what that "something" was.

The sun was starting to beat down and he realised that the time had come to stop and set up camp before the camel, who had been moaning since midnight, fell down definitively. But out of curiosity he forced them on a little further, stopping finally about one kilometre away from the object.

He put the canvas up over the animals and the man, who was now nothing more than a dead weight, checked that everything was in order and carried on, on foot, slowly. He forced himself to remain calm and not use up what little strength he had left, even though all he wanted to do was run over to the unidentified object.

Once he was about two hundred meters away he was just able to make out that the white object, crushed against the white plain, was actually the mummified skeleton, of a huge harnessed camel, totally intact still, due to the dry air.

He looked at it from a short distance away. Its sad smile of death revealed a set of enormous white teeth and there were deep sockets where its eyes had once been. Through the cracks in its skin you also could see that it was completely hollow on the inside.

It was on its knees, its neck pushed out along the ground, looking over in the direction from which Gazel had come, that is to say to the northeast, which meant it had come from the southwest, because camels, when they died of thirst, always took one last hopeful look towards their destination.

He did not know whether to be happy or sad. It was the skeleton of a mehari and an object that broke the monotony of the landscape that had accompanied them so far, for days on end, but if it had died there, it also revealed there was not a trace of water behind it.

His lame camel would die there soon, less than one kilometre away from it. His camel, having made the same journey but from the opposite direction would also end up mummified and staring over to the other dead camel, without seeing it, the two corpses marking the middle of the road.

In death they would unite the "lost land" of Tikdabra north with Tikdabra south, those poor desert beasts that had reached the limits of their capabilities.

What hope would there be for him? He, who had to continue ahead with two exhausted, fading mounts and a man that he was only just managing to keep alive. He preferred not to think about it since he knew the answer already and wondered instead where the white mehari's master was.

He studied the skin and pieces of exposed skull.

In most places in the desert he could make an accurate guess as to how long an animal had been dead for, but there, with that heat and dryness, in that terrain where not a drop of water had ever fallen or any being ever survived in, for all he knew, it could have been dead three years or one hundred.

It was a mummy and Gazel did not know much about mummies.

He realised that the heat was starting to intensify, so he made his way back.

He was pleased of the shade and stopped to look carefully at Abdul-el-Kebir's face. He was panting, almost unable to breathe normally. He slit the throat of the camel and gave him some blood to drink and the rest of the almost putrefied liquid from its stomach, barely six fingers deep in the saucepan. He was glad that he was unconscious, because he would never have drunk the rotten liquid otherwise and he did also wonder if it might actually kill him, given that he was not used to drinking putrid water like the Tuaregs were.

'Still it was better to die of that than to die of thirst,' he reflected. 'If he can take it, it will keep him going for a little longer,' he thought outloud.

He lay down to sleep, but instead of falling straight into a deep slumber, as he usually did, exhausted by the long journey of the previous night, he lay there awake.

He could not stop thinking about the skeleton of the dead camel, so completely alone there in the heart of the plain and he wondered what crazy notion had driven a Targui, who must have come from Gao or Timbuctu in search of a northern oasis, to travel through Tikdabra.

The mehari still had its harness on, but had lost its saddle and load along the way, which meant that its master must have died before it and the animal carried on in search of a salvation that it had never found. The Bedouins, like the Tuaregs, would always remove the harness of a beast that was about to die, out of respect and as a way of thanking it for its loyal services.

If its master had not removed it, it was because he had been unable to.

He expected to find the body that night or the following day on the plain, his hollowed eyes also staring out northeast, towards the end of that interminable plain.

But there was not just one body, but hundreds of them. He tripped over them in the darkness and could just make out their forms in the ghostly half-light of a new moon. The following day, he woke to see that they were surrounded by men and beasts for as far as the eye could see. It was at that moment that Gazel Sayah, inmouchar of the Kel-Talgimus, known amongst his own people as "the Hunter," realised that he was the first human being ever to have found the remains of the "great caravan."

Shreds of fabric hung off some of the guides' and drivers' bodies and many of them were still clutching their weapons and empty gerbas. The faded saddles that the Turaegs used were still attached to the camels' bony humps, with their silver and copper tacks, from which huge, broken bags of merchandise hung, that had, over time, emptied their precious contents onto the hard, sandy floor.

There were elephant tusks, ebony statues, silk that disintegrated at a touch, gold and silver coins and in the bags of the richest merchants, diamonds the size of chickpeas. There it was, the legendary "great caravan;" the ancient dream of all desert dreams; one thousand and one riches, that not even Sheherazade herself, could have dreamed up.

This discovery, however, did not fill him with joy, just a profound sense of uneasiness and he was overcome with an indescribable anguish. He just stared at the mummies, at those poor beings with their expressions of terror and suffering and it felt as if he was looking at himself in ten or twenty years time, maybe one hundred, one thousand or one million years. He imagined how his skin would also turn to parchment and his eyes to empty hollows, staring into nothing, his mouth open, in search of that last drop of water.

And he wept for them. For the first time since he could remember, Gazel Sayah cried and even though he realised it was stupid to cry for these people who had been dead for so long, to see them there, before him and to understand the desperation of those last few moments, broke his heart.

He set up camp amongst the dead and sat down to look at them, wondering which one was Gazel, his uncle, the mythical warrior-adventurer who had been contracted to protect the caravan from bandit attacks and ambushes, but who had been unable to protect them from their real enemy: the desert.

He spent the day awake, keeping the dead company. It was the first bit of company they would have had since death had carried them away and he called on the spirits, who he believed would be wandering through that land for eternity, to show him the route out of there, the route they had not known to take while they were still alive.

And the dead spoke to him from their hollow mouths, their bony hands grasping at the sand. They could not tell him which way to go, but the long, never ending line of mummies that snaked southwest as far as the eye could see, was evidence enough that the route they had followed was incorrect and would lead him to nothing more than days and days of solitude and thirst, from which there would be no return.

There was then only one hope, to head east and then to veer south and hope that by taking that route they would reach the end of the "lost land" more quickly.

Gazel knew the Tuareg guides well and that if they took a wrong turning they would carry on and pay the consequences. That one mistake usually meant they had completely lost their notion of space and distance and that they no longer knew where they were. There would be nothing else for it but to push forward and pray for salvation in the hope that their instinct would lead them to water. The Tuareg guides hated changing their routes unless they were completely convinced that they knew where they were headed, because centuries of tradition had taught them that there was nothing more exhausting or demoralising to man than wandering aimlessly from one side of the desert to another, without a concrete destination. It was without doubt then that, for reasons that would never be known, once the guide of the "great caravan" had realised they were in the unknown universe of the "lost land," he had continued blindly on, putting all his trust in Allah to make their journey short, which, in one sense, it would have been.

And there he was now, mummified by the sun, teaching Gazel a lesson, a lesson that Gazel would accept.

Evening fell and once the sun had stopped its angry assault on the land, he abandoned the shade of his refuge and filled his pockets with gold, money and large diamonds.

Not for a moment did he feel as if he were robbing the dead of their belongings. According to the unwritten law of the desert, everything there belonged to the person that found it. It was understood that the souls who entered paradise would be well provided for and have no need of them, while the evil souls condemned to eternal wanderings had no right to do so with their pockets full of riches.

Then he divided up the rest of the water between Abdul, who did not even open his eyes to thank him and the youngest of the camels; the only female that still had a few days left in her. He drank the blood from the last animal and tying the old man onto the saddle, he started off again without even taking the fabric that they used for shade with them as this time it would just be an unnecessary weight. They would not be stopping again, either by day or night, since their only chance of salvation now was to get out of that inferno.

He said his prayers, for him, for Abdul and for the dead, then took one last look at the army of mummies, checked his direction and set off, leading the camel by the halter. She followed him without protest, in the knowledge that only a blind confidence in the man who was leading her could save her now.

Gazel was not sure if that night was the longest or the shortest one of his life. His legs moved automatically and his super-human strength of will turned him once again into a stone, but on this occasion, he was a "travelling stone," like the ones that you saw in the desert. They were heavy rocks that moved myste-riously from one side of the flat land to another, leaving a wide track behind them. How they moved was anybody's guess. Maybe they were pulled along by some strong magnetic field, or by the spirits condemned to eternity or maybe the phenomena was just another of Allah's whims.

Corporel Abdel Osman opened his eyes and immediately cursed his bad luck. The sun was already a quarter over the horizon and was heating up the earth, or better said, the white, hard, almost petrified sand on the plain. He sighed as he took in the torturous terrain before him. They had already been camping on it for six days now, in the most unbearable heat that he had ever experienced, in all his thirteen years of service in the desert.

He turned onto his side, tilted his head slightly and looked over at his fat companion, Kader, who was still sleeping and snorting restlessly, as if unconsciously trying to remain in the world of dreams and avoid waking up to the painful reality that surrounded him.

Their orders had been categorical:

'Remain here and keep watch over the "lost land" until someone comes to look for you. That might be tomorrow, in a month or even a year. Move from here and you will be shot.'

There was a well nearby full of dirty, smelly water that gave them diarrhoea. They had been able to hunt up where the "lost land" ended and the high plateau of the hamada began, with its rough stones and tumble weed and old river channels through which, many thousands of years ago, water would have rushed on its way to the distant Niger and Chad rivers. As good soldiers, they were expected to survive there, in those conditions, for as long as it was considered necessary.

Whoever had given the orders had not taken into consideration the possibility that they might go completely mad in such solitude, in that relentless heat and it was clear that those orders had come from somebody who knew nothing about the Saharan desert.

A drip of sweat, the first of the day, ran down his thick moustache and slipped down his neck and onto his hairy chest. He sat up reluctantly and remained there, his dirty blanket still wrapped around him, squinting into the sun as he searched the white plain mechanically.

Suddenly his heart leaped and he reached for the binoculars, fixing them on a point almost directly ahead of him. Then he shouted out impatiently:

'Kader! Kader! Wake up you useless son of a bitch!'

Mohamed Kader opened his eyes reluctantly, but without taking the slightest bit of offence to his companion's abusive language. He had already got used to the fact that the corporal was unable to say his name without throwing in an affectionate insult or two.

'What the hell is going on?'

'Look. What do you think that is?'

'A man and a camel?'

'Are you sure?'

'Sure.'

'Dead?'

'It looks like it.'

Captain Abdel Osman, who had been rummaging in the back of the jeep, leant back against the machine gun and looked through his field glasses again, trying to keep them steady, even though his pulse was racing.

'You're right,' he said finally.

'A man and a camel.' He paused as he looked around. 'The other one's not there.'

'I'm not surprised,' the fat man said as he calmly started to gather together the blankets they had been sleeping on and set up the small burner they had been using to cook with in order to make some tea. 'What's surprising is that "this one" has managed to get this far.'

Osman looked at him questioningly and a little uncertainly: 'And what do we do now? I say we go and look for him.'

'That Targui is very dangerous. Incredibly dangerous...'

Kader, who had finished putting all their stuff into the vehicle, pointed to the machine gun that the other man was leaning on.

'You point it and I'll drive. At the slightest movement, you fire.'

His companion hesitated for a moment, then nodded in agreement.

'It's better than hanging around here just waiting. If he's really dead we can get out of here today. Lets go!'

He positioned the gun, while the sweaty and obese Mohamed Kader started up the jeep and they set off slowly towards the two bodies.

When they were about three hundred meters away they stopped. The man in the back picked up his field glasses, while the captain kept his eyes firmly fixed on them.

'It's the Targui for sure.'

'Is he dead?'

'You can't see if he's breathing with all those clothes on. The camel's dead, it's started to swell up.'

'Shall I shoot the bastard?'

Mohamed Kader shook his head. Even though the captain was his superior he was obviously the more intelligent of the two, well known in the regiment for his calm head and cold blood, or better said for his acute laziness.

'It would be better if we got him out alive. He might be able to tell us where Abdul-el-Kebir is. The commandant would like that.'

'We might get a promotion.'

'Maybe,' the fat guy said unenthusiastically, not even vaguely moved by the idea of a promotion and the possibility of any more responsibility. 'Or maybe they'll give us a month's leave from El-Akab.'

The captain was spurred own.

'Right, let's move in!'

Once the were no more than fifty meters away they were able to see that the Targui did not have a weapon on or near his body and that his hands were open and perfectly visible. It was as if he had fallen down about ten meters away from the camel that he had been trying to follow, his strength having finally failed him.

They stopped some seven meters away from them, pointing the machine gun at his chest and ready to fire at the slightest movement. Mohamed Kader jumped out of his seat, picked up his submachine gun and circling around the camel so as not to be in Captain Osman's line of fire, went over to the Targui, whose turban had fallen to one side and onto his dirty veil.

The fat man stuck his gun into the recumbent body, which did not move or make a sound. He then prodded him again with the butt of his gun and finally knelt down in order to listen to his heartbeat.

The captain who was still in the car by the machine gun was starting to get impatient:

'What's going on? Is he dead or alive?'

'More dead than alive. He's hardly breathing and he's completely dehydrated. If we don't give him any water he won't last another six hours.'

'Check him over!'

He did so carefully. 'He hasn't got any weapons on him,' he assured him and then stopped as he opened up a leather bag and a cascade of gold and diamonds fell out onto the sand. 'Fuck!' he exclaimed.

Captain Abdel Osman jumped out of the vehicle and in the

blink of an eye was at his side, grabbing at the money and handfuls of large stones that lay all around them.

'What's this? This son of a bitch is rich! Fucking rich!' Mohamed Kader put his gun to one side as he put everything back in the bag again, then, without lifting his head up he said:

'Only he knows about this.' He paused. 'And us now.'

'What are you trying to say,' he said, looking at him straight on.

'Are you completely stupid? If we hand him over alive they might give us one month's leave, but once he's recovered he'll want his money back and it won't be long before the commandant comes looking for us.'

He paused. 'What would happen if say, we hadn't found the body for another few hours?'

'Have you got it in you to leave a fellow dying like this?'

'We'd be doing him a favour,' he noted. 'What do you think is going to happen to him once they get hold of him after everything he's done? They'll beat the shit out of him and end up hanging him. Or not?'

'This isn't my scene. I just do what I'm told.' He leaned over to pull down the veil that covered the unconscious man's face, which was haggard and lined and half covered with a wiry, white beard that made him look even older. He wanted to turn away but there was something about his face that puzzled him and suddenly he shouted out:

'This guy's not the Targui! This is Abdul-el-Kebir!'

In a flash it dawned on him that they were still in danger and he went to grab his weapon, but almost simultaneously two shots, only two, rang through the air. Captain Abdel Osman and the soldier Mohamed Kader flew through the air, as if they had been picked up by an invisible hand and fell back to the ground, the first one falling straight onto Abdul-el-Kebir's body and the second man falling flat on his face.

A few seconds passed in silence. The captain tilted his head painfully, saw the face of his companion with a hole through his forehead and felt a sharp pain sear through his chest, mouth and stomach, but he still managed to turn over so that his face was upturned, in order to find out who had shot them

He could not see a soul. The plain continued on as always to infinity, desolate and flat, with no possible hiding place for a marksman. But suddenly, before his very eyes, which were already starting to blur over, a half-naked, tall, strong, man covered in blood, like a being from another world, a gun held firmly in his hand, emerged from the dead camel's belly.

Once he had checked that the man who was still alive no longer presented any danger to him, he walked around the animal, over to the fat man and pushed his gun away with his foot. Then he walked quickly over to the jeep, which he proceeded to search frantically, until he found the water bottle and then drank from it at length, all the while keeping his eyes firmly fixed on the wounded man.

He drank and drank, allowing the liquid to run down his throat and his chest, glugging it back until he almost choked, but continuing to drink as if his life depended on it. Finally and only once he had drank the last drop, he let out a loud belch and leant for a minute against the spare tyre, in order to regain his breath after the huge effort.

Then he took another water bottle and walked over to Abdul-el-Kebir, held his head up and made him drink as best he could, even though most of the water ended up all over his face, rather than down his throat.

Then he wet his face and turned to the wounded man:

'Do you want water?' Corporal Osman nodded. The Targui went over to him and grabbed him by the shoulders, pulling him into the shade of the vehicle where he gave him some water and even helped him drink it.

'I think you are going to die,' he said. 'You need a doctor and there isn't one anywhere near here.'

Osman nodded and then asked with difficulty:

'Are you Gazel? I should have remembered that old hunting trick you used. But the clothes, the turban and the veil confused me.'

'That was my intention.'

'How could you be so sure that we would come?'

'I saw you with the first light of day and I had time to prepare myself.'

'Did you kill the camel? Did you find the "great caravan?"'

Gazel nodded and looked back over his shoulders.

'It's back there, three days walk from here.'

The other man shook his head in amazement almost in disbelief. Finally he closed his eyes and his breathing became laboured. Then he was silent and ten minutes later he was dead.

Gazel remained still, squatting down before him in quiet respect of his agony and only once the man's head had dropped onto his chest did he get up and using the last of his energy, dragged Abdul-el-Kebir into the back of the vehicle.

He rested for a while because the exertion had been too much for him, then stripped the unconscious Abdul of his clothes, his veil and his turban and got dressed again.

When he had finished, he sat down exhausted. He drank again and then lay down in the shadow of the jeep, next to the body of Captain Osman and fell asleep immediately.

He woke up three hours later to the cries of the first vultures.

Some had already pulled out the entrails of the dead beast, while others were moving towards the dead soldiers tentatively.

He looked up at the sky. There were already dozens of birds of prey up there even though they were still keeping to the edge of the "lost land." It was as if they had appeared by magic from out of the tumbleweed and bushes of the nearby hamada.

Their presence worried him. A circle of vultures in the sky could be seen for many kilometers around and he did not know how far away the next patrol point was.

He looked at the sand. It was hard and even though there were pick axes and spades in the back of the vehicle he did not feel capable of digging a hole big enough for two bodies and one camel. Then he studied Abdul's face and saw that he was breathing more easily, but was still, however, some way off from regaining consciousness. He gave him water again and checked that there were two full cans still, as well as one full of petrol and another with food. He meditated for some time. He knew that he had to get out of there as soon as possible but he had no idea how to work the jeep, which in his hands was nothing more than a useless pile of metal.

He tried to remember. Lieutenant Razman had been driving an identical one and he had watched how he had pulled the steering wheel from one side to the next and how he had pushed the pedals on the floor and constantly moved a stick with a black ball on the end that was over on his right.

He sat down in the driver's seat and imitated all of the lieutenant's movements, turning the wheel and pressing down hard on the brake pedals, the gear and accelerator pedals and pushing the black ball from side to side, but the engine still did not make a sound.

Then he realised that they were the movements you needed to drive the vehicle with, but first of all he had to start the engine.

He leaned over and studied the small sticks, keys, buttons and indicators on the control panel. He beeped the horn, which startled the vultures and he managed to squirt the windscreen with water, which was immediately wiped down by two mechanical arms, but there was still no sound of the engine.

Finally, he saw a key inside a lock. He took it out, but nothing happened and then put it back in, still with no luck. Then he tried to turn it and the mechanical monster revved to life, coughed three times, jumped along for a while then became silent once again.

His eyes lit up as he realised that he was on the right track.

He turned the key with one hand and moved the wheel like a madman with the other, but the result was the same, just splutters, shudders and silence.

He tried the key with the brake. Nothing.

The key with the pedal. Nothing.

Then using the key with the right hand pedal, the motor suddenly roared to life and continued purring gently as he eased the pressure off slowly.

He then tried out the brake, the clutch, the accelerator, the handbrake, the indicators and just as he was about to give up, the vehicle jumped forward, the back wheels running over Captain Osman, stopping three meters further on.

The vultures flapped around bad temperedly.

He started the whole process again and advanced another two meters. He carried on like that until the evening fell and when he finally decided to stop, he had only managed to put about one hundred metres between himself, the vultures and the dead.

He ate and drank, then made a soup of biscuits, water and honey, which he tried to make Abdul swallow and then the minute night fell he lay down on one of the blankets on the ground and fell into a deep sleep.

This time it was not the vultures that woke him in the early hours of dawn, but the cries of the hyenas and jackals, arguing over the carcasses. He listened for a while to them fighting, to the crunching of bones and the sound of meat being torn off the carcasses.

Gazel hated hyenas. He could put up with vultures and jackals but he had felt an uncontrollable aversion to hyenas ever since he had been a boy and found one morning that they had killed a newborn goat and his mother. They were repellent, stinking beasts that were cowards, traitors, dirty and cruel and in large groups, capable of killing an unarmed man. Why Allah had put them on this earth was something he had often asked himself.

He went over to Abdul who was sleeping deeply and breathing normally now. He gave him some more to drink and then sat down again to wait for the day to arrive, mulling over the fact that he, Gazel Sayah, would go down in the history of the desert and become a legend, as the first man to conquer the "lost land" of Tikdabra.

And maybe one day they would find out that he too had discovered the "great caravan."

The "great caravan!" They might have made it had one of their guides veered just slightly south, but Allah had not wished it so and only Allah knew what sins they were being punished for and why their lives had ended in that horrific way. He was in charge of giving out life and death and the only thing to do was accept it gracefully and Gazel thanked Him for showing such benevolence towards them and for saving him and his guest.

'Insh. Allah!'

He thought that they were probably in another country by now, out of danger, but the soldiers would still be their enemies and he did not feel that they had reached safety yet.

But there was no escape. The last camel was now being devoured by carrion beasts and Abdul-el-Kebir would not be walking for a few days yet. Only that lump of inanimate metal would save him now and take them away from danger. He felt suddenly very angry at his ignorance and impotence.

The simplest soldiers, the dirtiest Bedouin and even a freed Akli who had spent a couple of months with the French, knew how to get even bigger vehicles moving forward than that one and drove heavy lorries weighed down with cement. But Gazel, inmouchar, revered for his intelligence, his courage and his cunning, was like a stupid child in front of that undecipherable piece of twisted machinery. He loathed possessions, they were like the enemy to him and his nomadic life meant that he only possessed maybe two dozen objects, the bare essentials and even those he instinctively rejected. As a free man and solitary hunter all he really needed were his weapons, his water gerba and the harnesses for his mount. The days he had spent in El-Akab, waiting to capture Ben-Koufra, had been distressing, as he witnessed a world where real Tuareg men, who had once been as austere as him, were addicted to "things," or objects that they had never previously heard of, let alone had any use for. These "things," however, had apparently become as indispensable to them, as water and air.

The car and being carried by it from one location to another, for no apparent reason, had become, as far as he could work out, one of those indispensable objects. Young nomads were no longer content, as their fathers had been, to journey for days and weeks across the plains, in no hurry and free of stress, aware that their destination would still be there at the end of the road, as it would be for centuries to come, however slowly they travelled.

Now, by some strange twist of fate, Gazel who hated and despised these objects, who felt repulsed by every kind of mechanized vehicle, found himself at the mercy of a machine upon which his and his guest's life now depended. He cursed his ignorance for not being able to make it run across the plain towards a freedom that now lay within their grasp.

Dawn arrived. The hyenas and jackals had fled, but the vultures were still there in their dozens, invading the skies with their dance of death, using their strong beaks to rip the flesh off the two men and the beast, who only twenty-four hours ago had been full of life. Their presence, there on the edge of the hamada, was like an announcement to the world that once again, in the "lost land" of Tikdabra, there had been another human tragedy.

'It was here, on this very bed that you're sitting on now and round about this time of day, that your husband slit the throat of the captain and things started to get a little more complicated for him.'

Laila instinctively made as if to get up from the bed, but Sergeant Malik-el-Haideri pressed down firmly on her shoulder, forcing her to stay put.

'I did not give you permission to move,' he snapped. 'And you need to get used to the fact that at Adoras, until they send in another officer, you don't move unless I say so.'

He crossed the room and sat down on the old rocking chair that the recently deceased Captain Kaleb-el-Fasi used to sit on, reading for hours at a time and he pulled it towards her.

'You're very beautiful,' he said a little hoarsely. 'The most beautiful Targui I've ever seen. How old are you?'

'I don't know. I'm not a Targui, I'm an Akli.'

'An Akli, the daughter of a slave!' he exclaimed. 'Well I never. You do like you'd be very good in bed. Are you good in bed?'

He did not get a reply and neither had he expected one. He looked for a cigarette in the breast pocket of his shirt, lit it with the lighter that used to belong to the captain and smoked it slowly, watching the girl through a swirl of smoke, who in turn watched him, her look proud and defiant.

'Do you know how long it's been since I saw a girl naked?' he asked, smiling creepily. 'No, you wouldn't know, because even I don't know the answer to that, it's been so long.'

He nodded towards an old calendar that was hanging above his bed. 'That fat bitch, who must be about one hundred years old by now, is all I've had to look at all this time and I've spent hours looking at her, jerking off and dreaming of the day I would have someone in the flesh again.' He found a dirty handkerchief and started to dab at the sweat that was running down his neck. 'But now you're here, as if my prayers had been answered; more beautiful and younger than I could ever have imagined...' He paused and finally, without raising the tone of his voice, said softly, but firmly: 'Undress.'

Laila did not move, as if she had not heard him and only a trace of fear flickered across her huge black eyes as she dug her fingers into the thick, dirty mattress.

Malik-el-Haideri waited for a few seconds, finished his cigarette, put it carefully on the floor under the rocking chair, rocked forward onto it then lifted his face to look at her straight on.

'Listen!' he said. 'We can do this in two ways: in a pleasant way or an unpleasant one. I would prefer the first personally because it's more fun for both of us. You collaborate, we have a nice time and I'll make your stay here a bit more comfortable. If you resist then I'll have to do it by force and I won't bother to look after you or your people.' He smiled cruelly. 'Your husband's two sons are very pretty. Lovely adolescents! Have you seen how some of my men look at them? They've also been imprisoned here for years and there are at least eight of them who'd be very happy, were I to give them the go ahead, to get their dirty hands on those kids, while everyone's asleep.'

'You dirty pig.'

'No more than any other man who's spent as long as I have in this accursed desert.' He stopped rocking and leant back, looking at the high dunes that enclosed the oasis, through the small window. 'Things are different when you're out here because as the years go by you lose hope that you're ever going to get out of it. As soon as you realise that nobody will ever give a damn about you again or care a jot for you, you start to lose any caring instinct you might have once had and stop giving a damn about anyone else.' He turned to look at her again. 'They're not going to give me anything. What I don't take, nobody will offer me and I can assure you that as soon as the others see you, they'll try on the same. Undress!' he repeated and this time it was an order.

Laila hesitated.

She was still trying to hold off, as every bone in her body cried out against his request, but she had known from the minute she had set eyes on Sergeant Major Malik-el-Haideri, that he was capable of anything, which included letting his men enjoy themselves with her husband's sons, who he had taught her to love as if they were her own.

Finally and very slowly she got up, crossed her arms, lifted up the edges of her simple dress, pulled it over her head and threw it into a corner.

Her body was firm, young and dark, with small breasts and strong buttocks. Sergeant Malik looked at her, standing naked before him, for some time, as he rocked back and forth, prolonging the moment for as long as possible as he entertained himself with lurid thoughts, before finally getting undressed himself.

The sun was very high and the smell of rotting corpses had become unbearable. The vultures were gathered in the sky like a dark cloud and he was powerless to anything about it.

He saw the first column of dust rising up from the west and approaching fast and as he got into the jeep to try and work out how the machine-gun worked, he saw the grey outline of another slower, heavier vehicle coming from the south. This second one had a light, rapid-firing canon raised on top of a small turret.

He knew that it would be hopeless to try and put up any resistance, when he was up against that type of a weapon. He tried to console himself with the fact that he had managed to cross Tikdabra, the desert of all deserts and had only been caught because he had remained loyal to his guest.

He picked up his rifle and walked to the edge of the hamada, without seeking protection from the rocks or bushes, leaving Abdul-el-Kebir behind him and out of range of the bullets.

He got his gun ready and then waited, trying to work out how far away the jeep would be from him, when it came into range. But just as the soldiers came into view and he lifted his gun to take aim, unsure whether to shoot the driver first or the one manning the machine gun, there was a loud crack as a mortar bomb flew through the air and hit the vehicle. The jeep stopped dead, as if it had struck an invisible wall and simultaneously exploded into tiny pieces.

One mangled corpse flew for almost forty meters, the other disintegrated as if it had never even existed and a few seconds later there was nothing left of the jeep other than a pile of smoking scrap metal.

Gazel Sayah, inmouchar of the Kel-Talgimus people, also known as "the Hunter," stood rooted to the spot, surprised and perhaps, for the first time in his life, unsure of what do to next.

Finally and very slowly, he turned round to face the second vehicle, the caterpillar tank that was still approaching him steadfastly. It stopped about twenty metres away at the exact point where the hamada and the "lost land" met.

A tall man with a well-groomed moustache, a sandy coloured uniform and stars on his cuff got out quickly and walked resolutely over to the Targui.

'Abdul-el-Kebir?' He enquired.

Gazel pointed behind him.

The officer smiled as if a great weight had been lifted off his shoulders.

'In my own name and in the name of my government I would like to welcome you to our country. It will be an honour for me to escort you to the military post and to personally accompany President Kebir to the capital.'

They started to walk slowly over to the vehicle and as they did so Gazel could not help looking over his shoulder at the remains of the jeep that was still smoking in the distance. The new arrival noticed and shook his head.

'We are a small, poor and passive country, but we don't like people invading our borders.'

When they reached the body of Abdul-el-Kebir, who was still unconscious, he examined him carefully, checked that he was breathing regularly and then, once he seemed certain that the man was out of danger, lifted his face and turned to look at the infinite plain that opened up before them.

'I would never have believed that anyone, at least anyone from this world, was capable of crossing that accursed place!'

Gazel smiled.

'A piece of advice,' he said. 'Stay away from Tikdabra.'

After they had been on the road for about three hours, he tapped the officer's arm lightly.

'Stop,' he said.

The other man did as he had asked and stopped the jeep, holding up his arm to tell the tank to stop as well.

'What's wrong?' he asked.

'I'll get out here.'

'Here?' he said in a tone of surprise, as he looked uncertainly around him at the stony, bushy plain. 'What are you going to do here?'

'Head home.' the Targui said. 'You're going south. My family is over there, far away, to the northwest in the Huaila mountains. It's time I went home.'

The army man shook his head, almost as if he were unwilling to believe that he really wanted to get out there.

'On foot and alone?'

'Someone will sell me a camel.'

'It's a long journey that borders the "lost land" all the way.'

'That's why I have to set off as soon as possible.'

The officer turned around and nodded towards the sleeping body of Abdul-el-Kebir.

'Aren't you going to wait until he wakes up? He'll want to thank you personally.'

Gazel shook his head as he got out of the jeep, taking his

weapons and water gerba with him.

"He's got nothing to thank me for."

He paused briefly. 'I wanted to cross the border and I've done that. He's your guest now.' He looked over at him affectionately. 'Wish him luck from me.'

The other man realised that his decision was final and that nothing was going to persuade him otherwise.

'Do you need anything?' he asked.

He shook his head and pointed to the plain: 'I'm a rich man now and there's good hunting here. I don't need anything.'

He stood very still as the vehicles drove passed him, heading south and only once the dust had settled and the noise of the motors had become a distant hum, did he finally take a look around him. He searched for direction, even though there did not appear to be any natural pointers on that wide and empty plain. Then set off, unhurriedly, with the air of somebody who was taking a gentle stroll in the countryside in the soft afternoon sun, taking time to admire his surroundings, to appreciate every bush, every rock, every mosquito and every slithering snake.

He had water, a good rifle and ammunition. This was his world, the heart of the desert that he loved and he was ready to enjoy the long journey ahead that would eventually take him to his wife, children, slaves, goats and camels.

A light breeze blew and as darkness fell the animals on the plain ventured out of their lairs to scamper around the low thicket. He shot a beautiful hare for his supper, which he ate by the light of a fire he had built using wood from the Tamarisk shrubs. He looked up at the stars that were gathering to keep him company and allowed wave after wave of pleasant memories to wash over him. He pictured the face and body of Laila and the smiles and games of his sons. He thought about his friend Abdul-el-Kebir's meaningful and intelligent words and the beautiful, passionate and unforgettable adventure he had just experienced at the very threshold of his maturity. An adventure that would mark his life forever and that the old men would tell of for years to come, enthralling their listeners with the stories of his heroic deeds and the fact that he was the only man to have ever challenged an army and the "lost land" of Tikdabra, all in one go.

He would tell his nephews how he had felt on the day that he had spent with the spirits of the "great caravan" and how he had spoken to them of his fears and of how scared he was that he might die, as they had, on that plain. He would tell them of how the drowned voices of the mummies with their bony fingers, had showed him the right way and how he had carried on for three days and three nights without stopping once, since he knew that if they stopped during time, then neither himself nor the camel would have been capable of resuming their journey. Thanks to their insuperable will, they had become like automatic, mechanised beings, immune to the heat, to thirst and to fatigue and had made it out of the inferno.

Now, there he was, lying down on the white sand, feeling the sweet contact of his damp gerba filled with water under his hand, the remains of the hare still smoking next to the fire and a bag of gold hanging from his belt. He felt at peace with himself and with the universe that surrounded him, for having proved that nobody, not even the government, could get away with breaking his people's laws and customs.

He thought about what the future might now hold for him, far away from the grazing grounds and places he had known as a child. The idea of emigrating over the border did not bother him, since the desert was the same for thousands of kilometers all around, whichever country one chose to live in. He did not worry either that someone might come and challenge his authority, or move him on from the sands, rocks and stony plains that he chose to inhabit, because he was quite aware that the number of people who chose the desert as a way of life was diminishing by the day.

He did not want any more wars or struggles and he yearned

for the peace of his jaima, the long days of hunting and the beautiful evenings spent by the light of the fire listening, each one of them, to old Suilem's stories. Those stories that he had heard as a child and that he would continue to listen to and never tire of until his faithful slave was silenced forever.

In the afternoon of the third day, he discovered an encampment of jaimas and sheribas next to a well.

They were Tuaregs, spear people, who were poor, but friendly and hospitable people. They agreed to sell him their best mehari and then sacrificed a lamb in his honour, which they added to one of the best couscous dishes he had tasted for some time and then invited him to a party the following night.

He knew that he would offend them if he turned down their offer and so he took a heavy gold coin out of the red leather bag that hung around his neck and put it down in front of him.

'I will only attend if you let me pay for the lambs,' he said. 'That is my price.'

'There aren't many of these left,' he pointed out. 'It's mostly dirty notes now, the value of which changes from day to day.'

'Who gave that to you?'

'An old caravan driver,' he replied without exactly lying, or telling the truth either.

'Have you got many of them? This is what they used to pay the guides and camel riders with,' the other man said knowingly. 'Did you know that?' he said, adding later with an ironic smile: 'I signed up with the "great caravan" but ten days later I started spitting blood so they rejected me saying that I wouldn't make it to Tripoli.' He shook his head as if he still found it hard to believe how fate had intervened. 'I'll be ninety soon,' he continued. 'But there's nothing left of the "great caravan."'

'How did you manage to cure yourself of tuberculosis?' Gazel asked. 'My eldest son and my first wife both died of it.'

'I made a pact with a butcher in Timbuctu,' the old man said. 'I worked for him for free for one year and in exchange he let me eat the raw humps of every camel he slaughtered,' he said, laughing.

'I became as fat as a barrel, but I stopped spitting blood. Almost two hundred camel humps!' he exclaimed. 'I haven't gone any where near one of those damned animals ever since. I'd rather walk for three months than get up on one of those things.'

'You're the first Imohag I've ever met that's not keen on camels,' Gazel remarked.

'Maybe,' he added smiling. 'But I'm probably the first Imohag to have survived tuberculosis.'

The beautiful girl with fine plaits, pert breasts, jewelled hands and red, painted palms, tuned the one string on her violin and plucked at it. The instrument let out a sharp wail, which sounded like both a lament and a high-pitched laugh in one. Then, looking directly at Gazel, the visitor, as if she were dedicating the story to him personally, said:

'Allah is great. Blessed is He.'

She paused. 'They say, although this did not happen in the land of the Imohag, or in Tekna, Marrakesh, Tunisia, Argel or Mauritania, but way over there in Arabia, near the saintly city of Mecca - which all believers must make a pilgrimage to at least once in their lifetime - that a long time ago in the prosperous and populated city of Mir, the glory of Califas, there lived three cunning merchants. Now these three men had managed after many years of doing business together to amass a sizeable fortune, which, they decided, they should use to start up a new business with.

It turned out, however, that the three merchants did not trust each other and so they put their riches into one bag and gave it to the mistress of the house in which they were living, to look after, with express instructions that she should not give any of it to any one of them, unless all three of them were present.

A few days later they needed to write a business letter to the neighbouring city and were in need of a piece of parchment. So one of them said:

"I will go and ask our good woman for one, she is sure to have some."

But when he went into the house, he asked instead for the money bag that they had given her and she said: "That I cannot do as your other friends are not present," and even though the other insisted, she continued to say no until the cunning merchant said:

"Look out the window and you will see my companions there in the street below. I'll go down and ask them."

The woman did as she was told and watched as the merchant went outside and whispered to his partners:

"She has some parchment, but she does not want to give it to me unless you ask for it as well."

Not realising that they were being tricked, they shouted up to the woman to do as he wished and so she gave him the bag and the thief fled the city.

When the men realised that they had been tricked and that the money had gone, they blamed the poor woman and took her before a magistrate in order to seek justice.

It turned out that the judge was a fair and intelligent man, who listened well to both sides of the story and then, after some deliberation said:

"I see that you have reason enough to make these demands and it is only fair that this woman returns the bag to you, or at least the value of its contents. But according to the pact that you all agreed on, it is imperative that all three of you are present when she returns it to you, so I believe that your time right now would be better spent in search of him. When you have found him, bring him here and I will make sure that the agreement is honoured."

And justice and reason triumphed, thanks to the cunning judgment of an intelligent magistrate.

As Allah would have wished.

Blessed be his name.'

The girl played a note on the violin as if to put a full stop to the story and then, without taking her eyes off Gazel, added:

'You, who seem to have come from such a long way away. Why don't you tell us a story?'

Gazel looked at the group of about twenty boys and girls, all gathered around the fire, over which two, big lambs were cooking slowly, emitting a sweet and intense aroma and said:

'What kind of story would you like to hear?'

'Yours,' the girl replied quickly. 'Why are you here, alone and so far from your home? Why do you pay with these ancient coins? What mystery are you hiding? Even through your veil you can see in your eyes that you are hiding a huge secret.'

'It is only your eyes that want to see a secret where none other than tiredness exists,' he assured her. 'I have made a long journey. Maybe the longest journey that anyone has ever made on this earth. I crossed the "lost land" of Tikdabra.'

The last one to have arrived at the party, a strong boy with a shaven head, a slight squint and a long scar that ran from his cheek to his throat, suddenly asked in a quivering voice:

'Is it you, Gazel Sayah; inmouchar of the Kel-Talgimus, whose family was settled in the guelta of the Huaila mountains?' His heart missed a beat.

'Yes, that is I.'

'Then I have some bad news for you,' the boy said with a tone of regret. 'I've come from the north, from tribe to tribe, from jaima to jaima,' he continued. 'The soldiers have taken away your wife and children. All of your own. Only the old Akli has escaped and it was he who said that they were waiting to kill you in the guelta of Huaila.'

He had to make an extreme effort to stop himself from crying out as he struggled to contain his emotions, an effort that took much more strength than anything he had had to confront whilst in the depths of the "lost land."

'Where have they taken them?' he said in a voice that did not betray his panic.

'No one knows. Maybe to El Akab. Maybe even further north, to the capital. They want to exchange them for Abdul-el-Kebir.'

The Targui got up and walked slowly over to the dunes as everybody watched in respectful silence. The cheer of the party had disintegrated and no one in the group had even noticed that one of the lambs was burning. The gri-gri of misfortune had spread through the flames of the fire and its fetid breath had dampened the suggestive looks and sparks of desire that might otherwise have led to happy unions later that evening.

Gazel collapsed onto one of the dunes in the darkness and buried his face in the sand as he struggled not to cry out loud, burying his nails in the palm of his hand until he drew blood.

He was no longer a rich man on his way to the peace of his home after a long adventure. Nor was he the hero who had rescued Abdul-el-Kebir from his enemies' clutches and crossed the "lost land" with him, carrying him to safety across the border. All he was now was a stupid fool who had lost everything he had in the world, due to his stubborn insistence that his old fashioned laws, which no longer meant anything to anyone, be respected.

'Laila!'

A shiver, like a river of cold ice, ran down his back as he imagined her in the hands of those men in dirty uniforms, with their thick belts and stinking, hard boots. He remembered their faces as they had pointed their guns at him at the door of his jaima and their filthy camp and the abusive way they had treated the Bedouins in El-Akab. A deep groan escaped from his lips, against his will, making him bite down hard onto the back of his hand.

'Don't do that. Don't keep it in. The strongest of men have the right to weep at a moment like this.'

He lifted his face. The beautiful girl with long plaits had sat down next to him and reached out her hand to stroke his face, like a mother might do to her son.

'It has passed,' he said.

She shook her head firmly.

'Do not lie to me. It has not passed… These things don't go away. They stay buried inside, like a bullet that's lodged itself deep within you. I know because my husband died two years ago and my hands still search for him at night.'

'She is not dead. No one would dare do her any harm,' he said, as if trying to convince himself. 'She's only a girl. God will not allow any harm to come to her.'

'The only God that exists is the one you want to,' she said firmly. 'You could leave it to Him if you want. But if you have managed to cross the "lost land" of Tikdabra then you are capable of getting your family back. I am sure of that.'

'How can I do that now,' he said despondently. 'You heard; they want Abdul-el-Kebir and he isn't with me any more.'

The girl looked at him fixedly under the clear light of a full moon that had climbed high in the sky, turning night almost back into day.

'Would you have accepted that exchange had he still been with you?' she asked.

'They are my children,' came his reply. 'My children and my wife - the only things I have in this life.'

'You still have your pride as a Targui. I remember her. And from what I know of you, you are the proudest and bravest of us all.' She paused. 'Too much so, perhaps. When you warriors go off to fight, you never stop to think about what might become of us women that stay behind, who suffer the brunt of your actions but take no slice of the glory.'

She clicked her tongue as if to stop herself. 'But I am not here to admonish you,' she conceded. 'Fact is fact and you had your reasons for what you did. I came, because at a time like this a man needs company. Would you like to tell me about her?' She tilted her head to one side.

'She's just a girl,' he sobbed.

The door flew open and Sergeant Malik-el-Haideri jumped up from his bed and grabbed the pistol lying on the table, but stopped as soon as he made out the shape of Lieutenant Razman, silhouetted in the doorway against the violent light that came flooding in from outside.

Even though he was half naked, he still tried to maintain a military air by standing to attention and saluted as he clicked his heels together, which actually made him look quite ridiculous. But it was clear from the lieutenant's grim expression that the business he had come about was no laughing matter. As soon as his eyes had got used to the darkness he went over to the windows, opened the shutters and pointing to the next hut with his whip, said:

'Who are those people you have locked up in there, sergeant?' he asked.

The sergeant felt himself break into a cold sweat that started to seep out of every pore, but still struggling to keep his composure he said:

'The Targui's family.'

'How long have they been here for?'

'One week.'

Razman turned to face him as if unable to believe what he was hearing and reiterated:

'One week...?' He was clearly horrified. 'Are you trying to tell me that you kept women and children locked up in this heat, in this inferno, for one week without having informed your superiors of this fact?'

'The radio was broken.'

'Liar! I have just spoken to the operator, you gave an order of silence. That's why it was impossible to communicate with you before I arrived here.'

He stopped suddenly as his gaze fell on the completely naked figure of Laila, who out of fright had scurried over to the furthest corner of the room, where she was curled up on top of a threadbare blanket. His eyes flicked alternately from the girl to Malik-el-Haideri and finally, as if he could hardly bear to hear the answer, he asked hoarsely: 'Who is that?'

'The Targui's wife. But it's not what you think...' he said trying to absolve himself. 'She did it of her own free will. She agreed!' he repeated, extending his hands out in front of him, as if begging for mercy.

Lieutenant Razman went over to Laila, who tried to cover herself up with a corner of the blanket.

'Is that true. That you agreed to this?' he asked. 'He didn't force you?' The girl looked at him fixedly and then turning round to face the sergeant said firmly:

'He said if I didn't agree he would give my children over to the soldiers.'

Lieutenant Razman nodded his head silently, then turning slowly round and pointing to the door, he shouted to Malik:

'Get out.'

He tried to grab his clothes, but the lieutenant shook his head firmly:

'No! You are not fit to wear that uniform again. Get out of here as you are!'

Sergeant Major Malik-el-Haideri went out, followed by the sergeant, but stopped in the doorway as there, watching them expectantly, were all the men from the outpost, accompanied now by Razman's wife and the enormous Sergeant Ajamuk.

'Over to the dunes!'

He obeyed, despite the fact that the sand was burning the soles of his feet and he walked on in silence, his head hung low, without looking at anyone, until he reached the start of the dunes.

As soon as he realised that he could not go any further and that he would never make it up the steep slope, he turned around and was not surprised to see the lieutenant taking his regulation revolver out of its holster.

One shot was all it took to blow his brains out.

Razman stood still for a moment pensively, contemplating the body and then he slowly put his weapon back, retraced his steps and stood in front of everyone present. Nobody moved a muscle.

He looked at each one of them, trying to read their thoughts and then finally took a deep breath, as if preparing to say something that he had been holding inside for too long and said:

'You are the scum of the army. The kind of men I have always hated and soldiers I never would have chosen to be in command of: thieves, murderers, drug addicts and rapists and riffraff!' He paused. 'But in the end, you might be nothing more than victims, or a reflection of the country we have become under this government.' He let them reflect a little on what he was trying to tell them and then, raising his voice, he continued: 'But the time has come for things to change. President Abdul-el-Kebir has managed to cross the border to safety and made his first appeal to the people who want to see a return to democracy and freedom, to unite and fight.' He paused again, this time more theatrically, aware that to rouse the men his speech needed to be dramatic. 'I am going to join him!' he finally said. 'What I have witnessed here today has convinced me and I am ready to break with the past and start the fight all over again with the man in whom I really trust. And I'm going to give you a chance! Whoever wants to, can follow me across the border to join up with Abdul-el-Kebir.'

The men looked at each other in astonishment, unable to believe that their prayers had been answered and that they were being given the chance to escape from that inferno. They were being freed from Adoras and being given the option to flee the country. Moreover, it was the very officer in charge of keeping them imprisoned there, who was offering them this freedom on a plate.

Many men before them had tried to escape, but they had always been captured and shot, or imprisoned for the rest of their lives. But suddenly this young lieutenant in his well-pressed uniform, who had just arrived there with his attractive wife and a colossal, but good-natured sergeant, was trying to convince them to do something, that only yesterday, would have been considered the most heinous of all crimes. Now, if they chose to leave that hellhole they would suddenly, as if by some crazy twist of fate, be committing a heroic deed.

One of the men almost burst out laughing, while another jumped for joy. Then Razman, quite sure of what he was doing and of what that bunch of criminals would choose to do, asked those of them who wanted to join him to raise up their hands. A sea of hands bounced into the air in unison, as if they had been pulled up by some invisible, mechanical spring.

The lieutenant smiled and looked at his wife, who smiled back at him. Then he turned round to Ajamuk:

'Get everything ready. We'll be leaving in two hours.' He pointed with his whip to the hut where Gazel Sayah's family were, watching the events unfold through the latticed window. 'They're coming with us,' he added. 'We'll take them across the border to safety.'

It was a long journey. He was unsure of which route to take home, not being exactly sure of where his home was and in search of his family, but not sure whether he still had any family.

It was a long journey.

First he went west, putting a day's distance in between himself and the start of the "lost land" and then, once he knew it had ended, he veered north, aware that he was crossing the border once again and that the soldiers that seemed to plague his waking hours, might appear at any time.

It was a long journey.

And a sad one.

He had never, not even during the very worst moments of his journey through Tikdabra, with death as his only companion, imagined that this would happen. Being a warrior from a race of noble warriors, death was always considered to be the ultimate defeat. But he had suddenly realised, like a punch in the face, that dying was nothing compared with the hideous reality that your family had become the victims of your own personal war. This was truly the defeat of all defeats.

Images of his children and the voice of Laila came into his head and scenes of their peaceful and solitary lives at the encampment, at the foot of the large dunes, tortured his thoughts.

The cold dawns when Laila would curl up against his stomach

in search of warmth; the long, beautiful, bright mornings they would spend hunting, full of expectation and fear: the soporific midday heat and the sweet siestas; the flaming red skies in the afternoons, when the shadows would stretch out to the horizon and the intense and fragrant nights spent by the fire-side, listening to well-known legends being told over and over again; their fear of the harmatan wind and of drought; their love of the windless plain and the black cloud that turned the desert into a green carpet of acheb flowers; the goat that died; the young camel that finally became pregnant; the cry of the little one; the smile of his eldest son; Laila's cries of pleasure in the half light. This was his life, what he yearned for, all he had worked for and everything he had lost because he had not been able to live with the fact that his honour, a Targui's honour, had been offended.

Would anyone have blamed him for not seeking revenge on the army? Who would blame him now for having done exactly that and for losing his family along the way? He had not considered the size of his country. He had ignored the number of people that lived in it and stood up against it, against its soldiers and its governors, without thinking of the consequences or of what his actions might lead to.

Where was he going to find his wife and children in this huge country? Who, out of all its inhabitants, would be able to give him news of them? With every day that took him further north he became increasingly aware of how small he was, even though that very same desert, in all its immensity, had never made him feel powerless in all the forty years or so that he had spent in it.

Now he felt powerless, not in the face of nature's grandeur but in the face of the vile people that lived in it, people who were capable of involving women and children in a war between men. He did not know what type of weapons one used against those people. He had no idea how to play their game and he remembered a story that the old black man Suilem had told them once. It was a tale of two families at war who hated each other so much that one of the families buried the other's small child in the sand, causing the mother to go mad with sorrow. But that was the only story of its kind in the whole history of the Sahara that he could remember. It had shocked his people so much that its memory had lived on and been carried through the centuries by word of mouth, only to be recounted night after night as a warning to adults and as a lesson to the children.

'See how hate and fighting lead to nothing more than fear, madness and death.'

He could repeat from memory every word the old man had said and maybe only now, after years of listening to it, did he really understand its true significance.

So many men had died since that dawn when he had first headed off into the desert with his mehari, in search of his lost honour, that it should really have come as no surprise to him that of all that blood shed, some of it would eventually trickle back to tarnish his life and the lives of his family.

First there was Mubarrak, whose only crime had been to head up a patrol, having taken over from another man who nobody had heard of. Then there was the sweaty captain, who had defended his position by saying that he was just following orders. There were those who had not been able to defend themselves at all - the fourteen sleeping guardians at Gerifies - whose only crime was to have been asleep and in his way. There were the soldiers who he had killed on the edges of the "lost land" and the men who had been blown into the air before they had even known what had hit them.

They were too many and then there was him, Gazel Sayah, with only one life to offer up in exchange - one death to compensate for so many.

Maybe that was why they were using his family, as part payment for this huge debt.

'Insh. Allah,' Abdul-el-Kebir would have said.

The image of the old man came to mind again and he

wondered what had become of him and if, as he had promised, he was struggling for power once again.

'He was a mad man,' he muttered quietly. 'A crazy dreamer, born to be on the receiving end of life's blows and with the gri-gri of bad luck stuck to his side and hidden in his clothes. His gri-gri was so strong that I got swept up in it too.'

To the Bedouins, a gri-gri was an evil spirit that brought with it illness, bad luck or death. The Tuaregs tended to dismiss it as a superstition that only the servants or slaves believed in. Even so, many of the most noble inmouchars had been known to avoid certain regions that were famous for their bad spirits, or certain people that they knew attracted them.

It was a sad and tragic fact that when a gri-gri fell in love with you there was no hiding from it and nothing in the entire universe could protect you from its malign spirit. Even if you buried yourself in the deepest of dunes or sought refuge in the depths of Tikdabra, the gri-gri would still search you out and stick to your skin like a tick, or a smell, or the dye from your clothes. The Targui felt sure that the gri-gri of death, the most loyal and insistent spirit of them all, had taken hold of him. A warrior could only be freed from that kind of spirit when he came face to face with another warrior whose own death spirit was still more powerful.

'Why have you chosen me?' he would ask it at night, when by the light of the fire he imagined he could almost see it sitting there on the other side. 'I did not summon you. It was the soldiers who brought it with them when they came to my home and the captain shot the sleeping boy.'

From that day on, from the very moment that his guest had been shot under his roof, it only seemed logical to accept that the gri-gri of death had consumed the master of that jaima, in the same way that the gri-gri of adultery would settle inside the wives-to-be, who cheated on their husbands in the month prior to their wedding.

'But it wasn't my fault,' he protested, as if trying to banish it him from his side. 'I wanted to protect him and I would have given my life in exchange for his.'

But as Suilem used to say, the gri-gri was deaf to human pleas and threats. Those evil spirits had their own criteria and when they loved someone they loved them to the end of time.

'There was once a man who fell victim to the locust gri-gri. He lived in Arabia and year after year, without fail, a plague of them would demolish his crops and the crops of his fellow citizens.

'In desperation, his neighbours took him before the caliph and begged that he be executed, otherwise, they said, everybody would die of hunger. But the caliph, realising that it was not the man's fault, defended him by saying: "If I kill you, then the locust gri-gri, who will continue to love you beyond death, will still visit your grave once a year. So I order you now, while you are alive and tomorrow when you shall be a spirit, to travel, every seven years to the coast of West Africa, where you shall stay for seven years. In that way, we won't offend Allah, the locust being one of His creatures as well and we will effectively distribute the load in order to alternately enjoy seven years of misery and seven of abundance."

'So that is what the man did during his lifetime and his spirit continued that way too, long after he had died, which is why the plague visits us for a time and then returns, with the man's spirit, to his own country.'

Whether the legend was true or not, it was certainly true of the locusts and it was also true that the Tuaregs, being the more cunning of all the Arabian peasants, had solved their hunger issues in a much more practical way and one which did not demand the execution of an innocent man. They chose to eat the locusts in the same way that they ate their crops. Toasted over a flame, or made into flour, they turned them into their finest foods and when they arrived in their millions, blacking out the sun at midday, it was never a miserable occasion, but one of prosperity and abundance for months on end. Laila would turn the insects into flour, mix them with honey and dates and turn them into cakes as treats for the children.

He had loved those cakes too and now he yearned for the long afternoons when he would sit at the door of his tent, eating them with a steaming hot glass of tea and watching as the sun slipped below the horizon. Then, as the women milked the camels and the children brought in the goats, he would walk slowly over to the well and check its level from the parapet. He could not bear to believe that all that was now over and that he would never again return to his well, the palm trees there, his family or livestock, just because this invisible and malign spirit had become attached to him.

'Go away!' he begged once again. 'I am tired of carrying you around and of killing without knowing why I am doing it.'

But he knew that even if the gri-gri had wanted to go, the sad souls of Mubarrak, the captain and the soldiers, would never have allowed it to.

Every weekend, Anuhar-el-Mojkri would leave his comfortable and cool study in the government palace, get into his old Simca that he had left full of water and provisions in a small street round the corner and rattle his way up to the nearby buttress of a mountain that overlooked El-Akab. At the top of the mountain there stood the ruins of what had once been an impenetrable fortress and refuge for the inhabitants of the oasis, during times of war and unrest.

There was nothing left to explore inside the castle walls as many of the stones had been removed by the French and used in El-Akab's new buildings. Anuhar-el-Mojkri, however, had discovered in the caves and rocky walls of the narrow passages that ran to the back of the ruins, that by looking carefully and by gently removing the outer layer of millennia dust, you would find an infinite number of cave paintings that told the story of the Sahara's remote past and its people.

Elephants, giraffes, antelopes and leopards inhabited the drawings and under his expert hands, hunting scenes, love scenes, pictures of daily life and of the people that inhabited his land long ago, would miraculously appear. He cleaned each stone with infinite care and with the instinct of someone who had been born an archaeologist, seeking out the pictures in places where he would have logically chosen to draw them himself.

It was his big secret, his pride and joy and in his tiny bachelor apartment he had put together hundreds of beautiful, colour photographs that he had taken during more than two years of meticulous work. They were the photographs that Anuhar-el-Mojkri planned to use to illustrate his volume: 'The Frescoes of El Akab,' which one day he planned to surprise the world with. He was still waiting to find something else though, something he had been looking for, for a long time, even though he had no idea where it might be. He was after a replica of the Tassili Martians, huge figures that were over two meters high with their clothing and postures drawn in great detail, which would prove that they had visited, back in the dark ages, those regions which were now desert, but that would have been, back then, fertile and rich and inhabited by all kinds of exotic animals. For the governor's secretary to prove that the inhabitants of another planet had visited El-Akab, so far away from Tassili, would certainly have constituted the high point of his lifelong ambition and he would have happily sacrificed his promising political career for just one of those drawings, however crude it might be.

So, on that particular day, under the heat of a midday sun that beat down harshly on his large, floppy straw hat, he found himself sitting before a small hollow in the smooth face of a living rock, shielded from the wind and the rain. He was praying that the moment had arrived for to him to discover the thing that he had always hoped he would find. His body was overcome with a strange sensation, almost as if he was having a premonition and he realised that his hands were trembling as they traced the line of a deep incision that promised to be the vague beginning of one of those tall figures.

He wiped off the sweat that was running down his forehead and steaming up his glasses, marked the line with white chalk until it became visible, took a quick swig of water and gasped in horror as he recognised the deep and threatening voice that came from behind him:

'Where is my family?' He spun round, falling against the wall for support as he saw, only three meters away from him, the black arm of a gun and the svelte silhouette of the Targui, who, since their first meeting, had haunted his dreams.

'You?' was all he could say.

'Yes, me,' came his dry response. 'Where is my family?'

'Your family?' he said in a tone of surprise. 'What have I got to do with your family?'

'What have they done with my family? The soldiers took them away.'

Anuhar-el-Mojkri, realising that his legs were about to give way, sat down on a rock and took his hat off, wiping the sweat off his face with the palm of his hand.

'The soldiers?' he repeated incredulously. 'That's not possible! No, it's not possible, I would have known about it.'

'The soldiers took them away.'

He cleaned his glasses with a handkerchief that he had taken out of his back pocket with trembling hands, then looked him in the face, through his own, short-sighted eyes.

'Listen!' he said, his tone quite sincere. 'The ministry mentioned the possibility of seizing your family and exchanging them for Abdul-el-Kebir, but the general opposed the idea and I've never heard them discuss it again. I promise you!'

'What minister? Where does he live?'

'The Minister of the Interior. Madani, Ali Madani. He lives in the capital, but I doubt he has your family.'

'If he hasn't got them, then the soldiers have.'

'No,' he said with absolute conviction. 'The soldiers can't have them. The general is a friend of mine, we dine together twice a week. He's not the kind of man who would do that and even if he had been considering it, he would definitely have spoken to me about it first.'

'But my family isn't there. My slave watched as they were taken away by the soldiers and five of them are still there, waiting for me in the guelta of the Huaila mountains.'

'They can't be with the soldiers,' he insisted. 'They must have been police that were sent in by the ministry,' he said, shaking his head despondently. 'I can believe that son of a bitch would do something like that.'

He adjusted his glasses once again, which were now perfectly clear and looked at Gazel with renewed interest. 'Did you really cross the "lost land" of Tikdabra?' he asked.

Gazel nodded silently and he gasped, whether through admiration or plain disbelief, it could not be said.

'Fantastic!' he exclaimed. 'Really fantastic. Did you know that Abdul-el-Kebir is in Paris? The French are backing him and it's very possible that you, an illiterate Targui, might well have changed the course of our country's history.'

'I don't care to change anything,' he said, reaching out his hand and taking the water bottle, which he proceeded to drink from, only lifting his veil up very slightly. 'All I want is my family back and that they leave me in peace.'

'That's what we all want: to live in peace; you, with your family and me, with my drawings. But I doubt they will let us.'

Gazel pointed with a nod of his head to the drawings marked with chalk that he could make out on the adjacent wall.

'What are they?'

'The history of your ancestors. Or the history of the men that lived here before the Tuaregs took over the desert.'

'Why are you doing this? Why are you wasting your time up here when you could be sitting peacefully in the shade, somewhere in El-Akab?'

The governor's secretary shrugged his shoulders.

'Maybe because I am disillusioned with politics,' he remarked.

'Do you remember Hassan-ben-Koufra? They dismissed him so he went to Switzerland, where he had amassed a small fortune and a few days later he was run over by a lorry carrying fizzy drinks. It's ridiculous! In a few months he went from being the "viceroy" of the desert, to a man with broken legs, crying in a clinic somewhere, in a land that's covered in snow.'

'Is his wife with him?'

'Yes.'

'Well then, that's all that matters,' the Targui noted. 'They loved each other. I know because I watched them together for some time.'

Anuhar-el-Mojkri nodded in agreement.

'He was an authentic son of a bitch, an unscrupulous politician, a thief, traitor and a fox. But he had something good in him and that was his love for Tamat, so maybe he deserved to stay alive, if only for that reason.'

Gazel smiled vaguely, even though the other man was unable to see him doing so, looked at the drawings on the walls and then stood up, picking up his gun as he did so:

'Maybe your love of history and my ancestors has saved your life,' he commented. 'But do not move from here or try to give me away. If I see you in El-Akab before Monday, I'll blow your brains out.'

The other man had picked up his chalk, his brushes and his cloths and had gone back to his work.

'Don't worry!' he replied. 'I wasn't planning on doing so.'

Then as the Targui headed off, he shouted after him: 'I hope you find your family!'

The bus he found himself bumping along in was the filthiest, most rickety, clapped out, old vehicle imaginable. It gasped and chugged along asthmatically, through the bushy plains and rocky terrain, at a speed that could not have exceeded fifty kilometers per hour.

It had to stop almost every two hours, either due to a puncture or because the wheels had got stuck in the sand and the driver and the conductor would ask the passengers, with their goats, dogs and baskets of chickens to get out of the bus and either push, or sit down on the roadside and wait while they changed the wheel.

Every four hours they had to stop and refill the petrol tank, using the primitive method of attaching a hosepipe to an old drum that was tied to the roof. Every time they reached a steep hill, the men would be asked to get out and walk.

For two days and two nights they were squashed in there like dates in a rabbit-skin sack, sweaty and woozy due to the intense heat, not knowing how much more of the torturous journey they could take and longing for a change in the monotonous desert landscape.

Every time they stopped, Gazel felt the overwhelming urge to abandon the filthy vehicle and continue on foot, however long it might take him. But he also knew that it would take him months to reach the capital on his own and that every day and every hour he gained, brought him closer to Laila and his children.

So he stayed with the bus, despite the overwhelming repulsion he felt at being so hemmed in. This man, who loved solitude and freedom above all else, now found himself sandwiched between chatty traders, hysterical women, noisy children and pesky chickens. He could not turn himself into a stone in amongst that chaos as he had done so in the "lost land," cutting himself off from his surroundings by forcing his spirit to temporarily abandon his body.

Every pothole, every lurch forward, every burst tyre or human belch brought him sharply back to reality and he was unable to sleep, even in the dead of night. He longed to sleep, if only to return, in his dreams, to his family and draw on them for the strength he needed in order to endure that interminable journey.

Finally, on the misty dawn of the third day, which brought with it an insistent and warm wind that blew clouds of grey choking dust into the passengers' faces, making it impossible too see further than fifty metres ahead, they drove past a huddle of mud huts, a dry ravine and a filthy square, before finally lurching to a halt in the middle of what looked like an old, abandoned souk.

'End of the line!' the conductor shouted, stretching his arms and legs and looking around him with what seemed to be an expression of astonishment on his face. It was as if he could not believe that once again he had taken part in the mad odyssey of driving to El-Akab and made it there alive. 'Thanks be to God!'

Gazel got off last, gazed around at the old, crumbling walls of the souk that looked as if they might collapse around him at any moment and walked hesitantly over to the conductor.

'Is this the capital?' he asked.

'Oh no,' the man said with a smile. 'But we only go this far. If we took that thing on to the main road we'd get arrested as madmen.'

'So how do I get to the capital?'

'You could get another bus, although I recommend the train, it's faster.'

'What's a train?'

The man did not seem at all surprised by the question because Gazel was the first Bedouin he had seen on a bus in twenty years.

'You had better go and see for yourself,' came his reply. 'Go down this street and three blocks down you'll see a brown building, it's there.'

'Three what?'

'Three streets down, three blocks…'

He made a sweeping gesture with his hand. 'None of this exists where you live I suppose. Go straight on until you see the building. There's only one.'

Gazel nodded, took his rifle, sword and leather bag full of ammunition, a little food and all his belongings and set off in the direction that the man had indicated, but the conductor shouted to him from the roof of the bus.

'Oy! You can't walk around with all those weapons on you..! If they see you you'll get into big trouble. Have you got a license?'

'A what?'

'A license for the gun. No, I can see you haven't. Hide them or you'll end up in jail!'

Gazel stood stock still in the centre of the old souk, unsure of what to do. Then, on seeing one of the other passengers walking in the opposite direction with a bag on both shoulders and some rolled up carpets under his arm, he had an idea and ran over to him.

'I'll buy those carpets from you,' he said, holding out a gold coin to him.

The other man did not even reply, took the money, lifted up his arm to let him take them away and hurried off, as if he were afraid that the stupid Targui might change his mind.

But Gazel did not change his mind. He unrolled the carpets,

wrapped up his weapons in them, put them under his arm and carried on to the station.

The conductor, who had been watching him from the roof of the bus, shook his head and burst out laughing.

The train was even dirtier, more uncomfortable and noisier than the bus and although it had the advantage that its tyres did not burst, it had the unpleasant habit of filling up with smoke and ash and of stopping with annoying regularity in every city, village, shantytown and farmhouse along the way.

When he first saw it appear in the shiny station, grunting and belching out smoke like a monster, just as the old black man Suilem had described in his stories, Gazel had been overwhelmed with a feeling of panic. He had been forced to draw on all his strength as a warrior and all his composure as an inmouchar of the glorious veil people to let himself be carried along in the wave of passengers and then to be bundled in alongside them into one of the dilapidated coaches with their hard wooden benches and windows with no panes.

He copied everyone else, by leaving his carpets and leather bag in the luggage rack and then, huddling into a corner, he tried to convince himself that he was just travelling on a type of big bus that moved along iron rails in order to avoid the dusty roads.

But when the whistle blew and the locomotive lunged forward and the sound of grating metal, creaking rails and the driver's shouts filled the air, his heart leapt again and he had to do everything within his powers to stop himself from leaping back out onto the platform.

Later, as it hurtled downhill at almost one hundred kilometers an hour, the air and smoke rushing in through the windows, Gazel sincerely thought he might die of fright. He watched as electricity pylons, trees and houses whizzed past him, making him dizzy and desperate to get off, but he bit down hard on his veil to stop himself from shouting out and ordering them to stop the rollercoaster and let him off.

Then, in the middle of the afternoon, the mountains suddenly sprung up before his eyes and he thought that he must be imagining things. Not even in his wildest dreams had he ever imagined that such a mass could exist, such an impenetrable barrier, sheer and proud, its peaks brushed with white.

He turned round to a fat lady, sitting behind him, who had spent most of the journey breastfeeding her twin boys and asked:

'What is that?'

'Snow,' the lady replied with an air of superiority, as if she was privy to some inside information. 'I'd wrap up because you'll soon start to feel the cold.'

And a cold like the Targui had never known before descended as the freezing air and flurries of miniscule snowflakes invaded the coach, forcing the shivering, stricken passengers to cover themselves up with anything they had to hand.

Just as it was starting to get dark, they stopped at a tiny mountain station and the ticket collector informed them that the train would be stopping for ten minutes, which would give them enough time to go and get their supper. So Gazel, unable to contain the urge, jumped off the coach and ran out of the station towards the snow.

He picked it up with his bare hands and was more amazed by its consistency and texture, than by its coldness. The powdery substance had an indescribable, light, crunchy softness to it that fell apart in his fingers, quite unlike sand, water and stone, different in fact to anything he had ever touched before. It was some time before he realised that his feet, which were naked apart from a pair of light sandals, were starting to freeze.

He walked back slowly and thoughtfully, almost horrified by his discovery. Then he bought a heavy, thick blanket from one seller and some hot couscous from another and returned to his seat to contemplate the night and the snowy landscape that was disappearing into the shadows. He studied the coach's slatted wooden walls, which had been covered in all kinds of graffiti, no doubt the scribbles and scratchings of bored passengers, trying to while away their journey. It was there, at that station, with his feet in the snow that Gazel Sayah suddenly realised that the predictions of the old lady Khaltoum were about to be fulfilled.

The desert, his beloved desert where he had been born, was now way behind him at the foot of those mountains that were covered in green pastures and huge trees. He was, he realised, heading, blindly and ignorantly into unknown and hostile lands, with the aim of taking on world leaders with only the help of an old sword and a pathetic rifle.

He was awoken by a screech of brakes, a sharp jolt and voices that seemed to come from beyond the grave. Sleepy voices echoed around him as the train ground to a halt inside what looked like a huge empty cave.

He put his head out of the window and marvelled at the high dome made of iron and glass, made still larger by the reflections coming from hundreds of small light bulbs that were hanging from the ceiling and the dusty, neon signposts that lit the way.

The passengers who had been on board for the entire trip got off the train, their shabby cardboard suitcases in hand and ambled off sleepily, cursing the ridiculous timetable of the Methuselan train that always arrived at its destination about six hours behind schedule.

He got off last, carrying his carpets, his leather bag and his heavy blanket and followed them all as they disappeared through a large, opaque, glass door. He walked slowly, impressed by the grandeur of the station, in whose high ceilings bands of bats were flying around. The only sound that remained was the noise of the locomotive, snorting and sighing, as if it were trying to recover its breath from the long and tiring journey.

He crossed the large waiting room with its dirty marble floors and long benches, upon which entire families were sleeping, still clutching their pitiful luggage, found the exit and walked outside. He stopped at the top of a wide staircase as he took in the huge square that lay before him and the massive buildings that surrounded it.

He was completely taken aback by the wall of windows, doors and balconies that sealed off, almost hermetically, the area and he shook his head in disbelief, as a hideous assortment of smells assaulted him, like hungry beggars who had been waiting to pounce on him.

It was not like the smell of human sweat, excrement or dead and rotten animals, or like the stench of putrid water from old wells or a male goat on heat. It was more subtle, less notable, but equally disagreeable and intense for a man used to the smells of the open spaces. It was the smell of people crowded together, of thousands of different meals being cooked at the same time, of boxes of rubbish that had been emptied out by starving street dogs and sewer smells that came up from the drains, as if the city were, and in fact was, built on a sea of faeces.

The air was dense; still and dense on that hot night; humid, salty, still and dense and it tasted of sulphur and burnt petrol and of cooking oil fried a thousand times over.

He stood very still, wondering whether to enter into the sleeping city or go back and rest on one of the benches until it was light. Before he could make a decision a man in a worn-out uniform and red hat had walked over to him and stopped next to him.

'Is anything wrong?' he asked and when the Targui shook his head, he nodded in turn.

'I understand,' he said. 'It's your first time in the city. Do you have anywhere to sleep?'

'No.'

'I know of somewhere near my house. Maybe they'd take you in.' He realised that he was not making a move to accompany him, so he gestured with his arm for him to follow. 'Lets go,' he said. 'Don't be afraid, I'm not a faggot or a thief.'

He liked the man's face, which was tired and marked with

lines that told of a difficult life. His skin had an almost yellowish hue to it from working nights, his eyes were bloodshot and he sported a limp moustache that was stained with nicotine.

'Come on,' he insisted. 'I know what it's like to be alone in a city like this. I arrived from the cabila some fifteen years ago with less luggage than you and only a cheese under my arm,' he said, laughing. 'And now look at me. I've got a uniform, a hat and a whistle.'

Gazel went over to him and together they crossed the square towards a wide avenue that led off the other side of the square, down which a lone vehicle would drive from time to time.

Just as they reached the middle, the man turned to look at him intently.

'Are you really a Targui?' he asked.

'Yes.'

'And is it true that you only reveal your face to family and close friends?'

'Yes.'

'Well you're going to find that hard here,' he said. 'The police won't let you walk the streets with your face covered. They like to control us. Everyone has to have identity cards, with their photo and fingerprints on them.' He paused. 'I don't suppose you've ever had an identity card, am I right?'

'What's an identity card?'

'I thought as much.'

They started walking again, at a leisurely pace, as if the man in the red hat was in no hurry to get to wherever it was that he was going and was actually enjoying his nocturnal stroll and chat. 'Lucky you, for never having needed one. But what brings you to the city?'

'Do you know the minister?' he asked suddenly.

'Minister? What minister?'

'Ali Madani?'

'No!' he said quickly. 'Luckily I don't know Ali Madani and I hope you never have the misfortune of meeting him either.'

'Do you know where I can find him?'

'At the ministry I suppose.'

'Where is the ministry?'

'You continue down this avenue and carry straight on. When you get to the esplanade, turn right. It's a grey building with white awnings over the windows. But if I were you I wouldn't go anywhere near it. They say at night you can hear the screams of prisoners being tortured in its basements, although some say they are just the cries of souls who have been murdered down there already. At night they take the bodies out through the back door and throw them into a delivery van.'

'Why do they kill them?'

'Politics,' he replied with an expression of disgust. 'In this damned city it's all about politics. Especially since Abdul-el-Kebir escaped. There's going to be quite a rumpus!' he exclaimed. He pointed to a side street and they crossed over the main road to it. 'Come,' he said. 'It's over here.'

But Gazel shook his head and pointed towards the end of the avenue.

'No,' he said. 'I'm going to the ministry.'

'To the ministry,' the man said, surprised. 'At this time of night? Why?'

'I have to see the minister.'

'But he doesn't live there. He just works there, during the day.'

'I will wait for him.'

'Without sleeping?'

The railway worker was about to say something, but stopped as he became aware of the steely determination in Gazel's dark eyes, just visible between his turban and his veil. His gaze then fell onto the bulky roll of carpets that the Targui was holding against his body and he suddenly, without knowing quite why, began to feel quite uneasy.

'My, it's late!' he said anxiously. 'It's very late and I have to work tomorrow,' he added hastily.

He crossed the street quickly, almost colliding with a rubbish truck, before turning into a backstreet, looking back constantly to check that the Targui was not following him.

The Targui did not blink an eyelid. He waited for the stinking truck to disappear from view and then continued on along the wide, poorly lit avenue, the image his tall figure and billowing clothes, against the backdrop of tall buildings, dark windows and closed doors, somehow vaguely absurd. He was master of the sleeping city, aside from a few stray dogs.

A yellow car passed by and a woman whistled to him from a doorway. 'Pssst.'

He went over to her out of respect and was taken aback by her low neckline and split skirt that revealed a leg. As soon as he stepped out of the shadows and into the light of the streetlamp, however, she looked even more taken aback than he had been, as she took in his appearance.

'What do you want?' he asked, hesitantly.

'No, nothing. I got you mixed up with someone else.'

'Good night!'

'Good night!'

He had only gone another two streets further down when he heard a humming noise in the distance that, with each step, seemed to get louder and louder. It was a monotonous, constant noise that he did not recognise, but that sounded like a giant stone being repeatedly and rhythmically smashed against a smooth surface.

He crossed the wide walkway, which seemed to mark the city's limits and walked past a line of tall streetlamps that lit up a sandy, wide beach. He stopped, dumbfounded. Right in front of him, out of the blackness of the night, a monstrous mass of water rose up in front of him and he could hardly believe his eyes. He stood there transfixed as it swelled and gained height, then crashed back down onto the ground with a dull thudding noise, only to pull back again with a sigh and repeat the attack, all over again, with renewed vigour.

The sea!

He realised that this was the magnificent sea that Suilem had spoken so much about and what the more adventurous of his visitors had described to him, on the nights that they had spent at his jaima. Another wave, more daring than the others, crashed onto the sand impetuously, threatening to drench his sandals and the edge of his djellabah, but he was so taken aback by the spectacle before him that he did not even jump out of its way.

The sea. This was where his garamant ancestors had come from. The sea that washed over the Senegalese coast and where the great river that edged the southern desert, went to die. The sea where all the sands ended and the unknown began and that took you to far off places and to where the French lived.

The sea. That impassable frontier that the Creator had imposed on the sons of the winds - the eternal wanderers of the sandy, rocky lands - was something that even in his wildest dreams, he had never imagined he would behold. It was a concept so alien to him that he had always presumed that it was as far away from him as the furthest stars in the final galaxy were. He had reached the end of his journey and he knew it. That sea was the limit of his universe and its furious roar was the voice of Allah telling him that he had pushed himself beyond his own limits. He gone further than an Imohag from the plains was permitted to go and he realised that he was about to pay for the magnitude of this insolence.

'You will die far from your own world,' the old lady Khaltoum had predicted and he could not imagine anything further from his own world than this groaning barrier of white foam that rose up furiously, before his very eyes, beyond which lay nothing but the dark night.

He sat down on the dry sand, out of reach of the waves and

remained there, very still, remembering his life and thinking of his wife and his children and his paradise lost. He let the hours wash over him in that way until, with the first light of dawn, a greyish and uncertain light spread through the sky and he was finally able to appreciate the immensity of the great extension of water that stretched out before him.

He had imagined that the snow, the city and the waves, would have exhausted his capacity to be surprised by anything, ever again. But the spectacle of dawn, unfolding before him, only proved him wrong as the lead-grey, metallic colour of the unsettled, threatening sea, hypnotized him all over again. He entered into a profound trance that rendered him silent and unmoving, like an inanimate statue.

Then, he watched as the first rays of sunlight broke up the grey, turning the water a luminous blue, mixed with opaque green. The white of the foam became more intense and in the distance he saw a black, menacing storm cloud, approaching from the west. It was like an explosion of shapes and colours that he could never have imagined existed, however hard he might have tried. He would have remained there, rooted to the spot, had not the insistent humming of the vehicles behind him, pulled him sharply out of his revelry.

The city was waking up.

What had just been high walls, closed windows and random patches of dark vegetation by night, had, by day turned into a riot of colour. The violent red of the buses clashed with the building's white facades, as the yellow taxis and bright green, bushy trees all screamed for space against an anarchic background of loud, brightly-coloured posters that covered the walls for miles on end.

And the people.

It seemed to him as if all of the Earth's inhabitants had made an appointment to meet each other on that particular morning, along the wide esplanade. They hurried in and out of the tall buildings, bumping into each other and dodging each other in a kind of bizarre dance. Then, at a certain point on the pavement they would all launch themselves in unison across the wide road, as the buses, taxis and hundreds of different vehicles all screeched to a halt. It was as if an invisible and powerful hand had stopped them dead in their tracks.

Then, having observed the scene for some time, Gazel realised that this hand belonged to a chubby, apoplectic man, who was moving his arms up and down continuously, in a seemingly random and insane manner. He was also blowing on a large whistle with such insistence and fury, that it made the pedestrians stop dead, as if He himself had ordered them to do so.

He was an important man, without doubt, despite his reddened face and sweat-stained uniform, as even the biggest lorries stopped when he raised his hand and then only dared to continue once he had given them permission to do so.

And there behind him, protected by high railings and set behind a small courtyard with bushy trees in it, stood the tall, solid and elaborate grey building with white awnings that the railway worker had described to him.

The Minister of the Interior, Ali Madani, lived there, or at least he worked there. The man who had seized his family and children.

He made a snap decision, gathered together his belongings and crossed the road with a resolute step, over to the apoplectic, fat man, who looked at him in surprise but continued to wave his arms around and blow his whistle.

He stood in front of him:

'Does Madani the minister live there?' he enquired in his deep and serious voice, which startled the man even more than his strange clothes and veiled face.

'What did you say?'

'Does the minister Madani work there?'

'Yes. He has his office there and in about five minutes, at eight o'clock on the dot, he'll be there. Now go away!'

Gazel nodded silently, crossed the street again as the disconcerted policeman, who had momentarily lost his rhythm of work, watched him go, then stopped at the edge of the beach to wait.

Exactly five minutes later he heard a siren and two men on motorbikes appeared, followed by a long, black Sedan car. All the traffic on the avenue ground to a halt and the procession passed by unhindered, before turning majestically into the small courtyard in front of the grey building.

From afar, Gazel could make out the tall silhouette of an elegant and proud man. He watched as the figure stepped out of the car and was immediately surrounded by a rabble of porters and workers, all giving him small ceremonial bows. He then made his way slowly up the five marble steps that led into the wide entrance, flanked on both sides by soldiers, armed with submachine guns.

As soon as Madani had disappeared, Gazel crossed the road again over to the nervous policeman, who had been watching him all the while out of the corner of his eye:

'Was that the minister?' he asked.

''Yes it was! And I told you to get out of here! Leave me in peace!'

'No!' the Targui said in a tone that was dry, resolute and threatening. 'I want you to pass on some information for me: If, the day after tomorrow my family is not freed, and brought here to this very spot, I will kill the President.'

The fat, traffic policeman looked at him in astonishment, unable to respond at first and then stuttering stupidly replied:

'What did you say? That you'll kill the President?'

'Exactly,' he said. Then, nodding towards the inside of the building he continued:

'Tell him that I, Gazel Sayah, who freed Abdul-el-Kebir and killed eighteen soldiers, will kill the President, if they don't return my family to me. Mark my words. The day after tomorrow.'

He turned on his heel and walked away between the buses and lorries that had come to a standstill, all beeping their horns insistently, as the man in charge of directing the traffic stood there transfixed. It was as if he had turned into a salt statue, as he stared out with the eyes of a dead cow at the tall Bedouin, as he disappeared into the crowds.

Over the next few minutes the guard tried to regain his composure and get the traffic flowing smoothly again. He also tried to tell himself that what he had just heard made absolutely no sense at all, that it had been either a dumb joke or the hallucinatory effects of a stressful job.

But there was something in the way that the madman had spoken to him and the determination in his voice that had unsettled him, particularly the fact that he had mentioned Abdul-El-Kebir and his freedom. It was now public knowledge that he had escaped and was in Paris, calling on his supporters to mobilise themselves.

Half an hour later, no longer capable of concentrating on his work and aware that he was about to cause a total collapse in the city's traffic flow, or a serious accident, he abandoned his post, crossed the road and went into the ministry's small courtyard. Then, trembling at the knees, he walked into the wide reception with its tall marble columns.

'I need to speak with the head of security,' he said to the first porter he came across.

Fifteen minutes later he was sitting before the Minister of the Interior, Ali Madani himself, who was looking at him with a worried expression, his eyebrows set in an almost comical frown, from the other side of a beautiful, lacquered, mahogany table.

'Tall, thin and his face covered with a veil?' he repeated, as if to make sure that the man had not been mistaken. 'Are you sure?'

'Completely, your Excellency. A real Targui, the likes of which you and I only see in postcards. Years ago they used to hang around the kasbahs and souks, but since they've forbidden the use of veils you don't see them any more.'

'It's him, there's no doubt about it.' the minister concluded, as he lit himself a long, filtered Turkish cigar and appeared to drift off, lost in his thoughts.

'Tell me again, as precisely as you can, what he said,' he demanded.

'That if you don't return his family to him the day after tomorrow, leaving them on the corner there, free, then he'll kill the President.'

'He's mad.'

'That's what I said to him, your Excellency. But these madmen can be dangerous sometimes…'

Ali Madani turned to face Colonel Turki, director general of state security and his right-hand man and exchanged a look of profound uneasiness with him.

'What the devil is he talking about anyway?' he asked. 'As far as I know we haven't touched his family.'

'Maybe it's not the same one.'

'Come on Turki, there can't be many more Tuaregs in the world who know about Abdul-el-Kebir and the death of those soldiers. It has to be him.' He turned to the policeman and waved him away with his hand. 'You can go now,' he said. 'But not a word of this to anyone.'

'Don't worry, your Excellency!' he replied nervously. 'When it comes to matters of national security, my lips are sealed.'

'You'd better be,' came his curt reply. 'If you're true to your word then you'll be up for a promotion. Otherwise, you'll have me to answer to personally. Is that understood?'

'Of course, your Excellency, of course.'

Once he had left the building, Madani got up, walked over to the large windows and pulled open the lace curtains. He stood there for some time looking over at the sea and the beautiful effects of light and shadow that the rainfall, coming from a large black cloud in the distance, was making on it.

'So, he's here,' he said out loud, so that the other man could hear, but mainly to himself. 'That accursed Targui isn't happy with the million and one problems he's already caused us and has the cheek to turn up at our door and provoke us even more. It's an outrage! Ridiculous and outrageous!'

'I'd like to meet him.'

'Crikey! Me too,' the other man said enthusiastically. 'You don't often meet someone with balls like his.' He stubbed out his cigar on the glass of the window. 'What the hell is he looking for anyway?' he muttered bad-temperedly.

'What's this about his family?'

'I haven't got a clue, your Excellency.'

'Get in touch with El-Akab,' he ordered. 'Find out what's happened to this madman's family. Shit!' he muttered as the butt he had thrown out of the window landed on his car, which was parked at the furthest end of the courtyard. 'As if Abdul wasn't enough to be getting on with!' He turned to look at his accomplice.

'What the hell are your people doing in Paris?'

'They can't do anything, your Excellency,' the colonel said apologetically. 'The French have him completely protected. We haven't even been able to find out where he's hiding.'

The minister walked back over to the table and picked up a handful of documents that he proceeded to wave around accusingly.

'Look at this!' he said. 'Reports of generals that are deserting, of people crossing the border to join Abdul, of secret meetings in the garrisons of the interior! All I need now is a mad Targui, trying to hunt down the President. Find him!' he ordered. 'You know what he looks like: A tall guy dressed like a ghost with a veil that covers his face, revealing only his eyes. There can't be too many that match that description in this city.'

He found what he was looking for behind the façade of an old Rumi temple. They were curious churches that the French had built throughout the country, even though they must have known that they never had a hope in hell of converting one single Muslim into a Christian.

It had been built on the edge of what had been on the brink of becoming one of the capital's smarter neighbourhoods, by a luxury development on the edge of the beach, next to a stretch of high cliffs. But it was one of the first things to go when the revolution got underway. One night the building burst into flames and continued to burn until dawn, with no-one, not even the neighbours or the fire brigade, daring to put it out. Everyone knew that in the mists of the neighbouring woods, the nationalist marksmen were waiting to shoot, by the light of the flames, at anyone imprudent enough to go near it.

Over time it had crumbled into a blackened and dusty skeleton, home only to rats and lizards and a place that even the tramps avoided out of superstition, after one of them turned up dead on the night, coincidentally, of the tenth anniversary of its destruction.

The central grand nave had lost its roof and the damp wind that came in off of the sea made it an unpleasant place to be in. Right at the end, however, behind what must have the main alter, there was a door that opened into some small, sheltered rooms, two of which, still had most of the glass intact in their windows.

It was a peaceful and solitary place and what Gazel needed after the nerve wracking few days he had just had. He was confused and sickened by this deafening city and its crowds of people, all of which felt like an assault to his senses and his eardrums, having always been accustomed to peace and silence.

Exhausted, he stretched out his blanket in one corner and slept, clutching his weapons and consumed by hideous dreams where trains, buses and roaring crowds all seemed to be rushing towards him, bearing down on him until he became nothing more than a bloody and shapeless mass.

He awoke at dawn, shivering with cold but sweating profusely. He struggled to get enough air inside of him and felt as if a giant hand was bearing down on him and trying to suffocate him. For the first time in his life he had slept underneath a concrete roof and in between four walls.

He went outside. One hundred metres away the sea was blue and calm, quite different to the foamy, daring, monster it had been the day before with its silvery reflections dancing up and down under a brilliant sun.

Very carefully, almost ceremoniously, he opened up the packet that he had bought in a shop in the kasbah and emptied its contents out onto the blanket. He propped up a small mirror and gave himself a dry shave, as he had done so since he was old enough to think, using the sharp blade of his dagger. Then he took the scissors and cut his short, black, thick, hair until he no longer recognised himself. Later he went out to the sea and bathed, using a perfumed bar of soap to wash himself with, surprised by the bitter tasting water, how little foam it produced and the salt traces that it left on his skin.

Once he was back his hideaway he put on some blue, fitted trousers and a white shirt and felt ridiculous.

He looked sadly at his djellabas, his turban and his veil and was tempted to put them all back on again, but he knew that he could not since his normal clothes were attracting too much attention, even in the kasbah.

He had issued a threat to the most powerful man in the country and on that basis the police and the army would all be looking for a Targui, dressed in a litham that only revealed his eyes. He had to take advantage of the fact that nobody knew, not even remotely, what he really looked like and he realised that with his new appearance, not even Laila would be able to recognise him.

He hated the idea that complete strangers would now be able to see his face and he felt embarrassed, as if he was walking out onto the street and into the crowds naked. One day many years ago, when he was no longer a child, his mother had given him his first djellabah and later when he became a warrior, he was given the litham, for having completed the tasks that made him eligible for one. To get rid of both items of clothing was like becoming a child again, or like going back in time, to an era when he had walked around without them and felt no shame or offended anyone.

He walked through the room and into the wide nave, trying to get used to his new clothes. But his trousers pinched him with each long step and made it impossible for him to squat, a position that he found comfortable and liked to assume, sometimes for hours on end. The shirt rubbed him annoyingly and his skin itched, whether from the fabric or the sea, he was not sure.

Finally he got undressed again, wrapped himself up in the blanket and spent the rest of the day huddled up in a corner, lost in his thoughts.

He closed his eyes as soon as the room became dark and opened them with the first light. He got dressed, overcoming the revulsion he felt for his new clothes and found himself standing before the grey ministry building, just as the city was starting to wake up.

Nobody took any notice of him or looked at him as if he were naked, but he did notice some policemen armed with machine guns who seemed to be positioned at strategic points. The fat man in uniform was in his usual spot, waving his arms around, maybe a little bit more frantically than normal and making regular and furtive glances around him.

'They're looking for me,' he said. 'But they'll never recognise me in these clothes.'

A little later, at eight o'clock on the dot, with chronometric precision, the ministry's committee appeared at the end of the passage and Gazel watched as Ali Madani walked quickly down the staircase and into the building, not stopping to greet anyone this time round.

He sat down on one of the banks in the boulevard, like any other of the city's unemployed men, hoping that at any moment Laila and his children would appear from the same door. But he knew, deep down, that he was wasting his time.

At midday, Madani left the building again, accompanied by his fleet of motorbikes and did not return. As afternoon fell Gazel knew that the minister had probably never had the slightest intention of returning his family to him. So he left the bench and headed off, having reached the painful conclusion, that there, in the midst of all that confusion, in that enormous city, the chances of him being reunited with the people that he loved most, were very remote.

His threat to the President had fallen on deaf ears and he wondered what on earth they were doing with them anyway, if Abdul-el-Kebir was free and in Paris. They must have been carrying out some kind of stupid and cowardly revenge, because surely they could not take any pleasure in hurting such defenceless beings, who had not done anything wrong in the first place.

'Maybe they didn't believe me,' he reasoned. 'Maybe they thought I was just a poor ignorant Targui that would never dare to go near the President.'

And maybe they were right because in just a few days, Gazel had realised how little his own knowledge, experience and judgement were worth in the complex world of a capital city and how small he felt in its midst.

It was a forest of buildings that backed onto an enormous, salty sea; where sweet water gushed forth from every street corner, producing more drinking water in a day than a Bedouin would drink in a lifetime; built on a stony ground that at dawn was inhabited by thousands of rats. It had to be said that even the most cunning, brave, noble and intelligent Imohag of the blessed Kel-Talgimus people, would be as powerless as a humble akli slave in the face of all that chaos.

'Could you tell me the way to the President's palace?'

He had to ask five times and then listen very carefully to each answer because the labyrinth of streets all looked the same to him and he was unable to tell one from the other. Finally, after much persistence and just as night was falling, he arrived at a big park and there, surrounded by high railings on all four sides, stood the grandest building he had ever seen.

A guard of honour in a red tunic and an elaborate feathery helmet was marching up and down, obediently obeying his orders. He was later replaced by some proud sentinels, who stood on each corner rigidly, looking more like statues than men of flesh and blood.

He studied the majestic park carefully and his gaze fell on a group of tall date palms that rose up and over the main entrance, taking up an area of about two hundred meters.

In the far away desert, Gazel had once hidden for days in the cups of those palm trees, tied to one of their thick leaves as he had laid in wait for a herd of onix, which, had he been hiding anywhere else, would have immediately smelled his human presence.

He checked the distance between the railings and the date palms and estimated that if, during the night, he was able to get into one of the trees without being seen, then he had a good chance of being able to shoot the President on his way in or out of the building.

It was just a question of patience and patience was something a Targui always had plenty of.

He knew as soon as the telephone rang that it was the President, since he was the only one who had a direct line to him.

'Yes, sir?'

'General Al Humaid, Ali...' He was clearly struggling to keep calm and his voice was notably strained. 'He has just called me, begging me "with all due respect" to call an election as soon as possible and avoid bloodshed.'

'Al Humaid!' Ali Madani realised that his voice had become equally strained and that he was trying, without much success to maintain a calm that he most certainly did not feel. 'But Al Humaid owes everything to you. He was just an obscure commandant that never...'

'I know Ali! I know!' he interrupted him impatiently. 'But he's up there now, the military governor of a key province and he has our biggest tank corps under his command.'

'Get rid of him!'

'That'll just get things going. If he rises up, the provinces will follow. And a rebel province is all the French need to call for a provisional government to be put in place. You know that the mountain cabilenos have never liked us, Ali. You of all people know that.'

'But you cannot possibly accept his demands...' he pointed out. 'The country's not ready for an election.'

'I know,' came his reply. 'That's why I've called you. What

news of Abdul?'

'I think we've located him. They're keeping him in a small chateau in the St-Germain wood in Maison-Laffitte.'

'I know the place. We hid in that wood for about three days once, as we prepared for an assault. What's your plan?'

'Colonel Turki went to Paris last night, via Geneva. He'll be getting in touch with our people as we speak. I'm expecting his call any moment.'

'Don't do anything until we're completely sure of success,' he replied. 'If we fail this time, the French won't give us a second opportunity.'

'Alright. Keep me up to date.'

He hung up. The Minister of the Interior, Ali Madani, put the receiver down slowly and sat quite still for a long time, lost in his own thoughts, mulling over what might happen if Colonel Turki failed and Abdul-el-Kebir continued to rally the nation. General Humaid was the first, but knowing him as he did, he doubted that he would have taken the initiative and challenged the President if he was not certain that there were other garrisons ready to follow suit. Going over the names in his head, he guessed that at least seven provinces, which held a third of the armed forces, would move over to Abdul-el-Kebir. From there, it was just a question of time before civil war broke out, especially if the French wanted it. They had still not recovered from their humiliating defeat some twenty years previously and had held on to the dream that they would one day return to claim back some of the country's riches, that for a century they had considered their own. He lit one of his lavishly adorned, Turkish cigars, stood up and went over to the window, from where he could see the calm sea, the beach that was empty at that time of year and the wide esplanade before it and wondered to himself whether the time had come for him to abandon the office that he loved so much, for good.

It had been a long journey to get to where he had done,

during which time he had seen the man who he had fundamentally admired, be imprisoned and then found himself entirely subservient to another man, whom he basically despised. A difficult road for sure, but one which had given him more power and strength than anyone else in the country so that no one, except for that damn Targui perhaps, could make a move without first receiving his consent.

But he was aware that this power was starting to weaken and he could almost feel it, like mud dried by the sun, crumbling through his fingers and the harder he tried to hold on to it, the quicker it disintegrated. He could not believe that this monolithic state they had built from so much sweat and blood could have ended up by being so fragile and that the simple echo of a name - Abdul-el-Kebir - had been enough to see its very foundations collapse. But recent events had shown this to be the reality and it was clear that it was time to face the truth and accept defeat.

He returned to the table, picked up the telephone and dialled his home number.

'Pack your suitcases darling,' he said. 'I want you to take the children to Tunisia for a few days. I'll tell you when you can come back.'

'Are things that bad?'

'I'm not sure yet,' he admitted. 'Everything depends on what Turki manages to get done in Paris.'

He hung up and sat there lost in thought once again, his eyes fixed on the large portrait of the President that took up most of the back wall. If Turki failed or deflected to the enemy, then all was lost. He had always had great faith in his efficiency and loyalty, but now he was overcome with the uneasy feeling that somewhere along the lines, his faith in him might have been a little misplaced.

He spent the best part of the next day going back and forth between the presidential palace and the kasbah, until he knew the route like the back of his hand and was able to go there and back to his hiding place with relative ease. He would never get used to the streets in the new town, however, because they were all the same, long and identical, lined with shops and only distinguishable by their names, which he was unable to read.

Later that afternoon he bought a supply of dates, figs and almonds because he was not sure how long he would have to spend hidden in the top of the date palms and a large water bottle that he filled up at the nearest fountain. Finally, he went back to the church ruins, checked the state of his weapons once again and waited patiently, leaning against the wall, trying not to think of anything else but the route he had to take between his refuge and the palace.

There was nobody in the kasbah, which was covered in an eerie mist and he crossed it in silence, startling the cats. A clock chimed three times, slowly and he came out onto one of the paved streets. He looked up at the luminous sphere that stared down at him, like the huge eye of a Cyclops, or a swollen moon floating just above the horizon, the tower behind it no longer visible, as if it had been swallowed up by the night.

The avenues were deserted. There were no night buses or rubbish trucks and the quiet of the city unsettled him, even though it was very late.

The silence was suddenly broken by the appearance of a black police car ahead of him with a flashing light on top and then the noise of a siren in the distance, somewhere on the other side of the beach, he guessed.

He started to walk faster, feeling more anxious by the minute, but had to dive into a doorway as another black car drove by, only about two hundred meters away from him, then stopped at the edge of the pavement and switched off its lights.

He waited there patiently, but soon realised that the men inside the car had no intention of going anywhere and had stopped to keep guard, probably since it was a strategic point and at the cross section of two streets. He decided to take the first street he came to and try and lose the obstacle, then come back out when he thought the car would be behind him.

But he had been forced to leave the route that he had spent so long trying to memorise all too quickly and before long, he realised that he was lost. All the streets started to look the same, lit up by the half-light of hundreds of identical, sad, street lamps and he could no longer spot any of the tiny details he had memorised during the day.

He started to get worried, because the longer he continued, the more lost he became and there was not a breath of wind or a twinkling star to guide his way and give him a sense of direction.

A police car drove past him with its siren on and he dived under a bench. Once it had gone he came up and sat on it, trying in vain to order his thoughts. He had to work out on what side of that giant, sprawling and filthy city the palace was now on and where the kasbah was and all those places that he had become vaguely familiar with.

In the end he had to accept that he had lost the battle that night and that he should return to his hideout and try again the next day.

He tried to retrace his steps, but going back was just as

difficult as it had been getting there and he wandered through the city as lost as ever, until finally he heard the sound of the sea and he found the esplanade, which came out right in front of the Ministry of the Interior.

He sighed with relief. He knew how to get back to his hideout from there, but just as he had started to quicken his step and was about to turn into a windy backstreet that led into the native quarter, a car parked next to the pavement suddenly switched on its front lights, dazzling him. A voice of authority shouted from within:

'Hey, you! Come here!'

His first instinct was to run away up the street, but he controlled himself and went over to the front window, trying to get out of the glare of the lights.

From the half light of the car's interior, three men in uniform looked out at him, a serious expression on their faces.

'What are you doing out in the street at this time of night?' the man sitting next to the driver and the one who had called him over, said. 'Did you not know that there is a curfew in place?'

'A what?' he replied.

'A curfew, you idiot. They announced it on the radio and the television. Where the hell are you from anyway?'

Gazel gestured to somewhere behind him.

'From the port.'

'And where are you going?'

He pointed with his chin over to a side street.

'Home.'

'Alright. Show us your papers.'

'I haven't got any.'

The man who had been sitting in the back of the car got out and walked over to the Targui slowly, dangling a submachine gun wearily at his side.

'Lets see now. How come you don't have your papers? Everybody has an identity card.'

The strong, tall man with a huge moustache walked over to Gazel with an air of self-assurance, but on reaching him, suddenly doubled over and cried out in pain as the butt of a rifle was shoved painfully into his stomach. Almost simultaneously, Gazel threw his carpets over the windscreen and ran off, turning round the corner and into a backstreet.

A few seconds later a siren started up, disturbing the quiet of the neighbourhood and just as the fugitive was half way down the street, he saw one of the policemen at the corner, who, without even taking aim, let off a short burst of gunfire.

The impact of the bullet propelled Gazel forward and he fell head first onto the wide steps, but he rolled over like a cat on to his back, fired a shot and hit the policeman in the chest, knocking him backwards. He loaded his gun up again, hid round a corner and waited, his breathing laboured, but still not feeling any pain at all, despite the fact that the bullet had gone right through him and blood was starting to soak through the front of his shirt.

A head appeared round the corner and shot without aim. The bullets went ricocheting through the night, bouncing off buildings and smashing glass windows.

He started to climb back up slowly, hugging the wall all the time. With just one shot he had made his pursuers realise that they were dealing with a superior marksman and they had abandoned the chase, rather than risk getting their heads blown off.

A few seconds later, as the Targui disappeared off into the darkness and lost himself in the kasbah's labyrinth of windy, narrow alleys, the two policemen who were still standing, glanced at each other briefly, then without a word, went over to the wounded man, put him in the back seat and headed to hospital.

They both knew that it would take an army to find a fugitive in the dark, complex world of the native quarter.

It looked like the old black lady Khaltoum had been right again. He was going to die there, in a dirty corner of a ruined Rumi church, in the heart of an overpopulated city. With the rumbling noise of the waves behind him, he could not have been further from the solitude of the desert, where the only sound was that of the wind as it whistled through the silent plains.

He tried to dress his wound by covering up the two holes with his long turban, which he tied around his chest. Then, wrapping himself up in a blanket and shivering with cold and fever, he huddled up into a corner and fell into a disturbed half sleep, alone with his memories and only the pain and the gri-gri of death as company.

He no longer possessed the strength to turn himself into a stone or the will to try and thicken his blood, until it stopped soaking through his turban. He was no longer able to depend on his strength of will or his wholeness of spirit, as his will had been broken by the weight of a heavy bullet and his spirit crushed, by the realisation that he might never see his family again.

"...See how wars and fighting lead to nothing, because a death on one side will be paid for by the death from another..." The wise words of Suilem came back to him and it was always that same story. The truth of the matter was that, while the centuries moved forward and the landscapes changed, man remained the same. He continued to play the leading role in that same tragic story, over and over again, irrespective of the changes that were happening around him in time and space.

A war might start because a camel had crushed a sheep, belonging to another tribe. Another war might erupt because somebody had failed to respect an old tradition. It could break out between two families who were equal in strength or, as in his case, between one man and an entire army. But the result would always be the same: the gri-gri of death would take hold of a new victim and carry on pushing him slowly into the abyss. And there he was now, on the edge of this abyss, resigned to the fact that he was about to fall in, but still sad because whoever found his corpse, would see that the bullet had gone into his back, whilst he, Gazel Sayah, had always fought his enemy face on.

He wondered whether or not his actions would allow him entry into eternal paradise, or whether he would be condemned to wander eternally through the "lost lands." His heart grew heavy with the thought that his soul might end up alongside the lost souls of the "great caravan."

Then he dreamed that the caravan of mummified camels and skeletons, with bits of tattered fabric hanging off them, had started up on their journey once again, across the silent plain and that later they would cross the station and enter in to the sleeping city. He shook with fear, banging his head against the walls because he was certain that they were coming for him and that very soon they would come marching into the great empty nave where they would wait for him, patiently, to join them.

He did not want to go back with them to the desert, to wander through the "lost land" of Tikdabra for centuries on end and he called out to them weakly, telling them to go back without him.

In the end he slept for three long days.

When he woke up, his blanket was drenched with sweat and blood, but he had stopped bleeding and the bandage had become a hard crust attached to his skin. He tried to move, but the pain was so unbearable that he lay down again for a few hours, before trying again to pull himself up and inspect his wound. Later, he managed to reach over to his water bottle, which he drank from until it was empty and then fell asleep again.

For how long he had hovered between life and death, between a lucid state and an unconscious one, between dream and reality, nobody, least of all him, could have said. Days, maybe weeks had passed. But finally, one morning he woke up and realised that he was breathing fully again and without pain. He looked around. Everything looked the same, even though he felt that half his life might well have passed him by whilst he had slept between those four walls and that maybe he had been there, in that city, for hundreds of years.

He ate the nuts, dates and almonds that he had left hungrily and drank the rest of his water. He got up, even though it was very painful and using the wall for support, took a few tentative steps. But he soon became dizzy and had to lie down again. As he lay there, he looked around him, even called out loud, until he felt confident that the gri-gri of death had finally left his side.

'Maybe Khaltoum, the old black lady had been wrong,' he thought to himself. 'Maybe in her dreams she only saw me wounded and defeated but did not imagine that I was capable of overcoming death.'

The following night, half walking and half crawling, he managed to get to the nearest fountain, where he washed with some difficulty but succeeded in removing the bandages that had almost become part of his skin.

Four days later, anyone who had dared go into the burnt-out old church would have been horrified by the sight of a ghostly, unsteady, skeleton of a man, dragging himself up and down the nave. Gazel Sayah was making an almost superhuman effort to overcome his tiredness and nausea, to regain his balance and return to the land of the living. He knew that each step took him further away from death and a little closer to the desert that he loved so much.

He gave himself another week to fully recover his strength, until he had nothing left to eat and he knew that the time had come for him to abandon his refuge forever.

He washed his clothes and himself in the fountain, in the darkness and solitude of his quarter. Then, the following morning, when the sun was already high in the sky, he set off, with only his heavy revolver, the one that had belonged to Captain Kaleb-el-Fasi, in his leather pouch, leaving his sword and his gandurahs, that were now in rags, reluctantly behind him.

He stopped in the kasbah, where he ate until he was about to burst and drank some strong, sweet, hot, tea. He felt the strength slowly start to return to his body and he bought himself a new shirt in electric blue, which made him feel momentarily happy.

Feeling much better he set off once again, stopping only briefly to look at the steps, where he had been shot and at the marks that the bullets had made in the wall.

He came out on to the wide avenue once again and was surprised by the amount of people gathered there on the pavements and when he tried to cross over the road towards the station, a policeman in uniform stopped him:

'You can't cross,' he said. 'Wait.'

'Why?'

'Because the President is about to pass by.'

He did not need to see it because he could already feel its presence. The gri-gri of death was back. Where it had come from, or where it had been hiding all that time, he had no idea, but there it was, clinging to his shirt once again and laughing at him for thinking that, even for one minute, he might have been free of it.

He had forgotten about the President. He had forgotten that he had sworn to kill him if he did not return his family to him. But now, as the station appeared before him and just one hundred meters stood before him and his return to the desert, it was as if fate had come to play one last mocking hand and make fun of his good intentions. The gri-gri of death was back to play one last tragic trick on him, as it dawned in him that the man who was responsible for all of his problems, for all of his wrong-doings, from beginning to end, was about to pass by in front of him.

'Insh.Allah!'

If that was His will, then he had to fulfil his oath to kill him. He would kill him because he, Gazel Sayah, despite being a noble Imohag from the blessed Kel-Talgimus people, could not stand in the way of the will of the heavens.

'Insh.Allah!'

If He had decided that on this day and time, his enemy would come between him and the life he had chosen to return to once again, then it could only be because the powers from on high would have this enemy destroyed and that Gazel Sayah was the man, the chosen instrument, to make this happen.

'Insh.Allah!'

Two motorbikes went by with their sirens on and almost simultaneously the crowds at the top of the avenue started to clap and cheer.

Oblivious to anything but his mission, the Targui put his hand into his leather pouch and felt for the handle of his weapon.

More motorcyclists, this time in formation, appeared from around the corner and then another ten meters behind them, a huge, slow, black saloon car appeared, which almost hid another open-top car behind it. In the back of that car, sat a man waving at the crowds.

The policemen struggled to hold back the cheering and clapping crowds and the women and children threw flowers and coloured paper out of the windows.

He gripped his gun tightly.

The station clock chimed twice, as if inviting him one last time to forget everything and go, but its echo was lost in the midst of the sirens, the cheers and the applause.

The Targui felt like crying, his eyes misted over and he swore out loud at the gri-gri of death. The policeman, who had his arms outstretched in front of him, turned to look at him, surprised by his words that he had not understood.

The squad of motorcycles passed by in front of them, the noise of their engines blocking out all the other noises, then the big black car and then at that moment, Gazel dropped the large leather bag, pushed the policeman sharply aside and leapt forward. In just two strides he was only three meters away from the open-top car, his revolver pointing towards it, ready to fire.

The man who had been waving to the cheering crowds saw him immediately and a look of terror crossed his face. He held up his hands to protect himself and cried out in horror.

Gazel fired three shots and was confident that the second one had gone through his heart, but looked him in the face still, just to make sure from his expression that he had died. Then he stopped, as if he had been struck by a divine ray of lightening.

A machine gun went off and Gazel Sayah, inmouchar, also known by his own people as 'the Hunter' fell onto his back, dead, his body destroyed and an expression of chaos on his face.

The open top car speeded up sharply, its sirens wailing in an attempt to clear the way as it sped off to hospital, in a vain attempt to save the life of President Abdul-el-Kebir, on that glorious day of his triumphant return to power.

B O O K S

O is a symbol of the world, of oneness and unity. In different cultures it also means the "eye," symbolizing knowledge and insight. We aim to publish books that are accessible, constructive and that challenge accepted opinion, both that of academia and the "moral majority."

Our books are available in all good English language bookstores worldwide. If you don't see the book on the shelves ask the bookstore to order it for you, quoting the ISBN number and title. Alternatively you can order online (all major online retail sites carry our titles) or contact the distributor in the relevant country, listed on the copyright page.

See our website **www.o-books.net** for a full list of over 500 titles, growing by 100 a year.

And tune in to myspiritradio.com for our book review radio show, hosted by June-Elleni Laine, where you can listen to the authors discussing their books.

mySpiritRadio